Chasing Catherine

By
Dana Bowen
&
Chloe Brogan

DCBNovels

Dedication

This book is dedicated to all of the people who made it possible. To our husbands Josh Bowen and Brock Brogan, who cheered us on and watched the kids when we told them we wanted to do this. To our parents Ginny and Todd as well as David and Laurie who provided a wellspring of knowledge and feedback, as well as acting as beta readers and babysitters when needed. To our friends who didn't blink twice when we told them our plans and offered support in any way possible. To our editor, Chris, who we loved from the start, and who really guided us to bring our dreams to reality.

From Dana: To Abbey B., JJ, Meggie, Leah, Abby H, Mom, and Josh. Without you guys, I never would have attempted this. Thank you for your help and undying support through all of it. To Chloe, thanks for seeing the potential in my crazy whirlwind of ideas and helping me turn it into something amazing. I never could have pulled this off without you.

From Chloe: To my Mom thank you for instilling the love of reading in me from a young age by reading me the best bedtime stories. To my dad—thank you for your endless support on this journey, and look I'm a writer just like you now! To my brothers for being there and supporting me from the start. To my husband that without his help we'd never had the time to do this. To my partner in crime Dana you saw me, my creativity and asked me to come along on this ride. I'm so honored to do this book and many more with you and there is no one I'd rather do it with.

Chapters

Dedication	3
Prologue	6
Chapter One	15
Chapter Two	21
Chapter Three	26
Chapter Four	35
Chapter Five	47
Chapter Six	58
Chapter Seven	77
Chapter Eight	92
Chapter Nine	104
Chapter Ten	117
Chapter Eleven	132
Chapter Twelve	141
Chapter Thirteen	149
Chapter Fourteen	156
Chapter Fifteen	170
Chapter Sixteen	189
Chapter Seventeen	204
Chapter Eighteen	223

Chapter Nineteen   237
Chapter Twenty   250
Chapter Twenty-One   261
Chapter Twenty-Two   274
Chapter Twenty-Three   287
Chapter Twenty-Four   302
Chapter Twenty-Five   310

Prologue

I sit at our dining table. I check my phone once again, a picture of Marcus and I at Unicoi State Park is my home screen. It flashes a '7:13 p.m.' on it. We look so happy, his arm wrapped around my shoulders and big grins on our faces. No one would ever know that we had just been arguing about how I couldn't finish the hike he planned. My knees gave out. I wanted to finish, but Marcus thought it was best to give up because I wasn't trying hard enough.

At 7:15 p.m I'm starting to get worried. He usually gets off at 5:00, the latest 6:00 p.m., but. I don't want to interrupt him if he's in a meeting. I hear our door handle wiggle and jump out of my seat to greet him.

He looks exhausted, his normally perfect blonde hair is messy, his clothes look disheveled from his normal wrinkless attire. I run up and hold him tightly. I can feel his strong runner's body under his clothes. I love how much he takes care of himself; it's something I try to keep up with, but it's hard to keep up with someone who has the body of a Greek god.

I look up at him and peck him on the cheek. He recoils slightly. I try not to take his actions personally, given how late he is tonight. Maybe something is wrong? "How was your day? I missed you so much! I'll reheat dinner. I expected you home a little earlier." I pause, unable to read his expression from the corner of my eye. "Where were you?"

"Why does it even matter to you?" The words leave his mouth slowly, but they cut razor sharp.

I can tell from his tone that I hit a nerve. I do my best to give him a reassuring look, pushing down the unease bubbling up from my stomach. "I was a little worried. You're really good at being so punctual."

He shoulders his way out of my embrace and I do nothing to stop him.

My arms fall lamely to my sides.

"Worried? Oh, so worried, huh, Kitty? I can tell by the fact that my phone is blown up with texts and calls. Oh, wait…there aren't any." He's already untucked his button down shirt from his slacks, but as he pulls his charcoal grey Nordstrom sweater over his head, I get a small peek of his six pack and the deep 'V' of his lean torso. He hangs his sweater over the hook by the door. His pressed white button down shirt fits perfectly over his toned body.

I try not to stare too intensely as he unbuttons the top button of his shirt and loosens his tie. No matter how long we have been together, I can't help but admire his physical attractiveness. "I'm sorry, I just didn't want to interrupt if you were in an important meeting."

He looks so tired. I shouldn't have said anything. I feel heat creeping up my neck as a flush of pink cascades across my face.

"Yet, if you were actually worried, you wouldn't have cared and still called. Don't hit me with your fake concern. I could've been in a wreck. What would you have done then? Sit at the table till midnight while I die in a ditch? I feel like shit knowing you couldn't even be bothered to call." He's right in a way, but I can feel my own irritation building up.

The emotion in my chest is slowly pressurizing. I hate that I feel like I can never keep up with him.

"I'm so sorry. Last time I did call, you were in a meeting and got upset. Are you okay? Did something happen?" I feel so bad. He must've had a horrible day at work.

He cuts me off. "Of course, now we have to turn it back to me. It's my fault you couldn't be bothered. It clearly doesn't matter what happened—if it did, you would've called." He starts to head to the dinner table. He sits at the head of the table like he always does and dives into the lasagna I made. "Uck! It's cold." He pushes his plate away. "See, if you would've called, you would've known I was going to be late. Now our food is cold." He glares at me like he's trying to burn through me with his eyes.

"I'm so sorry. I'll reheat it." I walk over to grab his plate. "Let's start over, I messed up. What were you up to this evening?"

Our small oak dining table seems miles away. I reach

his plate and pick it up. He has his head hung over the back of the chair. He keeps his eyes fixed on the ceiling. A memory of my younger half-sister doing something similar when she doesn't like what my dad says to her passes through my mind. I do my best to keep my face placid as I turn with the food and head to the microwave above our stove.

"JESUS, why does it even matter? You don't need to know my every fucking move, Kitty," he snarls at me.

"Seriously, Marcus? I'm just trying to talk to you about your day, and you're acting like I'm attacking you."

"Seriously, Kitty, you can be ridiculously controlling." He rolls his eyes at me.

"What? You were just mad at me because I didn't care enough, now I'm controlling?" I don't understand. He is so hot and cold sometimes.

"Don't overreact, Kitty. you are making this a bigger deal than it is." His tone becomes so nonchalant. I don't understand how he can turn it on and off like he does. One moment he has so much to say, and other times he can't seem to be bothered.

"I'm making a big deal? YOU WERE JUST MAD AT ME FOR NOT MAKING A BIG DEAL!" I can feel the heat rising over me. It's so unfair that he always puts it on me. I never know when I need to say something and when I need to keep quiet. I feel like I'm constantly playing a game of catch-up. I set the lasagna down on the stovetop before I do something stupid like throw it on the floor.

"Calm down, Kitty, you are acting irrational." He turns to me and crosses his arms. "I'm the one who had a bad day, and here you are making it about you once again." He kicks his brown loafers back and forth under the table.

"ARE YOU KIDDING ME? This is how it always goes. YOU pick a fight and then act like you didn't do anything." My ears are burning with frustration. I'm so exhausted. It's been fight after fight lately.

"Wow, sorry for expressing my feelings to my fiancée. My bad. I'll remember next time to keep them bottled up like you do, Kitty Cat." His sarcastic tone hits me like a ton of bricks.

Before I even know what's happening, I can feel something snap inside me. The gates open and there is no going back now. Fire and fear replace the exhaustion, simmering together inside of me. "THAT'S NOT WHAT I SAID! You're twisting my words, Marcus!" I cannot tell which emotion is going to win. As angry as I feel, there is an undeniable defeat that will come. I know how this is going to end. I'll cave, say,.'I love you' and he'll win.

"Now here we are again. I'm the bad guy. I'm always the bad guy, aren't I. If I'm so awful, why are you even with me then, Kitty?" He acts so cool. He knows exactly how this will end—with me rolling over.

Then something happens. Somewhere in me, all the anger, hurt, and fear bubbles out. Whatever broke inside of me moments ago has refused to give in this time. The fear in my chest mingles with the other twisted emotions running through me. This is supposed to be the rest of my life? This is supposed to be my happy ending?

"I don't know anymore." I hear myself say the words as if I'm watching from the outside.

His face is as shocked as I feel. His brows furrow and his voice is low and boiling. "What the fuck are you saying?"

"I can't do this. We need a break. I think I should go to my aunt's. All we do is fight. I don't want the next fifty years of my life to be fighting. I need time." My hand twists around the back of a chair so tightly I think I might crush it.

He clearly is in shock. I can't believe these words are coming out of my mouth. I sit down realizing the weight of what's going to happen. My stomach rolls and threatens to lose the half glass of wine I was nursing while waiting for him to come home.

"I don't understand, Kitty. We are getting married in a MONTH." I can see the veins in his forehead popping and pulsing as he tries to control himself.

I sit with my hands cupping my face, looking at his brown Louis Vuitton loafers as he paces angrily back and forth across the white kitchen tile in front of me. I flinch when he looks at me, his eyes full of so much fuming rage. His pupils had dilated so much I could see my own pained expression in them.

"I can't do it. I cannot marry you, right now," I say quietly, my legs trembling under me.

"FINE. You can go for a week to get your shit together,

but I'm booking your return flight for next Wednesday," he demands, grasping for a leash to reign me in.

"No, I need time. I will come back when I'm ready to come back. This--we—aren't working right now." I start towards our room to pack a small travel bag.

"Are you breaking up with me? What do you think you are going to do without me?" He picks up the plate of lasagna from the stove and throws it. It sails by my head, smashes on the wall, and then shatters on the tile that leads from the kitchen down the hallway

I squeeze my eyes shut. I keep moving forward toward the bedroom because if I stop moving, I'll fall into this trap again.

"You would have nothing if it weren't for me! I took you under my arm when you were just an intern at work. Even when everyone said you would be shit at your job, I pushed for you to have a chance. When you felt like there wasn't enough room for you at your dad's house, I moved my life around for you to live here. I introduced you to my friends! I hate to break it to you, Kitty, honey, you're not ex- actly easy to love. Do you think you would have the friends you did if it wasn't for me?"

The rage in his voice sends daggers into my heart. His words leave me feeling like the broken plate and lasagna that lay smattered behind me on the ground on the tile of the hallway.

"Those clothes you are packing? I bought you those clothes. I gave you this life. You would have no friends without me. If you leave, they won't care what you say. I will make sure none of them talk to you again."

I pull some clothes out of the closet and toss them in a Versace backpack Marcus got me for our last anniversary. Five years together. Five years of being blamed for everything.

I zip up my bag as he stands in the doorway and glares at me. I throw it over my shoulder and stare him down, hoping he'll move out of my way and I won't have to get too close to him while we're both angry.

"I need time. I need space. I want to feel loved again. I am tired of the fucking fighting all the damn time." I will my voice to stay quiet, trying desperately not to mirror the rage radiating from him. I have to stand strong on this. If I don't walk out the door now, I never will.

"I love you." He moves aside as I reach the bedroom door. His voice is quieter now, but the sincerity isn't there.

My heart breaks at the words. I pause in the hallway.

"I don't know if I love you, Marcus. I need to figure that out." Fear trickles down my spine. I have to stay strong and keep moving. I know exactly what my words do, and I can almost feel the ripple of his anger searing through my body like a build-up to a nuclear explosion.

I love you. Those words follow me to the front door, trying to pull me back in.

As I pull the door closed behind me, willing myself not to look back again, I can hear him screaming, "YOU'RE JUST A STUPID LITTLE WHORE FROM A HICK TOWN!

YOU ARE FUCKING NOTHING WITHOUT ME!"

I pull up my rideshare app on my phone while I stand in the hallway outside our second story apartment and get things rolling. Luckily, a car is close and on its way. I reach the end of the bare white space to the elevator. I can hear crashing coming from our apartment. The elevator can't come quickly enough. I'm terrified of Marcus's rampage spilling into the hallway after me.

DING! The doors open and, with a deep breath, I step in.

I walk through our lobby to the front of the apartment building where my rideshare driver is already waiting. I climb in with my Versace backpack and watch the building get smaller as he pulls out of the drive. When I can no longer see it, I bend forward and rest my head on the headrest in front of me. Only then do I feel the hot tears that were streaming down my face.

Chapter One

I stand silently in the middle of the road. A single humming street light hangs over me, illuminating the road before me. Snow falls heavily around me as I stand listening to the sound, like the sweet silence of falling feathers. The small puffs, like cotton, are continuously muffled by the next flake. The sound relieves my anxieties as I breathe the frigid air deep into my lungs. The cold burn reassures me that I am, in fact, still alive.

I watch as the winter wisps continue to fall steadily around me. Glancing back, I see the snow already starting to fill the tracks I had made down the center of the road. The stark quiet the night provides is both unsettling and peaceful. I can hear everything and nothing. As I tread forward again, I imagine the crunch of the snow under my boots slowly stomping out the stress of the last few weeks from my mind. A piece of my memories slip away with every step.

"What do you think you're going to do without me?!" A plate sails across the room above my head.

Crunch.

"You would have no friends without me. If you leave they won't care what you say."

Crunch.

"No one will ever love you."

Crunch.

My nose and throat burn from the cold night air. Before I realize it, I am stifling a sob.

Crunch, Crunch, Crunch.

My legs feel like lead and my eyes sting. Frozen tears leave a trail down my cheeks. I come to a crossroad and look around. I have no idea how long I've been out in the cold. As much time as I spent here in Bethton Grove with my Aunt Cici, I have a hard time recognizing where I am with everything layered in white. It takes me a moment to recognize a mailbox on one side of the street, a roofline on the other. I know where I am now. I pull my scarf up over my nose, using the already damp fabric to wipe my eyes as I turn to the left and keep walking.

When I pull my scarf down and readjust it around

my neck, I feel a tingle down my spine; I realize I am not alone. Ahead of me, their footsteps muffled by the blanket of snow, is another wanderer with their back towards me. The figure walks slowly and heavily, shoulders hunched with hands shoved deep into coat pockets as if to send a warning signal to stay away. I hold my breath, willing my feet to fall softer on the ground as I continue down the road. The snow seems to fall heavier as we both trudge down the road, like the weight of both our worlds is falling on us along with the snow.

The sound of my phone ringing in my pocket startles me. I quickly yank it out of my jacket pocket as my aunt's face flashes across the screen. I fumble to pull a glove off and touch the screen to answer the call.

"Kitty, DOLL," Aunt Cici's voice seems like she is shouting through my phone as I stand in the dim light of the street. "I just got home. Where the hell are you? It's time for *Crime Stoppers!*" She groans, and I know it is because I am throwing off her evening routine. Then her tone softens a bit. "Are you okay?"

"I'm fine. I decided to take a walk because it started snowing. It's been so long since I've felt fresh snow, ya know? I'll be back soon."

"Okay, I don't need you starring in our next episode!" My aunt's voice comes out in a low chuckle, but I can also hear her concern beneath the joke.

When I called her three weeks ago and asked if I could live with her for a while, she hadn't hesitated. I know she had a feeling something was wrong. She hadn't asked as I helped her clear out the guest bedroom in the basement of her house, but I felt the weight of her concern as she watched me settle in. She isn't one to stay quiet long, but I am grateful for the space she's given me the last few weeks.

She sounded like she was walking around while she talked on the phone. "Welp, I'm going to take a shower. I brought home leftovers from the bar tonight, so you better hurry if you wanna eat. You know I have absolutely no self-control! The patrons were fucking horrible I'm gonna blow up with all the stress eating."

"Well, be thankful the drunks are filling up your pockets along with increasing your dress size. Thanks, I'll be back soon Aunt Cici." I end the call, taking another deep breath, the cold air hits the bottom of my lungs. Aunt Cici is always a splash of frigid water that wakes me up.

As I face forward to continue my walk, a pair of dark intense eyes stare at me, haloed slightly by the glow from the streetlight behind me. My breath catches in my throat. The gaze feels analytical and intrusive. My chest tightens and I am locked in place. I feel myself shrink back slightly. He is unwavering, his eyes never leaving mine. I realize in the moment that he has been listening intently to my conversation with Cici.

"Sorry. I'm not trying to intrude. I wasn't following you. Not that I would follow anybody." My instant reaction is to apologize. The stupidity of my words hit me in the gut before I even realize that I am speaking.

He doesn't move, his eyes staying trained on mine. But I think I see his brows relax slightly.

"Cici, like Cici's Pub?" he inquires. But his words feel more like an accusation than a question.

I take a breath to keep myself from shrinking back any farther. I didn't just escape one asshole to do this ever again. I need to listen to my gut and stand my ground. His tone annoys me.

"Uh, yes," I whisper, internally kicking myself for how small I sound. His eyes still don't leave mine and it feels like he is standing on my chest, making it hard to get any words out. I am taken back by his gaze, an opaque ebony in the dim light. His eyes seem to threaten to unravel me, his angular jaw set in agitated tightness. Regardless, he is handsome; tall, with broad shoulders and a thick dark mane that rests on his collar. If the situation were different, and we had met at a bar, I may have tried for his atten-tion. I may have stood a little straighter or given him a smile, but I am beat. Flirting is not in my repertoire tonight. Standing in the middle of the street, I feel more like a child being reprimanded.

He steps a little closer, his expression changing ever so slightly from annoyance to something more like resent-ment. "Lord, I hate that trash heap, just like you said—filled with drunks, " he snarls, his face darkening. His jaw tightens and I can see the muscles in his neck pull his shoulders up in anger as he hunches forward.

He starts toward me and I flinch hard. Before I realize it, he stalks past me, heading back the direction from which I had come.

"You should be careful heading home," he scolds. "The snow is getting worse."

"ARE YOU MY MOTHER NOW?" I yell at his back.

Just like that, he turns down a dimly lit alley and disappears. I stand there, confused, snow falling around me. It seems even more still than before, and I shiver. The peace that had almost overtaken me before is stifled. What am I even doing anymore?

I turned up the next street, heading for my aunt's house.

Chapter Two

I push through the front door of my Aunt Cici's two story farmhouse and hang up my coat. The chill of the night follows me in, causing shivers to rain down my back. I rub my hands together and place them on my cheeks, trying to gain feeling back in my face as I head into the kitchen where my Aunt is heating up food in the microwave.

My Aunt Ceceile is fifty and proud of it. Her long white curly hair falls down to almost the small of her back. Tonight she is sporting some sort of muumuu type dress. Aquamarine with sunflowers circling the neckline, it swishes as she dances from place to place. She has a lean, almost athletic build, and her coke bottle glasses sit crooked on her face as she hums "Welcome to the Jungle," an 80's classic rock song, to herself. She must be trying to bring summer early.

I take a deep breath, the smell of french fries and weed hit me, before finally greeting her. "Hey, I'm back."

Cici whirls on me. "For fuck's sake, Kitty! Are you trying to send me to an early grave? If so, I want to be buried in this. Charlie got it for me!" She twirls, shimmies her glasses up her nose indignantly, and I can't help but laugh a little.

My Aunt has always had a foul mouth that would make a sailor look like a saint and a quick wit that would make Einstein sound like a dolt. As a child, before my parents split, my mom would get so irritated with her when we would spend weeks at her house in the summer that you'd think we were staying with thugs. My mom hated to be teased and hated Cici's habit of smoking before family events. My mom was furious when I turned thirteen and she found Cici and me sitting in her car hotboxing one night before dinner. After that, we rarely went back to her house. Cici and I still kept in touch, though, and after Mom left a few years later, Cici took it upon herself to make sure that I still had a female figure looking out for me.

She is the comedic relief in my mess of a soap opera life.

"Did you enjoy your leisurely walk in the snow?" My aunt turns so one of her hips rests gently against the counter. She pulls out a wooden box, painted green with sunflowers on it, from one of the top cabinets. She pops it open and the scent of skunk and burnt marshmallows wafts out, filling the kitchen as she starts to pack a bowl. The sweet smell of her pot grows a lot stronger in the kitchen as she lights it and takes one long solid puff from the pipe.

Jesus! Does she have iron lungs?

"Yeah. I missed snow when I lived in Georgia. The

place is too hot and everyone there has a weird obsession with peaches." I watch her as she holds her breath for another few seconds and then exhales slowly, blowing out rings.

Ping! Ping! Ping!

She turns toward the microwave and pulls out some chicken wings and french fries.

"Some asshole at the bar sent back his meal tonight for some reason," she huffs indignantly. "Comes into my bar and insults my cooks. So what, Larry only has ONE arm? He makes damn good wings." She takes a big bite of one of the chicken wings like she's an animal. "Yep, it tastes fine to me. That asshole was just trying to show how big his dick is to his bitchy date."

She passes me the plate with the rest of the food on it and turns to walk into the dining room where she settles into one of the high-backed, hand-painted wooden chairs and crosses her legs. She lights her pipe again, inhaling deeply before setting the pink pipe and matching lighter down on the table. She waggles her finger, motioning for me to sit. I follow, slowly setting the food down in front of me before folding myself into a chair.

"The most handsome man walked into the bar to-night." She says shortly. "God he was such a dreamboat. If I wasn't quite so old…" She trails off and winks at me, cackling to herself.

I giggle as well. My aunt has always had a way with men, and she's always loved to look at them.

I have a brief flashback to a conversation we had a few years ago when she'd come to my college graduation. She pulled me aside after the ceremony, pressing her cheek to mine as we looked across the room.

"So that's Marcus, huh? Mmm. what a man."

I had blushed and giggled with her at the time. Now I cringe, my heart sinking a little lower into my stomach as I play mindlessly with the french fries.

I glance up, and Cici is watching me. Her glasses have slipped down her nose again, and she pushes them back into place with another deep breath of smoke. She pushes the pipe my way and I cautiously take it and inhale a small puff. The sweet taste hits the back of my throat and I cough hard twice, thankful for the tingling feeling that brings warmth back into my fingers and toes after my long walk. Her eyes seem to pierce me deeper with every second we sit in silence.

I wait for the question I know is coming.

"So," Aunt Cici begins slowly, bouncing the coils at the ends of her curly hair. "How is Marcus?"

Even though I expected this, I freeze and my eyes start to sting around the edges. Cici doesn't seem to notice as she sits, fiddling with her hair. She twists it one way around her finger, unwraps it, then twists it the other way.

"Catherine?" Her concerned voice jars me back to reality. "Kitty, what happened?"

My body slumps forward against the table and my head drops to my chest. My Aunt stretches out her hand to me and I take it. The concern on her face makes me feel worse, my own emotions and exhaustion sitting like rocks in my throat and making it almost impossible to breathe. I squeeze my eyes shut and count to ten, trying to calm the storm in my stomach.

"We called off the wedding. I called off the wedding." The words come out quietly, spilling from me and sending the rocks in my throat down to the pit of my stomach. I shake my head, unable to talk more.

My aunt squeezes my hand but says nothing. I am thankful for the quiet as we sit there, the clock ticking away on the wall behind me. My aunt glances back and sighs.

"Kitty, why don't you get some rest. It's almost 3:00 a.m."

As soon as she says, 'rest', my body suddenly feels like it's a million pounds. Maybe it's the hit, or the time of night, but suddenly I feel like it takes all of my willpower to peel myself away from the chair and head to my bed in the basement. As I walk into the guest room and strip down to my underwear, tossing my clothes in a pile next to my bed and crawling into the musty cotton sheets, I pull them up over my head and curl on my side into a ball.

Before I know it, I'm asleep.

Chapter Three

The next morning when my aunt pops her head into my room, I still feel like I can't move. My limbs are heavy and my mind is groggy.

"I brought you some piping hot coffee." Cici comes in and perches lightly on the edge of my bed, holding two steaming mugs.

I sit up, tugging the blanket up to my chest and adjusting the thin tank top I wore to bed last night.

"Thank you." I pick the mug with cats on it. *Marcus hates cats.* I wrap my fingers around the cup and take a sip. The hot liquid spills down my throat and I can feel it settle in my stomach, causing warmth to spread through my body. The heat seems to slowly release the stiffness from my joints.

"Now get your ass upstairs. Vacation is over. You need to pull yourself up by the bootstraps," she huffs at me and heads back up the steps.

I can't help but roll over and pull out my phone and start scrolling. "I don't wanna."

I hit a post from Marcus two months ago. It's a picture

of me kissing his cheek with the caption, *What would I do without you?* slapped with heart and wedding bells emojis. I shout from the bed. "Why is he acting like everything is fine? It's not fine!"

"Catherine Dahlia Martin, get your ass out of bed AND ACTUALLY GET DRESSED!" Cici shouts down the basement steps at me. She's so strong and independent she has never let a man hold her back while I sit here being a puddle of depression. I'm probably getting on her last nerve.

I shift and throw my legs over the bed. I've been wearing the same gross sweats for three days. I don't have many clothing options, but she's right. I can't just shower and throw these gray—now almost black—sweats back on. I grab the Versace backpack I came here with, forest green leather with the classic Versace pattern on it. I shuffle through the clothes I shoved in it while fighting with Marcus and pull out a black v-neck shirt and ripped up jeans.

I skip the shower and wiggle my butt into the jeans, realizing that my lack of working out may have made me go up from the size twelves I'm trying to squeeze into. I get into them, but just barely. I have to lay on the bed to get them buttoned and zipped. Annoyance and discomfort course through me. I look around the room, trying to ground myself from the anxiety over my weight.

The carpet is a classic 70's green shag, the walls are sky blue, and have pink and yellow flowers hand-painted

along the bottom three feet to look like they are growing from the shag. Cici did this so she can *'always have
spring'*. I've appreciated this illusion more than she will
know.

The bed is also something that Cici has customized
with her personal flair. I flip it up into its hand-painted
hideaway cabinet, and I start my ascent to the lecture I am
sure is awaiting me at the dining table.

At the top of the stairs, I open the door and step up
into the kitchen where Cici is pouring herself another pot of
coffee.

"I swear, Kitty, if I hear one more thing about Marcus
and his damn *Facebook* again, you need to delete that
shit. It's not good for you." Just like Cici—straight to the
point.

She's right. She almost always is.

"I just…I just don't understand how he can pretend
we're fine. He posted that we postponed the wedding for a
family emergency. That I'm a *'saint'* for coming to care for
a relative. That's not even close to the truth."

"More like your relative caring for you.," Cici scoffs.
"This is ridiculous. He will keep posting and living his life;
you need to fucking do something with yours."

"I'm soul searching right now. I'm looking for…some-
thing," I remind her.

"Soul searching? Looking? For what? The fucking
Sandman? Honey, I've have had sucky break-ups, too.
The only way to move forward is to actually move for-

ward." She responds with her typical accurate advice.

What I don't want to tell her is that I'm not sure if Marcus and I really broke up. We haven't spoken in a month and it feels like a break-up to me, but he's not acting like it. I want to explain it to her, but I'm not sure right now if I even know what to explain.

She takes a long drink of her coffee. "I'm going to head into town with Charlie in an hour or so to run some errands before I head to the bar. Larry is going to get there early to start prep and cleaning, so I don't have to be there until around 5:00 when the rush starts. You're coming with me, and I'm throwing your ass out at the college to at least meander somewhere other than your fucking dreams."

Charles, or Charlie as Cici calls him, is one of Cici's closest friends. He has worked with her at the bar for over fifteen years. I have always liked him, his face is handsome and his eyes set deep in a nest of crows' feet and smile lines. He's like the *Wish* version of *Colin Firth*. Where Cici is quick and lively, he is calm and good-natured. When I was a child I always thought Charles would be my Aunts husband someday, but years have passed and they never became any more than friends from my knowledge. They have settled into a routine together, he is steady and dependable and I understand why my Aunt keeps him around.

"When you're right, Cici, you're right," I say, clearly defeated. "When I was scrolling last night, I saw an ad for some jobs on campus. I might check that out." I pull my phone out to double check the ad, and Cici whips my phone from my hands.

"Are you kidding me? He's still your background? Well, I can fix that." She fluffs her curls, holds up the phone, sticks out her tongue, holds up a peace sign, and presses the screen with her thumb. She hands me back my phone. "Much better. Now delete social media, or I'll break your phone."

I know she means it, too. Once during my junior year, she found out I was messaging a twenty-six-year-old and threw my phone out the window of the car.

"Fine, jeesh! I'll delete it." I shrug.

"Now take a shower. You are not getting into *Ol' Bessy* smelling like that." She laughs a deep, hearty laugh.

I flash her what I hope is a decent smile, somewhat disappointed and somewhat glad at the same time that she didn't just fall for the clean clothes.

She smiles back, but I could tell I hadn't convinced her of anything.

I head back down to the basement. The jeans are a little easier to get off than they were to get on, but not by much. I throw them on top of the backpack and head into the bathroom.

As I step into the shower, an image of the broken plate and the mess of food all over the floor of Marcus's apartment floods my mind. If it had been any other time, I would have stooped to clean it up as Marcus raged behind me. It wasn't the first time something had been thrown, I was just happy that time it hadn't made contact with me.

I grimace, pushing the thoughts away and scrubbing vigorously at my body. I watch my skin turn pink under the washcloth as I struggle to wipe away the dirty feeling that comes over me any time I think about my life. I want to wash every part of the depressing thoughts off my body. I want my body to feel as raw as I am.

Stepping out of the shower, I dry off and examine my naked body in the mirror. There are still faint tan lines from the summer left on my shoulders, and my stomach is a shade lighter than my arms and legs. A few stretch marks span my hips and breasts, leaving slightly discolored tiger stripes on my skin.

Marcus had always told me if I would just work out a little more, and lose a bit more weight, the stretch marks would seem less obvious. He always offered to take me to the gym with him and even train me if I wanted. For a while I tried, I did the things he told me to do, I ate what he did, but after a while, I just didn't care anymore. I wanted him to be happy when he looked at me. I wanted him to love my body. But when nothing changed, he stopped asking. I was clay he tried to sculpt, but when it didn't turn out exactly as he wanted, he abandoned *Project Catherine*.

I sigh deeply, brushing my hands down my stomach and hips, turning to the side and examining myself a few moments longer before heading to my bedroom to get dressed. I slip on a pair of leggings and a sweater that hugs close to my neck. I'm not going to fight with the jeans again.

Winters back in Pennsylvania would take some time to get used to. I roughly blow dry my auburn hair. Marcus liked red heads and he picked out the color. I make a mental note to pick up some hair dye. Throwing on a coat of mascara for good measure, I make my way up the stairs to find Cici.

Today, she is dressed up in a pair of super high waisted jeans and a flowery shirt with a jean jacket that did not match the weather for this time of year. She has a pair of socks pulled over her light wash jeans and hiking boots that come up mid-calf. Her hair is a tousled mess like she hadn't brushed it after she slept on it, and her glasses hang around her neck on one of those beaded glasses strings. She has a light layer of makeup over her whole face and a shade of plum lipstick on that I am sure only she could pull off.

She turns when she hears me close the basement door and grins. On the counter are a few bagels and two to-go mugs full of more coffee.

"Sorry, I didn't really make any breakfast, but I figured you could probably use a bagel before we left."

My stomach agrees with her and she carries the bagels to the table. I refresh the cup of coffee she has brought me this morning with the last little bit of what was left in the pot, and then I follow her to sit down. We eat in silence, which I am thankful for. Mornings are not my best time. Cici takes a bite of her bagel and chews slowly as she plays some silly game on her phone. I spend my time on my phone as well, intending to delete my social media, but instead end up scrolling through my feeds, meticulously analyzing the posts from my friends back in Atlanta.

My chest aches seeing my friends living their lives. When I left Atlanta, Marcus hadn't wasted any time spreading the news of the *'postponed'* wedding. At first, I received a few texts from his family and a few friends, but they all seemed to be the same. They wanted to know what was wrong and what they could do to help my *'sick relative'*. I didn't know what to say or how to express what I felt, so I didn't say anything. I also didn't know what Marcus had already said, so it was easier to just allow his lie to live than to come out with the truth.

I retreat inward a little deeper, imagining the lies Marcus would spin to my friends when the truth does come out.

She cheated.
I realized she only wanted my money.
I caught her stealing.
She lied about her past.

I had run away. I know I'm not this person that Marcus would make me out to be. I had been desperate. I couldn't watch my life slip into where I was headed.

"What are you looking at? I told you that shit isn't good for you." My aunt stares at me quietly. "You're frowning pretty hard. Be careful your face doesn't get stuck like that." She laughs at herself. "Your resting bitch face is bad enough as it is."

I roll my eyes and, stealing myself, I delete the apps off my phone. I feel better right away, then anxiety over not knowing what Marcus is posting about me starts to creep back in.

I take a deep breath. I can do this.

"Are you ready to go?" Cici stands from the table and grabs her scarf, looping it twice around her neck, and grabs her purse.

I stand as well, dropping my plate in the sink, then I grab both to-go cups of coffee off the counter before following her. She takes them from me as I wrap my winter coat around myself and pull on a hat. She hands my cup back to me and we head for *Ol' Bessy,* her classic VW Bus.

Chapter Four

The college campus is bustling and beautiful. A few people with backpacks scurry back and forth between buildings, the snow from the night before piled haphazardly around the walking paths. I walk slowly through the campus and admire the big old brick buildings. The snow covers everything liberally, making the campus seem much bigger than it is.

My mind wanders back to sitting at the kitchen table last night with Cici. I know she wants me to talk to her. I feel like I've been so secretive since moving into her house, invading her sanctuary like a church mouse. I want to talk to her, I really do, I just don't know what to say. I don't know how to explain away the last three years. I am embarrassed to tell such a strong woman how weak I feel. Breaking off the engagement was the tipping point, but all of the little things leading up to that weigh on me. I feel the heaviness sinking into my legs.

As I trudge forward looking for the admissions offices, I am suddenly cut off by a familiar smile.

Larry. Oh, my god, seeing him always makes me happy.

"Hi!" he squeaks. "We are looking for volunteers for our fundraiser on campus for the library! Any chance you'd be willing to help?"

"What the fuck are you doing here, Larry? You literally haven't been in college for thirty years!" I laugh at the absurdity of the situation.

Larry gives me a stupid smile. "I was just walking through campus and this sweet little blond girl looked miserable. When I asked her what was wrong, she said she needed to go to the bathroom! I told her that was a silly reason to be miserable, so I would guard her table while she ran off to pee." He stands up tall, like he takes great pride in his momentary job. "Come to think of it though… she's been gone quite a while. Hopefully she didn't walk all the way home to go to the bathroom." He chuckles to himself. "Here, take one of these so that I can tell her that I handed some of these fliers out while she was gone."

He shoves one of the brightly colored pieces of paper into my hand. "And, I definitely gain sympathy given I am a one armed old man trying to get volunteers to help with the fundraiser." He laughs to himself.

Before I can respond, he has already turned away, stepping in front of another girl and handing out another flier, making a similar joke about his missing arm.

No one seems to really know what happened to his arm, and typically if you ask, he just comes up with an insane excuse. One time when I was eight, he told me that he lost it in a fight with a bear, and another time, when I was twelve, he told me it was a freak skydiving accident. I asked Cici about it once, and she said she didn't even know, but she did know he was a damn good cook and that was what mattered to her.

Taking another look at the brightly colored flier in my hands, I realize this might actually be something I would like to do. It was a fundraiser for the college library. Back in Georgia, I worked for a nonprofit and spent a lot of time helping plan events and volunteering. Since moving away, there seems to be a part of me that is missing. It isn't just the part of me that Marcus and my friends had filled. I miss my job; I miss helping people.

I decide on a detour and head toward the library to see if I can find a booth to sign up and help. I may not have money, but I have time, and I am damn good at organizing and carrying boxes. I veer toward the library, taking my time to appreciate the old architecture and big marble columns. There's a small sign in one of the windows directing me into the building to sign up to help.

As I approach the door, a man steps out and holds it open for me as I get closer. I slow my pace as recognition waves over me. I faintly remember the look of his profile and his broad frame. I'm sure at that moment that it's the same man from the night before.

I remember his hard expression and his stern eyes on mine after I hung up the phone with my aunt. And I very clearly remember the way he exhaled in disgust at the mention of her bar.

Rage fills me. Of all of the people to run into on such a dreary day, *why him?*

Before I can register the words leaving my mouth, I hear myself say, "You again? What are you doing here?"

His demeanor from last night seems to trail into today. Something about him really rubs me the wrong way.

Our eyes meet, and I feel as if the air is being pulled out of me. My stomach seems to implode on itself as his gaze rakes over my face and down my body before he meets my eyes again.

I'm aware of my smallness and straighten my shoulders the best that I can. I puff myself up like an animal trying to ward off a predator. The mix of mild annoyance and total disinterest in his eyes threatens to topple my resolve.

He says nothing, studying my face, making no move to back down from this situation I instigated.

I roll my eyes, feeling even more irritated at his lack of response. "Do you make a habit of verbally assaulting people in the middle of the night and then storming off, or did I just get lucky last night?"

He let's go of the door, realization and something else flashes in his eyes, but before I can get any type of read on him, his face smooths over.

"You're Cici's niece," he says matter-of-factly. He breathes deeply, and his shoulders relax slightly on the exhale. I can see the look in his eyes soften as he takes a moment to study me farther.

I feel the irritation inside of me stumble as he runs his fingers through his hair. "I'm sorry."

The sincerity in his deep, rough voice causes me to pause. *'Sorry'* is definitely not what I thought he was going to say.

Before I can answer, he continues. "Last night was not my best moment. I know you don't deserve the anger that I threw at you. I was walking to clear my head, and I should have just kept my mouth shut. But since my father tends to be one of those drunks who *'fills your aunt's pockets,'* I guess I lost my cool."

I dip my head and stare at my feet, feeling my own discomfort as he uses the words that I said to Cici last night. I understand that from the outside, that may have felt like a really low-blow kind of comment, but when I talk to my aunt, I rarely think to censor myself. I respond in a small voice. "I probably shouldn't have said that either."

He sighs. "It's okay. I understand the sentiment wasn't directed at me. Issues with my dad just tend to put me in a bad place, and I don't always pay attention to who I lash out at."

There's a very small hint of an accent or something that I can hear in his voice, but I can't quite make it out. I feel the fight leave my body as my stomach finishes its slow descent into my feet. I can remember the venom in his voice the night before. But the abrasiveness is gone today, in its place is a much gentler personality.

His gaze drifts down and my cheeks flush. I can feel

heat rush over me and my heart races when I think he may be staring at my breasts. I feel my head spinning, but then I remember the flier I have clenched in my hands.

His rough fingers graze mine, sending tingles up to my wrist. He studies the paper for a moment. "There's a table just inside to the left if you're looking to sign up." He extends his large hand and gives the paper back to me.

I take another second to study him. His skin is golden even at the end of January. His eyes are rimmed by dark soft looking lashes. And his body, even under his thick winter gear, looks toned and strong. I doubt he's sporting a full six pack or anything, but I can tell he's probably used to manual labor. His hands are large and callused, and his hair rests across his forehead casually and waves slightly at the ends. It looks soft and clean, and I wonder for a moment what it might feel like if I were to reach out and touch it.

I'm still unsure of how to process the man before me, but I ask, "What's your name?"

Something very slight changes in his face, possibly a smirk? He studies me again and I fight the urge to look at my feet. His gaze feels so unnerving and I feel like my body is growing heavier, weighed down by the attention he's giving me.

"Nathan Alvarez."

"Catherine Martin." I debate for a second if I should try and shake his hand or something but decide against it.

"Are you going to be in town long?"

I try to hide my surprise at his question. I wasn't prepared for anything to go farther and I feel my cheeks flush because I don't really know how to answer him. I meet his gaze full force as he waits patiently for me to answer.

Speak Catherine, you look stupid. "I don't know." *And you sound stupid, too.* My voice falls flat because I honestly don't have an answer to his question. "I guess, maybe, I came here today looking for a job or something to do."

He nods but takes what feels like an eternity to say anything else. "Well I guess maybe I'll see you around town then, sorry again."

And just like that he's walking away. I am caught off guard once again by his ability to say so little and yet throw me off so much.

I turn to head into the library and feel my phone vibrate in my coat pocket.

Marcus:
Kitty, you cannot avoid me forever. I've given you space. We need to talk.

My stomach drops into my feet and I suddenly feel like I need to sit down. I find a bench a few feet away and collapse into it. As much as I've tried to hide from the last month, I know I can't escape it. I knew my dad and Cici had talked. She assured him that I was safe and with her and that she would keep him in the loop the best that she could.

But she knew I needed space.

When I left Georgia, I didn't tell anyone. I couldn't bear the questions. If Marcus made his threats true, our friends wouldn't care what I had to say. I couldn't explain my way out of things. I picked the wrong way out of a bad situation, and this was how I was paying for it.

My phone vibrates, and I muster the courage to look again in case it's Marcus.

CiCi:
I'll be done soon, meet me by The Grove in 20 minutes.

I realize I still haven't made it inside the library to complete the sign-up for the fundraiser, nor have I made it to the campus admissions office to ask about a job. I type back a quick reply and scurry to the admissions office.

I step out into the winter sunlight and squint at the brightness of the sun reflecting off the snow. I make the slow walk through campus in the direction of The Grove where I am supposed to meet my aunt. My pulse is still thumping in my ears from the last few minutes I spent in front of the library with Nathan. I figure the short walk to the coffee shop will have to be enough to clear my head.

What the fuck was that?

Today the man I met in the library was definitely not the same man who lashed out at me in the snow last night. This man today was good natured and almost friendly. I can't help but kick myself for being the main source of the awkwardness in our conversation.

In that instant, I am grabbed from behind. Fear tears through my body, causing my throat to constrict and my eyes to sting. I feel the air rush out of my lungs

"Cat! OMG Catherine it is you! Gosh, I was so worried for a minute that I just grabbed a total stranger!"

My heart falls into my butt and I spin around to look my assailant in the eyes. Sarah Adams grins and hugs me again. I stare open-mouthed at my childhood best friend.

"You totally didn't tell me that you were in town! Aren't you like, getting married soon?"

I'm still reeling as well as seeing my friend for the first time in roughly two years.

"What are you doing here?" I ask stupidly.

"Oh, I'm back in school here! But you didn't answer my question. What are you doing here?"

I take a moment to study her features. She was always the prettiest in our little friend group. She has a 'girl next door' kind of smile, and a thin willowy frame that makes her look very much like a model.

"I moved back. I'm staying with Cici for now."

"Moved back? But what about your fiancé?" Her eyes seem mildly concerned and very curious.

I fight the urge to just walk away. I don't know how much of this conversation I can honestly handle right now. But at the same time, the sight of my friend brings so much nostalgia and relief. It brings me back to reality a little.

"We are taking a bit of a break, I guess," I say shortly. I

know from the look she's giving me that she's expecting a full-blown gossip session, but this single sentence is all I'm willing to offer.

"Oh man, girl I'm SO sorry!" Sarah hugs me for the third time, and the physical contact is making me uncomfortable. "Wait! So like, if you moved back, you can totally come out tonight with Ashleigh, Meghan and me! We were literally JUST talking about going to your aunt's bar tonight to hang out! OMG, you just HAVE to come with!"

I try to hide my cringe. I'm not sure I'm up for it, but before I can say anything else, Sarah has her phone to her ear. "Ash! You will NOT believe who I just ran into! Catherine! Yeah, that Catherine! I know!"

She pauses for half a second. "She's coming out with us tonight! It's going to be so, so, SO fun!"

She pauses again, and I catch myself straining to hear what Sarah's cousin Ashleigh is saying on the other end.

"Okay Ash, I have to go, I'll see you tonight at 7:00!" Sarah clicks the screen of her phone to end the call and spins her full attention back on me. "I'll see you at 7:00 as well! This is going to be so fun, I'm so excited! Okay, I have one more class today, so I'll see you later!"

She hugs me for a fourth time, but I'm ready now and I hug her back. "Okay, I guess I'll see you tonight, then."

She flashes me her million dollar smile and basically skips off in the other direction.

The bus is filled to the brim with paper goods and supplies for the bar when I hop into the passenger seat. I hand Cici a cup of coffee and turn down the classic rock music that is bumping through the VW Bus. She glares and says *"RUDE"* but doesn't turn it back up.

Cici takes a long sip from her cup, muffling her humming offkey to the song on the radio.

"Did you find what you were looking for?" Cici kicks the car into gear and heads out of the parking lot and off campus.

I hold up a thin paper folder and the flier from earlier. "I need to call the admissions office tomorrow to set up an interview."

She nods, keeping her eyes on the road. The snow has started to fall again, slowly tapping the ground. It's peaceful.

We pass a sign advertising the mall, a place where I hung out with Sarah during my teenage summers.

"Hey, do you think you could drop me at the mall? I think I really need to pick up a few more essentials to add to my wardrobe here."

"Yeah, I can. Do you want me to hang around?" She turns at the next light, and heads toward the small mall we have in town.

"No, it's alright. I won't be terribly long, but I know you need to head to the bar soon. I'll just walk back to the house."

"Okay, well if anything changes, you can always call me. You know, in case you go overboard on the shopping or something." She chuckles to herself.

"You're the only one who goes overboard." I give her a big cheeky smile.

Chapter Five

I wave a goodbye to my aunt as her VW Bus putters
away. I turn to the sad, outdated strip mall before me
and head inside. The creek of the automatic sliding door
reminds me a little too much of a horror film. The floor is a
dirty, cream colored tile, and the walls a bland white. The
clash is extremely off-putting. I turn to my right and see a
young mom arguing with her three-year-old at the gumball
machine. There are some preteens at the coin dispenser
for temporary tattoos, buying up as many as they can.
Probably to stick all over their arms like I used to.

I go through the second set of doors to a similar environment but with the added drama of the food court. I think
about high school and how this was the best place in the
world. Now, looking at the Pennsy WoK sign with the 'K'
flickering, I cringe. I walk past tables and see teen stone
age art carved into the tables. I wander aimlessly until I
find Sarah's carving of S+D 4EVA. We used to come here
after school almost every day. I kissed Kyle Lamaille for
the first time in front of Cami's Graphic Tees. Then Kyle
punched Devin in front of the cell phone kiosk next to the

sports pub in the mall after using our fake IDs to get wasted.

I see plenty of old stores that still look stuck in the 2000s and some new ones smattered here and there. I stand in front of the mall map feeling lost. I can't decide where to go. I've always been an awkward size, somewhere between plus size and regular size. Marcus always bought my clothes and gave them as gifts, and he kept me in shape, so obviously none of them were plus size clothes. I could go to JCP, but their larger sizes look like they are meant for elderly grandmas leaving for a Hawaiian vacation.

I stare down the map, finally knowing where I need to go but not wanting to admit it. I start towards the plus size clothing store I shopped at before I moved to Georgia, Marcie's. I pass by the old jewelry store, then a new skate shop. The feeling of dread comes over me as I dead end at two stores—Simple Image, the salon that has been around since the mall was built, and Marcie's. Two plus size mannequins stand in the window. The one on the left is wearing tight ripped up jeans, a white mickey mouse graphic tee and a leather jacket. The one to the right is in a pink winter peacoat and black leggings.

I start towards the door and see my reflection in the glass.

Disgusting.

I look myself up and down. I look like I'm about to burst from the seams. I can see my muffin top is overflowing from my pants. *'Doughy'* would be a kind way to put how I look, but I'm feeling far too unkind today. I turn my head to the right and feel down my neck, noticing a double chin I haven't seen in years. I feel tears start to well up in my eyes. I try to push down the feelings and it just doesn't work. I can't do this right now.

A little voice in my head creeps in.

What a pig you've become without Marcus.

I give myself a little shake and shove the feeling down harder. I am not dealing with this right now. I need a second. Maybe I should just go into the salon to set up an appointment instead and then try shopping again. I spin on my heels and walk straight into Simple Image.

The little bell above the door tings and I'm smacked in the face by an almost painfully white environment. To my left, there are six waiting chairs and a receptionist's desk. To my right is a wall covered in posters of hair models from the 80s.

When I walk in front of the desk, it's so tall I could rest my boobs on it. It's pretty busy at the moment and no one is at the desk. I take a moment to look farther into the salon. It's full of more weird old pictures of haircuts and a few posters with inspirational quotes. My eyes land on the one that says *'Life isn't perfect, but your hair can be.'*

I try not to roll my eyes. What an absurdity. Neither my life or my hair is perfect. As a matter of fact, I'm one more shitty situation away from just completely shaving my head.

I begin to fiddle with the gold pen holder when I hear, "Can I help you?"

I look up and see a familiar face. "Oh, Meghan! I didn't know you did hair!"

Meghan squints at me for a second and the realization hits her. "OH MY GOD, KITTY! You look so different with red hair!"

I haven't seen Meghan since the summer after graduation. She was one of my best friends, but we didn't keep in touch. "I'm not a huge fan of it, I was hoping to set an appointment with someone to help fix it."

"Well, I have an opening in two weeks? Is that too long? I can set you up with someone else, but I'm the only one here who really does color anymore," she states while looking at the computer on the lower part of the desk. I remember in high school when I was going through a rebellious streak, I'd always let Meghan play with my hair. I smile faintly to myself, remembering lots of late nights getting tipsy in her bathroom with Kroger bags thrown haphazardly over our heads. I can still remember the taste of the shitty K vodka we'd mix with lemonade.

"No that's fine! When I lived in Atlanta, Marcus would have to book my appointments a month out," I mention.

"Marcus…oh, yeah. Your fiancé, right? The guy you came out here with a couple of years ago?" she inquires.

It makes me realize that I haven't really said to anyone what's going on. What do I say? The panic sets in hard. I start to pull at the skin around my fingernails, a nervous behavior I've had since childhood.

"Oh, well, he's…" I feel stupid searching for the words, but today has me frazzled. "I guess he's sorta my ex-fiancé." I stutter out.

"Sorta?" She pushes for more information I'm not sure I have. I can't remember the last time Meghan and I talked. Although I know we are friends on social media, we haven't had a real conversation in years.

I feel hot and sick, is it fair to him to call him my ex? Do I want him to be my ex? "Yeah it's a long story I'm not sure I wanna hash out right now." *Redirect, Catherine. How do you redirect this topic? Talk about something else, anything else.* "Are you coming to the bar tonight with Sarah? If not, you should! I'm going." Solid save. I force some excitement into my voice and I think she's getting what I'm putting down.

"Yeah, Sarah texted me earlier, I guess Ashleigh is having issues with the guy who's cheating on his wife with her. Chick needs to fucking get a life."

"Oh shit, really? Ashleigh has never had the best choice in men, but seriously…a fucking married man?" This was definitely a topic that would hopefully keep our conversation from returning to Marcus and me.

Ashleigh is Sarah's cousin. None of us like her very much but we always tried to include her in school.

"Here's the thing, though. He's also her boss." Megan has always been a bit of a gossip but will keep your secret if she really likes you, and she does not like Ashleigh.

"Shut up! If things go wrong, she could lose her job!" How could she be so dumb?

"Here's the kicker—do you remember Dr. Whitfeild? The hot, young dentist?" She is nearly jumping over the desk to tell me. The giddiness in her eyes over the drama brings back so many memories of sleepovers and car rides home from school.

"No, she's not!" I can't believe it.

"YES! Except he's not so young anymore and has four kids and a wife!" Meghan is giddy with excitement, having someone else to tell about the impending explosion.

"Classic Trashy Ashy." We say in unison and both start laughing.

An alarm goes off on her phone "MARGE, YOU'RE COOKED! HOP INTO THE CHAIR! Well, it was great seeing you. We'll catch up more tonight, and I have you booked for two weeks out!" She does a tiny jog to a chair where a pudgy mid-forties woman, adorned with a foil crown, is sitting with her back to a shampoo bowl.

I see myself out, knowing I need to go to the next store to at least get clothes for the bar tonight.

I step out of the salon and look to my right where Marcie's waits for me, and I feel a sense of impending doom.

Get the fuck over it, suck it up and get some damn clothes.

I sigh. I wish it was that easy. My weight and I have a tenuous relationship. No matter what I've done, I have never been able to 'slim down'. It was the cause of quite a few fights between Marcus and me. He paid for trainers and nutritionists, but nothing really got me smaller than a size twelve. Even when I tried to starve myself, or rather 'Intermittent Fast,' I still couldn't seem to drop the weight where I needed to. In the end, I would just start binging in secret, hitting a drive thru before coming home from work, hiding snacks next to the tampons where Marcus wouldn't look. He found some Oreos once when I hid them in my closet, and that led to one of our biggest fights—that no matter what the secret was, I might as well be cheating because it was still a secret.

It's a recurring theme in my life. My mother was thin and beautiful, and I took a lot after my dad's side, which could be described as 'hefty.'. I was put on diet after diet until my mom left. Then in high school, I tried to keep up with it, but it was impossible, so I'd starve, binge, starve, and binge some more. My dad took me to a therapist for a few weeks, but it wasn't a good fit, so I asked to stop and Dad let me. I struggled in college, then I took up the internship and met Marcus. Marcus invited me to work out with him and drop pounds like nobody's business. I felt great for a while, then I plateaued and Marcus found out about the secret binge eating.

Before I realize it, my hand's on the door of Marcie's. I pull the door open and pop punk is blaring through the small boutique. Suddenly my thoughts go quiet, and all I can hear is the sound of my own blood pumping through my body. There are racks of clothes everywhere, mannequins dressed in a variety of cute spring attire, and left-over winter clothes. I walk aimlessly through the maze of clothes and accessories until I find the clearance rack off to the side near the back of the store.

"Hi!" A curvy petite blonde basically hops up to me. "Can I help you find something specific?"

I try my best not to stare at her cute cleavage and tightly fitted dark blue graphic tee. The print on the shirt says *'Anti-Social Club,'* and I find the irony amusing, since she's gone out of her way to come over here to ask if I need help. I work for a minute to swallow the lump that's forming in my throat.

"Uh, I just need some new jeans, I think." I hate how small my voice sounds when I feel awkward or embarrassed.

"Okay! Come with me!" Perky Boobs Blonde bounces over to a rack of dark black distressed jeans.

I follow her slowly.

"These have been flying off the rack recently! The mom jeans look is totally coming back into style! Do you know what size you are?"

My heart sinks. This is the question I've been dreading. "I honestly don't know. Somewhere between a twelve and fourteen I think."

Perky Boobs Blonde turns and thumbs through the jeans on the rack. "Well, here's one of each. Let me get you a dressing room and you can figure out which one fits better!"

She doesn't even hand me the jeans, just turns on her heel and skips away to the fitting rooms. I follow slowly, mentally preparing myself for the task of trying on clothes. By the time I've made it over to her, she already has my jeans hanging up in a fitting room.

"Here you go! I'll be back over in a minute to check on you!"

Five minutes later, I'm standing half-naked staring at myself in the full length, illuminated mirror. Neither pair of pants fits. I'm desperately trying to have an *Eat, Pray, Love* moment, remembering something about enjoying pizza and just buying a bigger pair of jeans, but I feel my eyes starting to burn around the edges.

"Hey, hon! How's it going in there?" Perky Boobs Blonde is back.

"Uh," my voice hitches. "Neither of the sizes fit." My voice cracks on the last word, and I think the girl on the other side of the door can tell I'm losing it.

"Oh, girl! Let me go grab you a few more things! Just sit tight!" I hear her retreating footsteps and try and muster the courage for whatever she is going to bring back.

I wait patiently, choosing to just sit in my underwear and stare at myself. How did I not notice how big my thighs have gotten in the last month?

"Those stupid sweatpants," I mutter to myself. *Marcus always hated casual attire for any time besides bedtime.* He always said it was unflattering, and they fit way too comfortably.

"Here," a stack of clothes comes over the top of the changing room door, "I hope you don't mind, I pulled a few different kinds of jeans, a pair of leggings, and a few tops that I think would look amazing on you."

I'm pretty sure the enthusiasm in her voice is more for me than anything, and a small amount of gratitude pools in my stomach.

I sort slowly through the pile of clothes, taking my time to look at what she grabbed for me. I'm surprised to find I actually like the things she pulled. They fall well into the style I always want to wear, even if Marcus wasn't the biggest fan of graphic tees and distressed jeans. I slip comfortably into the first pair of jeans. My stomach falls when I see a tag with the size, but I can't deny the fit is good. I trade the top that I have on for one from the stack, and again I am surprised that I like the way it fits. It's a t-shirt with a retro flower pattern across the chest area. The sleeves are cuffed slightly, and the neck hangs loose across my shoulders. I turn my back toward the mirror, trying to avoid looking at the areas of soft flesh below the band of my bra that squish out.

"How do they fit you?" I didn't even hear the girl come back.

"I like this shirt," I say simply.

"Let me see!" the pep in her voice sends my anxiety up, but I unlatch the door and step out of the changing room.

"Girl! Those jeans fit you amazing! Turn around!"

I turn slowly, closing my eyes, reminding myself this isn't supposed to be like pulling teeth.

"Your butt looks amazing in those!" She giggles and gives an enthusiastic nod of approval.

A small smile threatens to grace my face as I look at her. I can't help but wish my body mirrored hers, but the genuine look on her face makes me feel a little better.

"Go try on the rest, and I'll be here if you need anything else."

Thirty minutes later, I'm heading out of the store. Even though shopping was miserable, I'm glad I went. The new clothes may still give me a bit of anxiety, and I definitely know I need to work on my size, at least it all fits okay.

Chapter Six

When I step into the kitchen of my aunt's house, I realize she's already gone. I wander around aimlessly until I see the note my aunt left on the fridge.

Decided to not be a total asshole today and headed to the bar to help Larry and Charlie get ready for the day. If you're free later, come see me and have a drink. I want to hear all about your day of shopping. Wear something cute.

I can't help but roll my eyes as I read the note. I don't think any of the things I got today really constitute *'cute,'* but whatever. I lean against the counter, and exhaustion takes hold of me. The daunting evening of seeing friends is still weighing heavily on me. I know they're going to have questions, and honestly I don't feel like I have the glamorous answers they're probably expecting.

I think a nap might be good for me. My life in Bethton Grove is proving to be just as eventful as in Atlanta. I head to my room and toss my stuff to the floor and flop on the bed. I lay staring at the ceiling fan. I remember many nights staring at this same fan when running away from my parents' fighting.

Then I can't stop thinking about Nathan. I think of his dark eyes. I feel the heat from my ears travel all the way down. My eyes close slowly as drowsiness takes over.

§

I see Nathan, his eyes piercing into me. I stare at his full, rosy lips, beckoning him to me. He shoves me against the wall. His breath is warm and sweet. Chills run down my body. His left hand travels from the wall to my waist as he leans in close. His hands are strong, and they fit perfectly in my curves. His dark eyes call me in an almost primal way. Nathan brushes back my hair behind my ear, and sparks run up and down my spine.

Then, like a predator going in for his prey, he kisses me deep and hard. His lips are soft and sweet. My lipstick smears across his mouth. He starts kissing up my cheek, pressing his hips hard into me. My hands move on their own. I begin to unbutton his deep red shirt. I let out a primal moan as he begins to nibble my ear. It's so warm, I feel pins and needles in every inch of my body.

I unbutton down three more, revealing a strong chest, he pulls me in harder and I feel him. Every inch of his thickness rubbing through his black slacks onto my core. He trails kisses down the nape of my neck as I get his shirt undone. His hand moves from my waist to my breast, rough but in just the right way. His hand moves from my breast, running down my stomach. His large fingers reaching greedily for the hem of my dress....

§

BRRRRRING BRRRRRRING BRRRRRRING

I jump up from my bed, sleep being ripped from me. I whirl and grab my phone from the nightstand. "HELLO?"

"SORRY, were you sleeping? I need more tequila, and I have the good stuff in the basement. I fucking need you to bring it ASAP!" Cici ends the call before I have any time to respond.

Shit, Cici, I'd really rather not have a heart attack before thirty. Well I had to go to the bar either way. I just need to catch my breath. I check the time and it's a little after 5:00. I definitely didn't plan to accidentally take a three hour nap. I sit myself back down on the edge of the bed, rubbing my face vigorously to wipe the sleep from my eyes. When my eyes are closed, images from my dream dance across my mind.

Loneliness, sadness, and anger fight for the spot to be front and center in my guts, but I stomp them out.

I stand back up from my bed abruptly and head into the bathroom to fix my hair. Since I'm going to be seeing old friends tonight, I might as well get ready for the night before heading to my aunt's bar. I brush through my hair quickly, and the ends fizz a little. I'm reminded once again

I really want to change the color. The auburn waves make me feel as though I'm looking at a stranger in the mirror.

I need to change my hair soon.

Last second, I decide to pat a small amount of concealer under my eyes, throw on some mascara and my favorite lipstick. It takes me all of seven minutes, but I feel a little better looking at myself in the mirror. I haven't made a habit of wearing makeup since I've been here, but something about it tonight makes me feel a little bit like I'm seeing myself reclaim my old life.

I contemplate just wearing what I have on now to the bar, but then decide against it, digging through the bag of clothes I got at the store today to find a new pair of dark wash blue jeans and a black shirt that has roses the same color as my lipstick on the front. I throw a black knit cardigan over it, and then dig through my closet to find the pair of knee high leather boots I bought at the airport when I came here.

Marcus would have hated the fact that I bought the cheap boots in the airport, but I was desperate. When I got off the plane, I realized that the winter weather of rural Pennsylvania was not the place to only have a pair of tennis shoes and some ballet flats.

I hurry to find the tequila, and after texting my aunt a picture of the box and getting confirmation it's the right kind, I throw my coat on, and head in the direction of the bar with the box in my arms.

§

I haven't stepped foot in Cici's Pub since the last time Marcus and I visited my aunt right after we got engaged. I brought him home because he said he was dying to see where I came from. I remember the look of mild disgust on his face when we had stepped into the bar.

The place is *old*. Before Cici purchased the property, it was used as a storage area for an automotive supply shop.

The exposed brick walls are dark and dingy. Cici decorated the place with old band posters, pictures of places she has traveled, and random knickknacks and objects that her friends and regulars at the bar have brought her over the years. Two large hookahs sit in the corner on tables. They are rarely used, but every now and then my aunt will bring them out when people ask. I'm pretty sure over the years she and I have used them more than anyone else.

The bar is made out of a dark old wood, and it lines almost the entire back wall, taking up nearly half of the space in the room. It's worn and beaten up from years of cups being banged down and slid across its top. The finish is nearly destroyed from the alcohol that has been spilled year after year.

It's a slow night at the bar so far. Even though it's early in the day, most people aren't coming out to get trashed on a Monday night. Even with the bar sitting right on the edge of campus, most of the booths are empty, and only a few people sit on one end watching the big TV my aunt has mounted in the corner.

"Catherine!" Charles spots me standing in the doorway and flashes his warm smile my way. He hurries out from behind the bar and takes the box from me, setting it on a chair before wrapping me in one of the warmest hugs I've had in months. "Oh, dear. You are just as beautiful as always. I am more than thrilled that you are back in town."

I lean into his comforting embrace, his voice, and his slight British accent soothe me immediately. For all of my life, Charles has been a fixture of kindness and friendship for me and Aunt Cici. He is all of the things that my aunt is not, which somehow makes them better friends. He's mild mannered and cool tempered, he's terrible with sarcasm, and even after almost two decades, my aunt's dirty jokes make him flush.

For so many years I secretly wished that he and Cici would get married. And when I was in high school, I suspected they may have had a thing, but when I confronted my aunt about it, she had vehemently denied anything.

"Did you say Cat is here?" Larry pokes his head out of the kitchen and he gives me the best lopsided grin.

Charles releases his hold on me, and Larry wipes his hand on his apron and crosses the floor in four long strides to hug me as well.

"Since when do we let little girls in the bar?" Larry jokes good naturedly. He smells like the kitchen, like bar food and grease. "How old are you now? Last I remember you were fifteen!"

"That was over a bloody decade ago, you old fart!"

Charles and Larry share a laugh.

"Don't remind me! If Cat has the audacity to get older, that means I'm basically deceased!" Larry rakes his good hand through his shoulder length hair and shakes his head. "Did you find what you were looking for earlier on campus?"

"I think so. I'll have to go back tomorrow and talk to some people about a job, though." I smile at the two men, and for the first time in a while, I feel light. Their presence makes me think of the summers I spent with Cici during high school.

At that moment, my aunt walks out of her office, bringing with her an empty beer glass and an ashtray. "Can you at least wait until your shift is over before you kick off? People need to eat!"

"Yes, ma'am!" Larry shuffles himself back toward the kitchen, taking the glass my aunt is holding from her to put in the sink in the back.

"Don't fucking call me 'ma'am'! You KNOW I hate that!"

Charles chuckles to himself and heads back to the bar with the box of booze that I brought with me. I pull off my coat and hang it on the rack by the door and walk to take a seat at the bar. The friendly banter back and forth between the three of them warms my soul a little more. My aunt smiles over at me and walks behind the bar to stand in front of me.

"Do you want a beer while you're here?"

Before I can answer, my aunt is filling a glass with a good IPA and sliding it over to me.

"Thanks." I take it and drain a third of the glass in one drink before setting it down on the napkin Cici has placed in front of me.

"Are you hungry?" Larry's face appears through the window behind the bar.

As if on cue, my stomach grumbles so loudly I swear they can hear it across town. I nod at him and Cici laughs lightly to herself. I'm pretty sure she just heard how hungry I really am.

"Do you still like mac and cheese bites?" Larry asks.

"Do you still like to breathe?"

"I'll throw some in the deep fryer." He winks at me and disappears again.

Cici scurries around behind the bar, wiping things down and refilling a few drinks before she comes back over to me. "So, are you planning to keep crashing my cool, or you planning to leave?"

She loves to pretend like I'm the dweeby one and she's not a fifty-year-old mess.

"I know this is crazy, because I love you so much I would totally come down to the bar just to see you, but I'm also here to catch up with friends." I snark back.

"Oi! Since when do you have mates?" Charles quips.

"Oh, stop it! The poor girl has friends. I see you got

some new clothes. Did you have a good day?" Cici is working so I don't want to give her every detail, maybe just the sunnier ones.

"Yeah, I ran into Sarah and then Meghan. I'm supposed to be meeting them here with Ashleigh at 7:00. I also ran into Nathan Alvarez. I was wondering if you could give me the scoop on him?"

Cici raises her eyebrow. "That's his dad over there. He used to work at BGPD when your dad was training. Then Mr. Alvarez decided to go to Philly. " She motions over toward the TV to a Hispanic man sitting with two other guys.

For it only being about 6:00 on a Monday, they look like they've been having a good time, there's a row of shot glasses lined up in front of them, mixed with a few empty beer bottles.

My aunt sighs deeply, looking at him. "Depending on how long you're here tonight, you'll probably see your new friend a little later. He usually comes looking for his dad about 11:00."

I feel a slight blush creep down my neck and I hope to god my Aunt doesn't see it. At that moment, though, Larry pushes his way out of the kitchen with a steaming basket of fried food in his hand.

"Mac-and-cheese bites for the princess." He half bows dramatically like he used to do when I was a kid.

Joy surges up through my body and I can't help but laugh. My aunt rolls her eyes, trying to fake annoyance, but she can't help but chuckle a little as well. Larry winks at me again before heading to the other end of the bar to take food orders and joke with the men watching the game.

A lot of old memories bring up warm, fuzzy feelings. This was my favorite place to be all through high school, and some of college when I could get back here. My aunt, Charles, and Larry have been my rock through a lot of rough times. They cared for me and cheered me up. It was nice to be back here.

I settled in to eat my food, and realized it was already a little after 6:30.

"Sarah and them should be here soon," I say to Cici.

"Oh good!" Cici's face brightens slightly. "They're in here probably once a month. Sarah is always asking about you."

"Yeah, she was very insistent about me coming tonight."

"I'm glad she was," Cici takes another mac-and-cheese bite and pops it into her mouth. "It will be good for you to hang out with some people besides just me. Don't need you turning into a hermit. Or worse, my basement dweller." She fakes a shiver.

I roll my eyes at her, but honestly the more I sit here, the more I am excited to see them again. We always used to have so much fun together.

It's five minutes until 7:00 when Sarah and Ashleigh walk into the bar.

Sarah has dark hair that's pulled back into a loose

French braid. She has on a plaid pencil skirt and green sweater. She's totally killing the teacher vibe. A few pieces of hair have fallen from her braid over the day and they hang loose around her face. She's honestly beautiful. In high school, I was always jealous of her thin willowy frame and long straight dark hair.

Ashleigh is her cousin. She and Sarah definitely look related. They have the same willowy bodies, and the same eyes. Ashleigh's hair is dyed the shade of black you get in a box from CVS, and she has a thick, hot pink streak behind her ear. Her hair is chopped shoulder length and perfectly straight. She's about a year older than all of us. She never liked school, and went to school for dental hygiene, and finished in about two and a half years. As far as I can remember, she has disliked everything about her job.

They both see me and smile. I slide off my bar stool and walk toward them as they hang their coats by the door. Sarah throws her arms open to hug me, and this time I embrace her of my own free will. Ashleigh follows suit and hugs me as well, but hers is considerably quicker and not nearly as warm.

"Should we find a table?" Sarah asks as if all the tables aren't empty.

I wonder if she feels as weird as I do about seeing each other for the first time in so many years.

I point up to the bar, "My stuff is there, but if you want to grab a booth, I'll meet you over there. Do you guys want me to order drinks while I'm up at the bar?"

"Jager and Pepsi for me," Ashleigh demands coldly, already heading to a booth.

"I'll follow you up." Sarah threads her arm through mine like she used to do when we were in high school. "I'll help you carry everything."

I order myself another beer along with Ashleigh's drink, then quickly finish the beer I already have while we wait for the drink order. Sarah orders Meghan a Long Island iced tea and soda water and lime for herself. As we carry the drinks to a booth back by the corner opposite the TV, Meghan walks in a few minutes late.

She sways over to the table, setting her purse in the seat next to Ashleigh.

"Oh, it's so good to see you twice in one day!" Meghan hugs me tight.

"I know right! I miss you all so much." I smile a big smile. I feel a real happiness I haven't felt in a while.

I hand Ashleigh her drink, and we all sit at the table. Two minutes of uncomfortable silence pass as we all take a few sips of our drinks. Sarah has an uncomfortable smile plastered across her face while Meghan checks her phone really fast and Ashleigh stares at her glass on the table.

"So," Ashleigh looks right at me, and I mentally prepare myself for the conversation that I know we need to get out of the way. "Why are you back here?"

"ASHLEIGH!" Sarah and Megan say in unison.

Ashleigh sighs. "Ugh, what? She has a nice fucking life in Atlanta and she's back in this podunk college fucking town. Like, we all know that it doesn't, like, make sense."

Megan smirks and retorts, "Well, what doesn't make sense is why you're sleeping with a married man."

Ashleigh glares at her.

"Cool, glad we established we should keep things light and non-attackative," Megan declares.

We sit quietly another moment before Ashleigh speaks again. "It's just weird, okay? Marcus is posting all this stuff, and you haven't commented anything on any of it, not a like or anything from you." Ashleigh continues to pry despite Meghan's warning.

"You're friends with him on social media?" Meghan turns in the booth to look straight at Ashleigh.

"Yeah." Suddenly Ashleigh is studying her glass again like it's the most interesting thing she's ever seen. "He sent me a request after that time they came to visit. Right after they got engaged and we met him. I figured he friended everyone."

My heart sinks as everyone slowly looks at me.

Yet another thing that he hid from me…

"Are you alright?" Sarah wraps her arm around mine again, and I reach for my beer with the other one.

"I will be. We broke things off…well, I broke things off, and I'm not sure if he's realized that. I deleted that stuff on my phone, so I haven't really checked." I think about what he could be posting. This is so embarrassing– *'Hey! Friends-I-haven't-seen-in-a-while! Here's my baggage.'*

Disgusting. Shameful. They must be so annoyed.

You're always such a bummer.

"Okay, well, we don't have to talk about it anymore tonight if you don't want to. We understand. I'm so sorry, Cat," Meghan adds.

I feel my shoulders slump a little farther into my chair. I really don't feel ready to talk about everything with anyone other than the conversation I had with Cici. The longer I'm away from him, the more ashamed of the whole situation I am.

This isn't the first time I have left…

§

"Kitty, enough of this! Your father already told me you're staying with him. You can't be barging in on them like this. That's not fair to them." Marcus lays on his thick parenting tone.

I mentally smack my father for telling Marcus that I'm here. I asked him to stay out of it. "My dad said I am welcome as long as I need to stay. I am tired of you controlling every aspect of my goddamn life, Marcus!"

"I don't know why you get like this… how am I controlling you? I just care for you! And right about now I miss you. I barely got any sleep last night after you left. I hate having the bed to myself."

My heart hurts. I lay across my bed, willing my voice to stay low when I answer. I don't want him to know just how much I hate everything about this conversation. "Marcus, everything you do is overbearing. I'm so tired of walking on eggshells, fearing that every time you come home, or I do something different, you're going to lose it."

"Kitty. Darling," his voice is laced with frustration. "I want what's best for you. I want you to be happy."

I can tell he's fighting for control.

"How can I be happy when every other comment out of your mouth is an insult to me!" My own fight for control ends, and I know my voice is louder than it should be.

"Lower your voice," he grits through his teeth.

"Marcus, I made you dinner last night. All I did was try a new pasta recipe. I was so proud of it, and it took me forever to make." I will my voice to stay steady as I continue. "I knew you'd had a busy week at work, life has been stressful recently, I thought..." I feel a silent tear escape down my cheek.

"Kitty, I know your intentions were good, but we've done so well dieting recently." Marcus's voice is void of emotion, and something inside of me snaps.

"THAT'S THE PROBLEM! MARCUS, I DON'T WANT TO DIET FOREVER. SOMETIMES I JUST WANT TO ENJOY MY DINNER WITHOUT YOU SAYING SOMETHING ABOUT MY WEIGHT."

"Jesus, Catherine, is that really what this whole thing is about?" He sounds amused, and it fuels me onward.

"No, that's not all that this is about. This is about how little you appreciate me, and how much you care about the wrong things! Sometimes I just want to enjoy time with

you. I don't want to be 'on' all the time. We don't relax anymore. We don't have Friday night movie nights anymore.
When was the last time you asked me about myself?
When was the last time you took me out somewhere, or
we did something together?"

There's a long pause, and for a moment I wonder if
he's hung up on me, but I'm still fuming, so I don't say a
word.

"Do you know how fucking childish you sound right
now? You're throwing a fit because I care about you? I
don't let you eat junk food all the time and take you places?" I hear him exhale sharply. His words whiz through the
phone and hit their mark like bullets.

My stomach plummets to my feet, and a hollowness
settles over me.

"I love you, okay. If you really need those things, then
fine," he huffs. "Will you please come home, though? I
want to see your face when we talk. I hate trying to express myself over the phone, and I'm sure your father and
his wife would like to have their space back. They have a
toddler, and jobs. It's unfair of you to drop in and disrupt
their lives. Just come home."

I feel like I can't feel my toes. My jaw is tight and my
stomach is churning, but whatever broke in me a minute
ago has also zapped my ability to fight anymore. I am
exhausted.

§

"Catherine?" Meghan gives me a concerned look.

I jump involuntarily and realize all three of the girls are staring at me. "What?"

"Charles was asking if we wanted another round of drinks, and we were waiting for you to say what you wanted, but you were pretty zoned."

I look up to see Charles's eyes on me, worry dancing on his face as he stares at me expectantly. Suddenly, I'm ready to drink. I had been sticking with beer with the expectation I wasn't going to get drunk tonight, but after the first five minutes of conversation with these girls, I feel my resolve crumble. I drain my cup and order myself a Long Island iced tea, telling myself it's fine because I'm walking home or riding with Cici. Charles raises an eyebrow, but he nods and comes back with drinks and a plate of onion rings.

"Larry said you lovely women looked like you needed something fried and wonderful."

We all enthusiastically send out 'thank you's back to the kitchen like school children, and finally the walls around our reunion seem to start to fall. We spend the next few hours catching up on everything. Each one of my friends takes their time filling me in on work and their families and love lives. We talk endlessly. After a while, I realize it feels so much like I never left. They all laugh and poke fun at each other. Sarah goes on endlessly about all of the kids in her elementary classes, and tells us all about some new romance she's trying out with one of the guys in her college lit class.

"He's so sweet." She blushes, stirring her tonic water with a straw.

"Yeah, but is he good in bed?" Ashleigh wiggles her eyebrows.

Sarah blushes even harder, the pink color spreading down her neck and onto her chest. "We haven't quite gotten that far. He says he wants to wait a little longer."

Ashleigh scoffs. "He's probably sleeping with someone else and doesn't want you to know."

Sarah deflates slowly into her seat. Clearly this thought hadn't crossed her mind.

"Shut up, Ash." Meghan chides. "Not all guys are heartless assholes like the ones you sleep with."

Ashleigh rolls her eyes but keeps her mouth closed.

We all sit in silence for another few minutes, sipping on our drinks. The girls all seem to decide without speaking that now is a good time to check their phones. I sit and play with the condensation on my cup. Without meaning to, my mind wanders to the weird dream that I had earlier about Nathan. I don't know how a total stranger could already be starring in my dreams. Especially in such an intimate way.

Just in that moment, almost as if it's fate, I see him.

I have to shut my eyes and breathe for a minute. I think the alcohol is going to my head too fast. I must just be seeing things. But when I open my eyes again, I am slammed by those dark eyes. Nathan Alverez is standing in my aunt's bar. He's wearing the same coat he had on the other night when I saw him on my walk, and the same dark expression he wore a few nights ago as well. I feel glued in place, memories of my dream racing through my head, the alcohol on my veins breaking down every mental barrier I normally have in place.

Chapter Seven

His hand wrapped around my hip, the other hand racing greedily along the hem of my dress, his mouth on mine, his body pressing against me, holding me in place against the wall. The feel of his tongue slowly tracing along my collar bone.

"Catherine, are you okay? You look pale." Sarah's concerned tone catapults me back to reality.

"Yeah, I'm fine. I think the alcohol just all went to my head at once." I give her what I hope is a convincing drunken smile.

"Oh gosh! Nathan! Heey!" Meghan is standing before I can compute what's happening, and she throws her arms around Nathan's broad shoulders. His face and posture relaxes slightly when she touches him, and I feel jealousy bubble up in my gut. "Nathan, come sit with us for a few minutes! Pleeaseee!"

Meghan has always been a huge flirt and I envy her alcohol-infused confidence tonight. Something inside of me is aching to know what it would feel like to curl myself around him.

"Hey Meg, I'm actually looking for my dad. He's usually here right now." Nathan's eyes scan the room

I find myself looking around, too.

"He left a little while ago." Charles says from behind the bar. "I tried to get him to sit and have some water, but he left with a few other people. Something about better food."

"As if there's better food somewhere else!" Larry calls out indignantly from the back.

Nathan nods, and looks at our table. Something in his gaze makes me uncomfortable. I feel exposed. My pink cheeks don't hide anything that I'm feeling. I just hope, more than anything, he doesn't think I'm just a drunk.

"I really should head out soon…" Nathan looks at Meghan pointedly.

"Oh, come on, Nathan. Come sit. Come tell me about your sisters! Sofia and I haven't managed to cross paths at the salon for awhile. How is everyone?"

She somehow manages to make him walk over to our table and pulls up a chair behind him so he can sit on the end. His knee brushes mine as he sits on the chair at the head of our table. He seems big and awkward sitting with us, squeezed onto the end of our tiny booth. His leg touches mine. He doesn't move it, and I don't think he realizes it's not the booth he's pressed against. Do I move mine? Or do I leave myself feeling his muscular legs against my chubby calves?

Nathan pulls his phone from his coat pocket and starts

typing on it under the table. For the moment, the girls go back to the idle conversation, talking about plans for the week and Ashleigh's birthday that is coming up.

I pull my leg away, praying he doesn't notice how jumpy I feel tonight.

"So," Nathan turns his attention on me. "Catherine, I didn't know you knew these hooligans"

There's a teasing edge in his tone tonight, and I don't think the girls are listening. I find myself smiling slightly at the way he refers to my friends. This is such a casual side I hadn't seen, he takes off his black pea coat to reveal a weight lifter's body, tight in a graphic tee. He's muscle bound with a thick core that resembles more a tree trunk than a slight athletic six-pack. I can't help but study the veins in his biceps.

"Catherine?" he asks.

Crap! I was caught staring. "Oh sorry, I blame it on the ADD. ha-ha" I laugh mechanically, but it just comes out sounding kind of crazy. I'm so flushed and embarrassed.

"Ah yes, anyways… Nathan, we're all just catching up! Catherine has been our friend since high school!" Meghan slurs the word *school* slightly, unable to hide the amount of alcohol we've all consumed so far tonight.

"She was living with her *fiancé* until a few weeks ago," Ashleigh cuts in.

I flinch at Ashleigh's words, looking down at my drink as hot embarrassment creeps across my face.

Ashleigh sniffed. "But now she's back."

Nathan doesn't take his eyes off me as the girls chatter for a few minutes about who knows what. I can't hear them, and I can't manage to meet his gaze either. I study the ice in my cup, slowly turning my glass around in the condensation that's pooling on the table. I take a few sips, contemplating whether or not I should slow down at this point. I decide finishing my drink is best. This has been an overwhelming night and I don't know how to act with Nathan's dark eyes seeing through me.

"Fiancé, huh?" Nathan says lightly.

I peer up at him through my lashes, taking a moment to study his face before I reply. I'm again struck by his strong features, but tonight his face is soft and friendly. "Ex-fiancé, actually."

"I see." His face is stoic, but his eyes dance with something I don't quite understand.

Meghan seems completely oblivious to my discomfort and the half-ass conversation Nathan and I were just having. She turns her full attention to him, leaning awkwardly on the table to speak. "How is Sofia doing? Like I said, I haven't seen her in the salon for a while."

"Oh, she's okay. The kids have been passing around a stomach bug, so she's been home a lot over the last two weeks."

"Oh no! Major bummer."

I take another long sip of my drink. I feel so out of place here right now. There are years where my life was so different that I have no idea where I fit in with these people now. I can't keep up with the conversation because I gave up the last four years of my life that I could have been living here to live in another city with a man whom I thought was my person.

I check the clock on the wall, and see it's coming up on 11:00. I'm not sure where the last few hours have gone, but I suddenly realize how exhausted I am. "I think I should get going, I have some job hunting to do first thing in the morning."

"I was just thinking that." Sarah yawns. "Regardless of how much sleep I get tonight, my kiddos will have just as much energy in the morning."

"Can I at least finish my drink?" Ashleigh looks at Sarah pointedly.

I have a weird feeling the three girls have something to talk about once I'm gone, but at this point I'm too buzzed and tired to care. I leave my drink unfinished and stand to head toward the door. I sway on my feet as I stand and feel a big hand take my forearm to steady me.

My face goes unbelievably hot when I realize Nathan is standing next to me and it's his hand on my forearm, steadying me.

"I'll walk you out, I should probably get going as well." Nathan nods and says his goodbyes to the girls.

I follow suit, waving and saying I'll talk to them later. I think Sarah says something about meeting for lunch during this coming week, and I nod at her when she says she will text me tomorrow. As I turn to head for my coat, I catch Meghan staring at me intently. Her eyes dart briefly between me and Nathan before she gives me a small smile that I don't understand.

I quickly say my goodbyes to Charles, Cici, and Larry, put on my coat, and head for the door. Nathan holds it open for me, and we push out into the cold night. I'm so physically aware of how close he is as we stand in the parking lot, I can't tell if I feel hot because of the alcohol, or from his gaze.

"How much have you had to drink?" he asks quietly.

"A few, not very many."

"You're not driving are you?"

"No, I walked. My aunt's house is only a few blocks. I'll be fine." I turn to walk and sway again, feeling another rush of the alcohol in my bloodstream. The earth threatens to topple and I feel Nathan's hand press into the small of my back. Lightning surges through me, momentarily sobering my mind as I concentrate on the pressure of his big warm hand holding me up.

"I walked, too. I'll go with you. Don't need you drunkenly stumbling into a ditch tonight." He keeps his hand on my back as we start forward, his touch giving me stability.

I allow myself to momentarily relish the safety he brings me on our quiet walk back to Cici's house. I don't quite understand why Nathan would care so much about how I get home, but I'm thankful for the company, even if it's nothing more than this handsome man walking next to me.

We walk in silence, slowly heading in the direction of my aunt's house. I realize I have no balance. I feel like a newly born colt. I stumble, nearly falling face first on the snowy sidewalk, my hands landing in the ice. They begin to sting as suddenly he sweeps me up and cradles me in his thick, muscular arms. He's so gentle.

"Here we go." He readjusts his grip under me. "How many drinks did you have? I thought the only drunk I signed up for was *mi papà*." A chuckle escapes from his chest, but it only makes me feel worse.

Oh, god how embarrassing. I manage to mutter out, "More than I thought I guess, thankssss." He's strong, and I wonder if he lifts? Is he a gym rat, or is he a hard working heavy lifting kind of man. I know nothing about him, yet I can't help but wonder what kind of man is Nathan Alvarez that he would carry a drunk he barely knows back to her home.

I can't help but think of Marcus, the times I made the mistake of getting too sloshed around him.

§

"Are you serious right now?" I'm pulled into Marcus as he hisses in my ear.

"What? I don't understand?" His grip tightens hard, his perfectly manicured nails dig into my bicep.

"You are making a mockery of me. You've had two glasses." His tone is terrifyingly calm.

"Everything good, Marcus? Catherine?" A friend at the party asks, her eyes holding genuine concern.

Marcus switches to what almost seems like a different personality.

"Oh, we're fine. We have an early morning tomorrow, so I think we'll be leaving." He grins wide. Just as his friend takes her first step away, his grip tightens again. He turns to me and it's like the switch is hit again. "I cannot have you behave this way in public. You are such a moron." His voice is cold and hard in my ear.

I make the mistake of jokingly responding instead of obeying like he expects me to. "Oh, stop it, silly, I'm just getting my confidence. I want to impress your friends, and I'm just a little nervous."

The glare I get from Marcus shows I made a horrible decision. He leans in. "You can only impress people by being a pretty face. No one wants to hear you talk. We are leaving now and going home before you ruin my reputation."

We walk to the door and he turns back towards the small crowd. "Adieu, my friends! I do hope we can do this again. Catherine truly enjoyed you all!"

We leave. As he shuts the door, I shout, "Bye!"

He turns to me. "What did I fucking say? No one what's to hear you. You're so obnoxious."

I look down and follow behind him.

We climb into his black BMW SUV. I sit down in the passenger seat and the tears begin flowing. "I don't un-

derstand, I'm barely tipsy. What did I do wrong? Did I say something?"

He looks forward as he turns the key.

"I'm sorry! What can I do? I was really nervous, I'm..." I can't finish my sentence. I begin sobbing hard.

We pull out of the parking garage. I'm crying hard and loudly. He doesn't even turn his head.

"IM SORRY! PLEASE, WHAT CAN I DO?"

Nothing. Not a turn to check, no comfort, not even a glare.

"MARCUS, I'M SORRY!" I'm screaming at this point and still he says nothing. I see his hands dig into the steering wheel. I choose to just cry to myself and stare out the window as the other cars and buildings fly by.

We make a silent trudge back to the building. We get to our door. He turns the handle, and like an angry father, he looks at me. "Bed, now!"

Like a child I walk to the bedroom without dinner, tears streaming down my cheeks like rivers.

§

"Catherine, are you alright?" Nathan's deep voice brings me back to reality. The hum of his chest against my cheek soothing my drunken nerves.

"Yeah, I'm okay. Sorry." I look around, struggling to lift my head from his chest. I recognize being close to my aunt's house. "You didn't have to carry me all of the way here."

"Well, I'm not sure if you remember, but your legs betrayed you earlier. This seemed quicker than dragging your drunk ass through the snow."

I try to laugh, but something in his eyes makes me suck the sound back in. I see a flash in his eyes that reminds me just how awkward this whole night has been. He sets me down in fron t of Cici's porch and pain seers through my left knee, and then I realize my hands burn, too. I grimace, looking down at them and see the scrapes from my fall a few minutes ago.

"Shit, are you okay?" The concern in Nathan's voice is almost enough to make the pain in my hands go away.

I give him a shaky smile. "I'm liquored up enough it doesn't really hurt." But even as I say it, the sting in my palms intensifies.

"Let me help you." He takes my hand and looks at the scrapes in the light of the streetlamp by the road. "This needs to be cleaned."

"I don't need you to take care of me." The words come out uglier than I mean for them to. I fumble through my purse for my keys, and then promptly drop them like an idiot when I look for the one for Cici's house.

Nathan bends to pick them up, and hands them back to me. My face heats as I step onto the porch to find the one that goes to the lock. He follows me onto the porch despite my arguing.

"It's no big deal," he says shortly. "But, given the last

half hour, I don't feel comfortable leaving you until I know you're safe inside and not bleeding all over the place."

"I'm not a child." Annoyance surges through my stomach.

"I never said you were."

I push through the front door and into the hallway, stumbling to take off my shoes and coat.

Nathan closes the door behind us.

I turn and almost slam into his chest. I reel back, suddenly off balance and disoriented from the closeness of our bodies and the faint smell of his cologne. He grabs my shoulders to steady me, but as his hands linger on my body, I wonder if he can feel how quickly my heart is beating. I swear for a second his eyes dart to my lips, and my breath catches somewhere in my chest.

"Does Cici have a first aid kit?"

I nod, unable to speak with his hands still on me. Heat radiates from where his hands are touching me, and I can feel it creeping across my chest and up my neck. He pulls his coat off and drapes it over a hook on the wall before walking past me into the kitchen. I find myself following dumbly.

"Wash your hands," he directs me as he starts opening cabinets.

I feel him brush against my back as he opens the cabinet above the sink. My heart fully stops. For a moment, I cannot do anything, and I feel my body threatening to sway again, dizziness surging through me with his front lightly grazing my back. His hand snakes to my hip as he lightly presses me back upright. I hadn't even realized my body had started to tilt.

"Woah, there," his voice has a husky undernote that sends shivers through my body. "One fall was enough for tonight."

Even after I'm steady, his hand stays in place for another three long beats of my heart. Time seems to both be frozen and also racing all at the same time. I turn in his arm, and before I can react, his other hand grasps my hip and he lifts me on the counter next to the sink. My eyes are heavy watching him check my palms. My left hand appears to be relatively fine, but my right hand must have caught some ice or gravel. There is a patch of raw, bleeding skin that traces a short distance from my thumb down my wrist.

He works quietly and carefully, rubbing disinfectant into the cuts. I hiss under my breath from the sting of his touch, and his eyes flick up to meet mine.

"Are you okay? Does your wrist hurt, too? It doesn't hurt when I move it, does it?"

"No, it's okay. It just stings a little." I know my voice betrays all of the muddled feelings I have. It comes out shaky and low. My heart jumps into my throat when Nathan brings the palm of my hand close to his mouth and blows gently on the cut. The coolness of his breath sends shivers up my arm and down my spine, and lessens the sting of the antiseptic.

"Okay, I just want to make sure nothing's broken." He takes his time bending each of my fingers and rotating my wrist. When he seems satisfied, he turns to my knee. "Sorry, you ripped your pants."

"No big deal. It adds to the aesthetic." I try and laugh. "It was my drunk ass that fell."

He gets down on one knee, getting to work wiping the scrapes through the rough hole in my new jeans. My breath catches when he wipes at the sensitive skin with a warm paper towel. When he stands again, placing a gentle hand on my thigh to place more disinfectant and a bandage on my knee, I think I might pass out. He bends to blow cool air on the cut after he places the antiseptic on the scrapes.

I'm suddenly so aware of how long it's been since someone touched me. I catch myself thinking about how easy it would be to wrap my legs around him and run my hands along his chest. My eyes settle on the shape of his strong shoulders and chest, the angles of his jaw, the stubble running across his cheeks. Before I can stop myself, my hand has gone to his chest, my fingers brushing against his broad shoulders and across his chest. His muscles tense under my fingers, and momentarily it feels as if we are suspended in time, connected by the places where our bodies are touching. I peer up at him with heavy eyelids, and his eyes are dark and piercing. My breath hitches in the back of my throat when his deep eyes study my face.

"Okay, you're almost good as new." The moment is gone, and Nathan steps away, gathering up the trash from the bandaids, and places the kit back above the sink.

"Thank you," I manage to squeak out. My body feels cold. I don't know what's come over me. My mind is racing and I can't seem to focus on anything but the feel of his fingers on my thigh a moment before.

He absently opens another cabinet and takes a glass, filling it with water and hands it to me.

Embarrassment from the night's ordeal is creeping into my mind and tightening in my chest, squeezing my heart. This is definitely not how tonight should have gone. "I'm sorry." I say finally. "I'm sure this is not how you wanted to spend your night."

He shrugs. "I could have been spending it picking my dad up off Cici's floor."

"Instead you picked me up out of the street." My face heats. I can't imagine what he must think of me right now.

"Yeah, but you're way prettier."

I meet his eyes, and he scans my face, the dark intensity seeming to grow more as he looks at me. I'm sure this time his eyes drop to my mouth and hover there for a few agonizing seconds. I resist the urge to reach for him again, clutching the glass of water with both hands to keep them from doing something stupid. He's still standing close enough to me that if I wanted to, I could touch him again.

After another long moment, he shifts on his feet and takes a step toward the hallway that leads back to the front door.

"I'll let myself out, I'm sure I'll see you again soon." His face smooths into a light, kind smile that sends my heart skittering through my chest.

I nod, trying to throw him a smile, but I'm not sure if it works. He turns, and I am left sitting in my aunt's kitchen, unsure of so many things.

Chapter Eight

BLARRRGHF

"Oh, god…" The splatter sound is almost as bad as the actual vomit exploding out of me.

BING! BING! BING!

My morning alarm goes off.

You can do this. You need to get up and look for a job. You need to build a life on your own.

I am having the worst morning. I definitely had worse than this at college, but I'm not in college anymore and I can feel it. Every inch of my body feels like it's been hit by a Mack truck.

I throw up for what I hope is the last time and stand up to look in the mirror.

Thank God you're already up. It's gonna take forever to fix your face.

I study my face deeply. I seem so tired. My dark circles would impress Dracula but I don't look as sad anymore. I'm starting to seem more like me again. I pull out my black makeup case and get to work.

I throw on a red shirt, my favorite black cardigan, grab

my purse and run out the door. Leaving now gives me a pretty good length of time to let the cold air really wake me up and help me shake off some of this hangover. Luckily Cici made a smart decision buying this house just within walking distance of the bar and campus. She's still sleeping when I leave, which saves me a lot of questions about my time with Sarah and Meghan and Ashleigh, and also Nathan walking me home. That's a topic I know Cici won't let go by, but at least I've escaped it for now.

§

I stand in front of the college administration office wondering if I really have the energy for a job right now. I'm tired of just sitting around, though, and I think if I don't get a job soon, Cici is going to turn me into one of the mice from *Cinderella* to do her laundry.

Standing outside the large glass doors, I'm startled by the secretary popping into her seat. She turns to her computer and starts vigorously typing away. Her eyes glance up at me quizzically, and I flush with embarrassment, realizing how creepy I must seem waiting there. I pull the door open. The office is modern, the secretary not so much. Her light brown hair is mottled with grey and twisted up on top of her head, wearing red cateye glasses, and a blazer to match.

Her lipstick creeps into her wrinkles as she greets me, "Oh, hello dear! How can I help you?"

"I'm here to turn in my application. I was hoping that maybe you have some openings available?" I felt hopeful to start my new life as soon as possible. I'm afraid if I wait too long, I may change my mind.

She shuffled through the pages of my application. "It doesn't pay much or offer many hours, but the campus librarian is hosting open interviews today at the library. His previous assistant graduated early. We usually keep the position to students, but you are more than welcome to go apply." She hands me my application back with a smile. "Take these with you, then you won't have to redo them."

I take the application, and slide it under my arm. A library position would be perfect. quiet atmosphere, slow pace, and maybe I could pick up a class or two while I'm here. Even though I've already finished school with a de-gree, I love learning. Even when I was in high school and my parents were struggling through their divorce, school was my safe place. Homework gave me a reason to avoid them, and I thrived off learning new things. Working at the college would give me a reason to take some random classes about things I'm interested in. I mean, it's not like I don't have the time.

I begin the leisurely walk from the administration building towards the library. Campus is beautiful, the trees touched by snow, the white blanket on the ground crunch-ing under my boots. I admire the statues of old important men that litter the grounds around me.

Approaching the library, an old three-story cobblestone

building with gables and leaded windows, I just have to take in the grandeur of it all. Two stone lions guard the heavy wood doors, and it is like walking up to a castle.

I pat the little lion for good luck and then pull open the large door. Life is finally looking up. I can imagine this place becoming my home again. The weight of the last few years slowly seems to lift away from me. Things are quieter in my head. The constant nagging of my inner voices seem to dimmer today after my talk with my aunt and after deleting the social media links from my phone. At least I'm not thinking of Marcus first thing when I wake up. I feel like I can breathe easier knowing that Marcus doesn't have a hold on me here. He doesn't get to make my choices anymore. I can be who I want, I can work where I want. I can have my own friends, my own life.

Nothing here has been touched by him.

The library has rows and rows of books. The center of the space is open to the floors of books above with a gallery railing going around all sides. The three-story building that seems like a castle on the outside feels more like a fortress from in here with each row of books holding the next one up, I feel safe and protected by the stories around me. The vast expanse of untapped knowledge makes my skin prick with excitement. A literary avalanche could happen at any moment, and I think that would be a lovely way to be buried.

I climb the stairs. The third floor is circled with office doors and more shelving filled with reference guides and encyclopedias. The carpet is a classic burgundy red that has never been replaced. I can see the well-worn trails where people have walked for years. I think it might be a requirement at all libraries. At my right is a glass case filled with trophies and old photographs and to my left was a large, solid semi-circle oak desk.

I walk up to the desk with a little kick in my step. A young blonde girl sits behind it with her nose in a book. I take a minute to study her face. She is petite and has cute, thin reading glasses that droop slightly down her nose. The book she is reading is titled *Alice's Adventures in Wonderland*. I take a mental note to talk to her if I get this job.

"Excuse me, I'm here for open interviews?"

She doesn't bother looking up and points to a tiny sign taped to an office door – *OPEN INTERVIEWS*.

I walk toward the door. It is cracked already, so I knock gently before pushing it all the way open.

My heart stops as my gaze is met with Nathan's dark, intense eyes, those eyes that seem to be piercing through me instead of just looking at me.

Breathe, Catherine. In, out. In, out.

"Fancy seeing you again," His voice is bland, but there is a playful glint in his eyes.

"I just can't seem to stay away from you." I fake a dramatic sigh, pouring sarcasm into every word as I say them, and roll my eyes.

He laughs, and I almost jump out of my skin at the

sound. He has a low, deep laugh, and his head tilts back slightly, his shoulders shaking. My cheeks flush hot, and a smile seems to tug at my mouth against my will. The sarcasm I tried to convey a moment before slips away and my stomach tightens with the same warmth I feel on my face.

I use the brief second he takes to control himself to steal a look at his face. His full lips are pulled into a smile as he turns to click something on his computer before he returns his attention to me. The intensity of his gaze paired with the good natured look on his face has me reeling. More than anything now, I feel the urge to do whatever it takes to see that smile as much as I can. The previous night doesn't seem to have put a damper on things, and I like the kind way he's looking at me.

"It's a good thing you're not an actress. That was a terrible performance." He motions for me to sit in one of the chairs in front of his desk.

I walk in slowly, pushing the door closed behind me.

"How are your hands and your knee today?" He stands and walks to the shelves pushed against one wall. He pours two cups of coffee and hands one to me.

"It's okay today. My hand is a little sore, but nothing I can't handle." I set my purse down under my chair before taking a big drink of the dark rich coffee.

Nathan takes a sip of his coffee, "How was your morning?"

I look absently out the window behind him, feeling the warmth of the coffee in my fingers. "Oh, you know, pretty much spent all morning on my knees."

Nathan practically chokes and coffee comes spraying back out from between his lips. "Excuse me?"

Nathan tries to control his facial expression, and all of a sudden my words register in my brain. Horror rises up in my throat, and I can feel it spread across my entire body.

"Oh, god. I didn't mean like that! I mean…Shit. I mean I was puking."

Nathan's face is red. I can see his pulse in his neck as he regains composure. "I'm sorry you had a rough morning." His voice cracks on the word *'morning'* and I want to die.

I want to crawl in a hole and never come back out.

We sit in silence. All I can hear is the beat of my own heart as I sip my coffee and try really hard to not make eye contact with Nathan. After who knows how long, he clears his throat and I pull my eyes away from my cup.

I take a breath. "So, the woman at admissions said there was nothing available currently with the school office. She said I should try here."

He nods. "That folder is your resume?"

I pull the few papers out of the folder and slide them across his desk. He skims his eyes over the papers, a little piece of his hair falling forward onto his forehead. I again have the urge to reach out and touch it, but I force myself farther into the cushion of my chair, trying to look around the room instead of staring stupidly at him. We sit in silence for what seems like an eternity, and I can't help but admire the way his face looks. The angles of his jaw, and his dark lashes. His eyebrows dip ever so slightly together as he reads, and when his eyes meet mine again, I resist the urge to squirm.

"Well, honestly, I haven't had a single other person in today, and your resume makes you seem more competent than any college student who may have applied, so if you want the job, you're hired. It's only part time, a few hours a day, usually in the mornings. Mostly you'll be putting books back on shelves and helping students find what they need. Can you manage?"

The last sentence seemed uncalled for, and I don't know why, but suddenly realizing I will be working with Nathan makes me feel all kinds of feelings in my stomach that I don't have time to unpack right now.

I surprise myself a little when my words come out borderline enthusiastic. "Sure, that sounds great! When can I start?"

"Well, I can show you around now if you want, and you can start tomorrow morning." He stands and walks easily toward the door of the office, pulling it open.

I realize he's holding it open for me, and I almost stumble over myself in an attempt to not make him wait.

As he steps behind me, pulling the door closed behind him, I am greeted with a sideways glance from the blonde receptionist, who earlier was reading Alice's Adventures in Wonderland.

"This is Amber," he says, walking up to her desk.

"You'll work with her or me over the next few days as you get used to the way things work here."

Amber looks up from her phone and smiles at me. Her reading glasses are pushed up on her head, holding her hair back away from her face.

"Hey, nice to meet you!" hHer voice is sweet and quiet. "Nathan, do you want me to show her around?"

"No, it's okay. I'll take her on the tour." He turns away and heads toward the stairs that spiral all the way down to the first floor.

Amber's eyes dart between me and him briefly, and something like mild confusion casts a momentary shadow across her face before she turns back to her phone.

I have to hurry to catch up to him where he is waiting by the top of the staircase that leads down. As we spiral down the stairs to the first floor, he slows at the bottom, matching my pace, and we turn toward the back of the library. He leisurely points out where books are returned, and where I can scan them back into the computer system. He shows me how to stack carts so they're easy to unload back onto the shelves, and then he grabs a cart and starts pushing it back toward the elevator. I follow him, taking in the toned muscles of his back that show through his fitted shirt. When he turns to look at me, warmth creeps up my neck because I can tell he caught me staring.

Something hot flashes in his eyes for a moment, and it sends a small shiver down my back. But this time, rather than feeling like backing away, I have to fight the urge not to step closer. The elevator door opens and I follow him on. Between the cart, me, and him, there is very little room left in the elevator.

As the doors close behind me, he turns to face me. I catch the scent of his cologne, and my stomach flutters. His eyes study me. He seems to be taking all of me in. I feel his gaze drag over me almost as if there is physical contact, and I cannot control the rush of heat to my face when I think I catch his eyes lingering on my mouth a second longer than the rest of me. I am overwhelmed by how close our bodies are in that moment, and I am hyper-aware of every inch of him. I can almost feel the heat off of his skin, and my stomach is doing complete back-flips.

"Are we gonna get off the elevator? Or just stand here all day?"

All of the butterflies in my stomach plummet to their deaths in my feet. I realize the door has opened behind me and I'm just standing there, stupid.

Turn, walk out. Breathe. In, out. In, out. Don't be an idiot, Catherine.

I take the first book off of the cart, and look at it. It's a book of poems by Max Ehrmann. I've always been a fan of poetry. Marcus never understood the appeal, but nonetheless, it has always been one of the small pleasures in my life. I flip through the book, looking for my favorite poem.

I find it in the middle of the book and skim the words on

the page. I remember at one point in my life finding comfort in those words, but then I grew up, and that comfort faded away.

Nathan's voice is soft in my ear. "*Therefore, be at peace with God, whatever you conceive Him to be, and whatever your labors and aspirations, in the noisy confusion of life, keep peace in your soul.*"

Nathan's body is mere inches away from mine, and my mind goes fuzzy momentarily from the feel of his breath on my neck. Goosebumps prick their way down my arms and legs reviving the butterflies that had died only a few minutes earlier.

"*With all its sham, drudgery, and broken dreams, it is still a beautiful world. Be cheerful. Strive to be happy.*" I finish the poem, realizing how breathless my words sound.

At that moment, I'm absolutely sure he can hear the sound of my pulse racing through my body. But just like that, the moment is gone, and he steps around the cart to grab another book and put it on the shelf to his left.

"'*Desiderata.*' I have always loved that poem," he says softly.

I catch my breath and look for where this book goes on the shelf. I step to the left as well, studying the rows of poetry books in front of me. My mind is still fuzzy, and I'm looking for the space where the book goes when he steps up to me again, his arm reaching around me, gently brushing mine as he points to a space between two other books. Electricity courses through me, starting at the point where his arm touched mine and my legs feel wobbly. I hope he can't tell when I step forward quickly to place the book where he pointed.

When I turn to face him, our eyes meet again for a brief moment, and I wonder if the glint of warmth I see in his gaze means he just felt the pull of the electricity like I did.

"Is 8:00 tomorrow morning okay to start?" He doesn't break eye contact, and I feel frozen again under his look.

I nod. Normally I never have a problem filling silence, but for some reason today, I cannot seem to find a way to speak.

"I'll be here," I manage to squeak out.

His mouth turns upwards slightly in a gentle smile. "Okay, dress is casual, just don't show up in PJs or anything skanky."

"But those are my two favorites!" I protest sarcastically, my confidence renewing slowly.

He laughs like he laughed before in his office, and I can't help but smile. The sound bounces off of the walls, making the whole library feel warmer.

"I'll see you in the morning," he says, turning back to the cart full of books.

I realize that is my cue to go, and I turn to find the stairs and head out of the building. I'm full of so many thoughts and emotions that I need to sort through before I show up in the morning to start my new job.

Chapter Nine

"Where were you?"

My head snaps up as I walk into my small bedroom to see Marcus sitting on my bed. His eyes rip over me, a look of disgust turning the corners of his mouth as he surveys my knee length dress and heels.

The contentment I felt moments ago after spending an evening with my friends instantly falls away.

"Out with friends. I told you I was going to dinner with a few people tonight." I sit in the chair in the corner of the room to slide off my low wedges.

It's September in Georgia and still an impossibly hot evening. My skin feels sticky after walking home from the bar right down the road from my house.

"I came over to surprise you with a movie night. I didn't realize you were going to be gone so long." Marcus seems unusually agitated.

"We decided to go for a few drinks after dinner. I didn't know you were coming or I would have said no." I set my shoes in my small closet and turn to face him.

He's no longer sitting but standing next to my bed, his eyes gleaming with more than irritation. "WHO exactly did you go with?"

I can tell he's trying to control himself. His voice rumbles from his chest, causing my heart to beat a little quicker.

"Uh, Lacey, Tanya, Jeff, and Brice. They're just friends from college."

In the next instant, Marcus's gaze is white hot. I feel as though my skin is catching fire under the fumes of his rage. I have never seen him act like this. I don't understand what's happening. "Marcus, what's wrong?"

"You didn't tell me there would be men at this dinner. Since when do you have dinner with other men without me?" He spits out the last few words like they leave a sour taste in his mouth.

"They're just friends, Marcus. It's not a big deal." I feel my own irritation rising in my chest. I grab a towel and walk toward my bathroom to shower this now shitty night off my body. As I open the door to turn the water on, Marcus's big muscular arms wrap around me, pinning my arms at my side and knocking the breath right out of my lungs.

"We were 'just friends' once, too, Kitty," he hisses into my ear. His voice is low and filled with rage. His arms dig into my chest, sending pain through my ribs. "Don't be ignorant and pretend like I don't see the way men look at you. And don't ever turn your back on me when we are having a conversation again. I fucking HATE it."

His grip softens around me until it's just his hands resting on my arms. He presses a kiss onto my shoulder, and then against my neck right under my ear.

The normally intimate action sends shivers down my spine in a way that makes my stomach lurch. Fear and anger fight inside of my chest. He rubs my arms slowly where he just gripped me so hard. There still doesn't seem to be enough oxygen in the room, and I close my eyes against the unsettled feeling that is unfurling beneath his hands and spreading through my body.

"I'm sorry. I didn't mean to yell. I'm just so afraid to lose you. You have no idea what you do to me." He kisses me again, and I feel his warm breath snake across my cheek and shoulder. One of his hands settles on my hip, and the other around my midsection, and he pulls my back to his front gently in an almost hug. He rests his chin against my shoulder and inhales deeply.

I try to will my body to relax against him, but it betrays me, and stays rigid against his touch.

After a moment, he plants another soft kiss on my cheek and then lightly steps around me to turn on the shower. "You take a shower, and I'll go find a movie. It's Friday, we can still have our movie night a little late."

I don't breathe again until he closes the door behind me. My hands shake as I slowly remove my clothes, trying to understand what just happened. I step into the shower, steading my breath, and only when the hot water *runs over my body do I find the willpower to relax.*

§

I startle awake, covered in sweat, I roll over and check my phone. Three missed calls, all from Marcus. Chills run down my back. I can't escape from him even in my dreams. I have a half hour to get ready. I must've slept through my alarm. I flop my body upwards and command it to get moving. I drag my feet over to the shopping bags of clothes I bought the other day. I just don't have the willpower or time to put them away right now.

I pull out a red knit sweater with black stripes and a pair of jeans. I pop my head through the neck of the sweater, birthing both a new day and some bed head. I tug the jeans over my legs knowing I need to hurry but don't have the energy to. I hate the way I feel. It's frustrating.

Do I even have the strength to head up the steps?

The smell of fresh coffee is coming from the kitchen upstairs. Now that's something I can move towards.

I drag myself up the steps to a familiar figure in a blue bathrobe. Charles's gray hair is messy and his house slippers tattered. The tall, slim man turns to me, flashing his classic smile and his bright blue eyes.

"Good morning, Love! I made a pot of coffee for you." His smooth, subtle British accent makes me feel at home.

"Good morning, Charles! Pour me a cup before I fall over from exhaustion." I flash a big smile. This house never feels complete without Charles. I am not even sure if he has his own place, he's here so often. Growing up, I swore up and down that he was my uncle, but my mom often corrected me that he and Cici weren't married, just best friends. My dad told me when I was older that Charles lost his wife and baby in childbirth, and his little girl would've been around my age at this point.

"Here you go dear. Off to work? Are you going to be okay? Do you need me to drop you off? Cici is still asleep. I wouldn't mind," Charles offers. He hands me a travel mug covered in pictures of myself in elementary school. My mom gave it to Cici years ago. I'm shocked that she still has it.

"I'm not sure if I am comfortable taking this to my first day of the job. It screams a little conceited, don't you agree?"

He looks at the mug I'm holding and laughs. Charles is so sweet and kind. No matter what my mom said he is family.

He takes the mug from my hands "Sorry, Kitty, love, That's the coffee I put together for your aunt. Let me find a better cup for you, then I'll drop you at work." He turns to the cupboard.

"No, it's fine. I'll pick up a coffee from The Grove, I also planned on walking since I've gained a few pounds. The walk will be good for me." I smile wide at him.

"Well, a few stones never hurt anyone. I think you look just as beautiful as always." He puts his hand on my shoulder. "You were and are beautiful. Please don't let a scale determine that."

"I am glad I have you, but I need to run and you need to wake up sleeping beauty. She'll be pissed if you let her sleep in too long." I hold my hand on his for a moment and squeeze it and he lets go.

"Oh, bloody hell, you're right!" He gives me a big hug and runs out of the kitchen.

I head to the door to get started on my new day. Leaving now gives me a pretty good length of time to let the cold air really wake me up and help me wake up. Luckily Cici made a smart decision buying this house just within walking distance of the bar and campus. I think she assumed I'd live with her and go to college here. I wish I had.

I make it to campus and stop in front of The Grove, the campus coffee shop, trying to decide if coffee is worth being late. I check my phone. Too risky. I trek on towards the library. The snow is less like snow on the sidewalks and more like slush. I walk up to the large wooden doors and swing them open. It's like opening the doors on a new, better life.

Amber is there staring at her phone behind the desk.

I use all my energy I have left for a very pathetic "Good morning Amber."

She looks up and with a big untainted smile "Good morning Catherine! Is that what you prefer to be called or something else?"

I do not have the energy for a conversation. "Catherine is fine. Or Catie. Or Cat, Really, as long as it's not, like,

'Fred' I'm happy."

She laughs. "Fred? That's so silly."

This woman is too much energy for me today.

I feel a tap on my shoulder. Nathan's wearing a red flannel with jeans and black loafers. He clearly didn't shave this morning, his stubble making him look a little lumberjack-ish. I feel so tired, but being around him brings me a little energy. I feel my spirits lift incrementally as he smiles at me gently.

"Good morning, Catherine. I have some books on the third floor that need to be put back, so you can start there." He eyes me carefully for a moment.

I can't quite understand the look on his face, but it makes my heart flutter slightly.

"Yes, sir," I say exhaustedly, nonchalantly saluting as I walk towards the elevator. I hit the 'UP' button and the silver doors slowly ease open. I walk in and the doors close. I hit the number '3' on the button panel then close my burning eyes and lean my face against the cool metal doors. The elevator shakes and begins to creep upward.

The cold doors feel good until, Ping I almost faceplant onto the third floor, but stumble and catch myself. My cheeks burn red hot, and I look to make sure no one saw that. This floor is completely empty, probably since most of these books are historical or research books.

I walk slowly toward the cart full of books, slowly push-ing it down an isle and starting to set books on the shelf. They're mostly historical literature, but I recognize some from high school and college. I'm thankful for being sent to the third floor. There are no people around and it's quiet. I can be miserable in peace. I am uncomfortably aware of how empty my stomach feels, and my head feels like it weighs a hundred pounds.

I hear the elevator doors ping behind me, and turn to see Nathan looking at me intently as the doors close behind him. Something like sympathy or pity shows in his eyes and it makes me uncomfortable.

"Come on." He motions toward his office. "I'll make you some coffee."

"My hero." I give him the best smile I can muster given how shitty I feel and follow him into his office.

He closes the door behind me and goes to start the coffee pot. We sit in awkward silence for all of five minutes while the coffee brews.

He stands and pours two cups of coffee, handing one to me before returning to his seat behind his desk. "How are you feeling this morning?"

Nathan's casual swing at conversation throws me off a little. I wonder if he has morning coffee in his office with many of the people that work here.

"Just a little tired this morning." I woke up feeling un-settled after the dream from last night, and the feeling is proving difficult to shake.

He nods, sipping his coffee quietly.

"So, you signed up to help with the fundraiser. Were you planning to help with setup only, or during the fundraiser itself?"

"Uh, wherever you need me I guess." The coffee is taking effect, and I am starting to feel alive again.

"Can I get you a little more?" Nathan stands and reaches for my cup.

I hand it over, grateful for his kindness this morning. When he takes the mug from me, his fingers brush against mine, and his breath hitches. But his face remains unreadable, so I think maybe I imagine it. He tops off my cup and sits back down. "If you want to come help with setup tomorrow, that would be great. We never seem to have enough people for that."

"Sure, I can do that. What time should I be here?"

"I'm gonna walk over here about 3:00 tomorrow. Cici's house is on the way, I'll swing by and we can walk together?"

I know that it's a question, but the way he asks makes me feel like maybe he wants to walk with me more than he's letting on.

"Okay, that sounds good then. Thanks for the coffee, but I think I'll get back to work now."

He nods, turning to some papers on his desk and I see myself out. I don't know what to do about the conversation I just had with my boss. I still feel mortified about my accidental sex comment. I don't know why I said it like that. Why didn't I just say I was hungover? Or even that I spent the morning puking? I guess some part of me thought it was kind of funny, but I definitely didn't expect him to react the way he did. Sometimes my mouth speaks before my brain can compute what I'm saying. It's a real problem.

I work the rest of the morning by myself, taking books from the back room, loading them on to a cart, and putting them away in their respective areas. I don't see Nathan the rest of the morning, but once when I walk by his office, it sounds like he is on the phone with a caterer about tomorrow.

When I run out of books to put away, I decide instead of finding Nathan, I'll see if Amber is still here. I find her sitting at the front desk by the main door with a laptop open in front of her. She looks up at me through her mascara-covered lashes and then holds a finger up, signaling to give her a minute. I clasp my hands behind my back and wait patiently for her to finish what she's reading.

When she closes her laptop and turns to smile at me, I find myself smiling back. After putting a few hours between me now and my bad dream-hangover this morning, I am ready to have a conversation.

"The books are done. Is there anything else for me to do?"

"You can come sit and keep me company!" she says cheerfully, patting the seat next to her behind the desk. "If anyone comes up with questions or a return, we help them. Other than that, we can just sit here and talk!"

"Okay, sounds good." I take the swivel seat next to her. She turns her seat toward me slightly and I follow suit. "So, uh, what do we do now?"

"To be honest, I just sit here. The last guy whom I worked with got an internship a couple weeks ago. He was super boring. All he ever talked about was his bug collection." She says in one breath then takes another big one. "So basically, anyone from entomology, archeology, thanatology—well, most of the studies that involve dead things—are super boring and ONLY talk about their dead stuff collections. Like, that's cool, but that can't be your whole personality. Like, I wanna be a literature professor, but I am not only gonna talk about books. That's not my whole life or dialogue. I hike and write, and I am super into coffee. I know it's a weird thing to be into, but coffee is so good! Like, I could drink coffee all day and I'll order weird coffee online to try." She takes another deep breath. "I also don't understand people who don't like coffee. You like coffee, don't you?"

I nod in fear as her tangent changes direction once again.

"Speaking of coffee, I go to The Grove often. Their coffee is meh, but I love Larry. He's so funny. Larry is the barista, but he works everywhere. If you meet him, don't bring up the arm. So, tell me about you." She leans forward slightly, taking a sip of coffee, leaning on the desk with one arm and uncrossing her legs.

I make a mental note—*Don't bring Amber coffee at work.* She seems to already have had way too much.

I smile as I answer her question. "Nothing really to tell. I'm really excited to be working with you, though. I noticed you were reading *Alice's Adventures in Wonderland*. I haven't read it myself, but I love the movies and the concept."

She perks up and I realize I may have made a mistake.

We spend the next two hours sitting behind the desk while Amber tells me about the in-and-out novelties of *Alice's Adventures in Wonderland*, looking through our phones, and scanning the few returns that students bring to us. It's easy, and I really enjoy her company. It's nice to not have to do any talking. Somewhere near the end of my shift, Nathan shows up carrying my purse.

"Hey, you forgot this in my office this morning." He hands it to me and smiles.

It's so genuine I feel my face heat. "Thank you."

"So, are you still good with tomorrow? Walking with me, that is?"

"Yeah, of course. What time was it?" I feel Amber's eyes on us, but I keep my attention on Nathan.

"Probably around 3:00…" he pauses. "Here, give me your number, and I'll text you when I'm on my way over to you."

He hands me his phone, and I type in my number. My fingers move mechanically, and I awkwardly hand his phone back to him.

"Thanks. I'll see you tomorrow."

I nod, unsure of how to feel about what just happened. It's not a big deal that he asked for my number. He has a perfectly valid reason. I mean, we also work together. It makes sense he would need it. I'm definitely overthinking it. Nathan disappears back up the stairs toward his office, and I start to pack up what little I had up on the desk and get ready to go.

"So, Nathan seems to really like you." Amber gives me a sideways look.

"What makes you say that?" I wrinkle my nose at her, unsure of what she means.

"I don't know, something in the way he looks at you." She looks casual.

I don't think she knows the turmoil her words stir up inside of me. I squirm, unsure of how to answer. But she's already opening her laptop back up. I try and push the feelings that are stirring back down into my guts.

"You'll be here tomorrow morning right?" she asks.

"Yep, I'll see you in the morning," I reply.

"See you then, Catherine." She smiles, and I feel myself smiling back. She may be one of the few people who has gotten a genuine smile from me since I've been home.

Chapter Ten

I get home from work a little before 1:00 the next day, and Cici is nowhere to be found. My morning was uneventful. When I got to work, Amber handed me a list of things to do and a cart of books before she skipped off to the front desk. Nathan was nowhere to be found.

I made myself busy, but by midmorning there was nothing left to do. Amber placed me at an information desk, and I spent the next two hours answering questions and showing college kids how to find the books or references they needed. But by noon, the library was close to empty and Amber told me I could leave if I wanted to since I was coming back that evening to help with the fundraiser.

I head to my room, and decide to shower. Working at the library definitely isn't hard work, but after walking there and back this morning in the cold, the warmth of the water is blissful. I also have time to dissect the few conversations I've had with Nathan over the last forty-eight hours. As the water runs over my back, I can't help but think about the way his body felt pressed against my back the other night when I was drunk. His strong hands steadying me while

I washed my hands. The way he lifted me so easily onto the counter. I've always been a bit of a bigger girl. I think *'Midsized'* is my middle name. I don't fit in with the skinny girls, and I'm not quite big enough, or curvy enough, to be considered fat. But the way Nathan carried me home the other night, he made me feel downright petite.

My face heats at the thought of him carrying me, more from embarrassment than anything else. I take my time washing my hair and conditioning. Then, when I get out I opt to blow dry my hair with a brush rather than my fingers, taking care to smooth the frizz away.

I don't know what I'm going to be doing. I just know I'm going to help set up for the fundraiser, and I'll probably sweat. But something about the way that Nathan looked at me when he said he would walk with me makes my stomach flip-flop. I don't know what's going on with me, but I can't help myself. I wonder if he feels what I feel. I remember the way his breath caught in his throat when he took my coffee cup from me the morning before. I swear I could see his pulse quicken by the base of his neck. The way his eyes caught mine this morning and he gave me an easy smile. His eyes trailed down my body slowly before he pulled his gaze away and walked into his office.

But maybe I'm imagining it all.

"Kitty! Are you home?" I hear my aunt's voice from the top of the stairs.

"Yeah!" I call back, hurrying to pull on a pair of maroon leggings and an old crewneck college sweater.

Cici walks into my room, lighting a joint and taking a long deep breath. She holds it out to me and I follow, taking a comparably smaller drag, feeling the thick smoke hit the back of my throat. For some reason, nerves have settled in my stomach over the last thirty minutes and I need to calm them at least a little if I plan to do anything productive the rest of the day.

"Where are you heading off to?" Cici lounges casually on my bed, resting her shoulders on my headboard, and setting an ashtray on one knee.

"To help set up for that fundraiser I told you about." I pause a breath before trying to casually add, "Nathan and I are walking over there together."

My aunt studies me as I walk back into the bathroom and throw some mascara on for good measure. "I saw you two leave the bar together the other night."

I walk back into my bedroom and perch on the edge of the armchair shoved in the corner of my room. "I had a little bit too much the other night. He was just making sure I got back here okay."

"That's weird," she knocks the ash into the tray before taking another drag. "I don't think he's ever walked someone out of my bar who wasn't his dad." She gives me a look, and the glint in her eyes makes me feel weird.

"He was just being nice. We are just friends."

"I never said you weren't. Just be careful, Kitty. His family is drama."

I have to fight the urge to roll my eyes at her. I am

about to ask what she means when my phone buzzes and I look down. It's an unknown number. For a moment my heart stutters and I'm afraid it's Marcus before I remember Nathan said he would text me.

Unknown:
I'll be out front of your Aunt's house in 5 minutes.

My heart does a little flutter. "I need to get my shoes on," I say absently. I send him a thumbs up emoji and then instantly kick myself.

That was stupid.

I walk to my closet and find a pair of black combat boots. I grab my socks from the dresser and throw them on.

As I'm pulling my boots up, I feel my aunt still staring.

"What's wrong?" I ask, pausing what I'm doing to look at her.

"Oh, nothing." She puts out the rest of her joint and lays it in the ashtray. "I just made some coffee. Want me to put some in a paper cup for you?"

"That would be great."

My pocket vibrates.

Trashy Ashy:
1 attachment

—pops up on the screen.

I slide my screen getting punched in the gut.

I thought you were over....

Underneath is a screenshot from her newsfeed showing a new post from Marcus of our engagement photo. He's on one knee, and I have my hands covering my mouth in excitement. The caption reads, *'One day soon!'* followed by ridiculous bride and groom emojis.

"Great..." I mumble under my breath and decide to just ignore Ashleigh's instigation. Cici sighs and walks out of my room. I stand alone for another second before running to the bathroom one more time to swipe some lip gloss on my lips, and I head upstairs.

§

I pull the front door closed behind me, and I am instantly met by the dark intense eyes that will someday probably be my downfall. Nathan is leaning against the passenger side door of an early 2000's blue Honda Civic. He would drive a major dad car. He finishes whatever he was typing on his phone and shoves it back in his coat pocket.

I clutch the paper cup in my hands and try for a smile that I hope doesn't look as awkward as I feel. He smiles back. It's easy and warm. I still can't wrap my mind around the change in his personality from the man I met a week ago. I wonder for a brief moment what his life outside of what I can see is really like.

"Hey." His eyes drop to my open coat, running down the front of my body. "I know I said we would walk, but I forgot I had a few boxes I needed to bring to the library." He finds my face again and something about the way he looks at me makes me feel exposed.

My face flushes and I can only imagine how silly I must look. I try not to squirm or fidget with my clothes under his eyes. I drop my eyes and take a sip of the coffee my aunt handed me when I came upstairs.

"What are you drinking?" He asks, pulling the passenger side door open for me.

He walks quickly to the driver's side door and gets in, starting the car. "Cinnamon-vanilla latte."

Ever since I started drinking coffee, Cici's cinnamon latte has always been my favorite. Before I catch my next words they're already out of my mouth. "You can try it if you want." I offer my cup to him, and without hesitation he takes it from me and takes a sip.

Something about the intimacy of sharing a drink causes butterflies to spark in my stomach. I feel my breath catch when he hands the cup back. He seems unphased, so I take another drink, trying desperately to catch the butterflies floating around my insides.

No big deal. I tell myself. *If this was another friend I wouldn't have batted an eye.*

His tongue runs along his bottom lip, and I am transfixed. He looks over at me and gives me a lopsided smile.

"What?"

"Your lip gloss is minty." His voice comes out deep and playful as his eyes rest on my mouth. This time he isn't shy. His gaze darkens around the edges as he looks over my face before meeting my eyes again. Nathan exhales deeply, emptying his lungs, and turns his attention back to the road in front of us.

We drive in silence the rest of the way to the campus. My pulse roars in my ears, every inch of my body aware of his closeness and the lust-filled way he looks at my mouth. The smell of his cologne fills my nose and sends shock-waves through my stomach and between my legs. I must be losing my mind. There is no reason for me to feel this unhinged just from sharing a drink.

After parking in the small employee lot behind the library and grabbing the few boxes Nathan has piled in his trunk, we head inside. We go through a side entrance of the library that takes us straight to a conference room where the fundraiser dinner and silent auction is going to take place tomorrow night. The room is bustling with activity as about twenty people run in different directions setting up tables and chairs. A few men are putting up a portable stage in the corner, and some other people are setting up what appears to be a soundboard next to it.

"Nate!" A woman calls, heading our direction. She's smiling widely. She's taller than I am, and middle-aged. Her dark black hair has a few grey streaks that frame her face, and her wide hips swing happily.

Nathan visibly stiffens as he is overwhelmed by a hug. "Hi, Mami."

Mom?

A teenage girl who could have been Nathan's younger twin follows closely behind the woman, She has one head-phone propped in her ear, and her hands are buried deep in the pockets of her sweater. She has the same dark eyes framed by dark lashes that I now can see come from his mother.

"How's my *hermanita*?" He says pinching his sister's nose affectionately.

She sticks her tongue out at him, but there's a glimmer of love that is unmistakable on her face.

"Where's Amaya?" He turns his attention back to his mom.

"She's with her friends," his mom says shortly, and some sort of understanding passes between them.

He nods, and looks at me. I feel awkward, like I'm eavesdropping on a conversation I shouldn't be hearing. "*Mami*, this is Catherine." His hand brushes my wrist when he says my name, as if encouraging me to step forward.

I follow his lead and extend my hand. I realize after I've done it how silly I must look. But she takes it anyway, seeming to overlook my awkwardness.

"Nice to meet you, Catherine. I'm Nellie. This is Nadia."

I wave timidly at Nadia, unsure of what else to do. "You look just like your brother."

She blushes a little and gives me a small smile.

"Looks like everyone has already gotten a lot done," Nathan says, studying the people bustling around the room.

"Yeah," his mom surveys the room with him. "I'm so proud of you, *gordito*." She says the word so affectionately, I don't understand Nathan's annoyance.

Just then Amber bounces over to us, throwing an arm around Nathan's waist in a casual hug.

"Hey guys!" Amber smiles warmly. "So the stage still needs to be set up and decorated, And I figured Cat could help me catalogue the silent auction pieces."

Her eyes are on me, but she still has her arm around Nathan, and something inside of me feels uneasy. I wonder what their history is. But as soon as I have the thoughts I backtrack on myself, I don't get to feel weird. Nothing is happening between Nathan and I, we are friends and I don't get to feel jealous or weird.

Amber and Nathan exchange a few more words, and then Nathan follows his mom and his sister away from us to where I'm assuming the stage will be set up.

"Come over here." Amber links her arm through mine in a gesture

"Okay, sounds good." We walk quietly over to a corner of the spacious conference room where there are auction pieces stacked into piles.

"So, tell me about you." She takes a stack of papers from the top of a box and hands it to me along with a marker. "I'll go through and find items, and when I find them you check them off on the list, then write the number on the note card along with the name of the item and set it aside."

"Sounds good." I flip absently through the pages of auction items, half reading, half trying to think of something to say back to Amber's initial question. "Uh, what do you want to know?"

She shrugs. "Are you from around here? Do you have family here? Why are you working at a library? Do you have any hobbies, or deep dark secrets?" She wiggles her eyebrows when she says *'secrets'* and I see a glimmer of playfulness in her eyes.

"Well, I grew up here, but I moved to Georgia my senior year of high school when my parents divorced."

"I'm sorry," she says, and for once I don't feel pitied telling someone my parents split. Her *'sorry'* seems more like a blanket of understanding rather than an apology for something she doesn't understand. "Did you move with your mom or your dad?"

"My dad. He got remarried not long after my parents got divorced, and his new wife's job took her down there. My dad is a cop, so he didn't have any trouble relocating somewhere else. My mom has been pretty checked out of my life for years. She moved, and went through the divorce process long distance."

"That sucks. Would you have gone with your mom if you could have?" She pauses and picks up a gift basket full of coffee samples and other things. "Coffee sample basket from The Grove."

I scroll down the list, checking the item off and writing a brief description in a note card.

"It was never an option," I say shortly. I haven't talked to anyone about my mom and my parents divorce since I told Marcus about it when we were dating. I don't know why I find it so easy to talk to Amber...something in her face. She feels open and receptive. So many people judge you so quickly. They make assumptions before you can even talk to them. But Amber seems unbiased. For the first time in a while, it feels like someone is listening to me without assuming what kind of person the details of my life make me.

"So, before your parents split, did you live around here?" She digs through a pile of what I assume are gift certificates and reciepts, throwing the question over her shoulder as she works. "I'm not trying to be nosy, I'm just curious about you. It's not often Nathan takes so much interest in someone. You must be awesome." She gives me some sort of knowing smile that I don't understand, and I make a mental note to ask her about what she means later.

"We lived about thirty minutes from here, but my aunt owns Cici's Pub. When my mom left, I spent most summers here after high school and during college until..." I pause. *Until Marcus decided he didn't like me spending so much time here.*

"Until what?"

"Life just got busy… My job… I was dating someone. You know." I shrug.

"So, Do you live with your aunt then? Why did you move back?"

I was running.

"Yeah, I live with her. I came back because…" I hesitate. I have no idea what to say to her about this. I still haven't really talked to anyone besides Cici about my break-up with Marcus, and I don't know if she will understand. "I came back because things were over with the guy I was dating. I needed somewhere to go to get a break."

I feel sick talking about everything. I still don't know how to tell people what happened. I just feel dirty.

She nods, understanding, filling her eyes. "When I was in college for my bachelor's degree, I was dating this guy. I thought we were going to get married." She studies another auction piece. "My sister and he were good friends for a long time, and I never thought anything of it. But they started to grow closer and closer. I was so busy with school I didn't notice. I wasn't present. Before I knew it, he was distant, and then he was leaving me for her."

Her eyes meet mine. I see so much sadness and regret in her eyes, I instantly feel for her. My heart seems to reach out of my chest, and I hope she sees how much I understand her pain.

"They got married last summer." She moves another box and starts rifling through it, organizing what looks like paintings and books inside.

"That really is horrible." I don't know what I can say to help. Nothing seems to sound good enough coming from me.

She gives me a dry smile and we work in mostly silence for a long while. She tells me the auction piece she is holding, I put a checkmark on the list and make a note card. But it doesn't feel uncomfortable. It's calm and warm. Both of us seem to be mourning something, and honestly it feels really good to not have to do it alone. Even though Amber still doesn't know everything, she seems to understand.

I take a few sips of my coffee, perching on the edge of one of the tables as Amber does a second run-through of the note cards, placing them on top of each item to make sure we didn't miss anything.

Nathan turns in our direction, striding easily across the room, his eyes locking on mine before slowly working their way down my body.

I almost do a double take, unsure of the way he's looking at me. He stops in front of me, slipping the coffee cup out of my fingers and taking two drinks. It's all I can do to make sure that my jaw doesn't hit the floor.

His lips part slightly, and I watch his tongue run along his bottom lip again. I wonder if he can still taste my lip gloss. His eyes haven't left mine the whole time. I chide myself again for finding something so inconsequential so absolutely unnerving.

Amber clears her throat and my neck just about snaps with how quickly I turn to look at her. She's eyeing us carefully, but if she thinks anything is odd about the interaction, she doesn't let it slip.

"All of the auction pieces are here and accounted for." She gives Nathan a smile.

"Awesome," Nathan says.

We all turn to look at the rest of the room. Everything's coming together nicely.

Nathan continues, "Once we get the table clothes, place settings, and center pieces on the tables, I think we will be done for the night. The sound crew just has to set some speakers up on the stage and then they said they'd put the decorations up there when they are done."

Amber and I both nod. Nathan hands my cup of coffee back and turns to head over to where his mother and sister are standing next to the stage.

"Why didn't you share any of your coffee with me?" Amber giggles and gives me a pointed look.

My face heats to an unnatural degree, and I turn back to look at him from across the room.

Nathan and his mom join up with us a few minutes later. His sister is standing back by the door with her nose buried in her phone. They say their goodbyes, and Nathan's mom hugs and kisses him sweetly.

Once they are out of the room, he turns to me. "It looks great here."

"Thanks. That didn't take as long as I thought it would.

I came with the full expectation for this to consume my night."

"Well, If you want to waste a little more time, we could go to dinner for a bit. My treat."

I flush. *Is he asking me out? Is this a date?* "Sure? I could really use a good burger and fries!"

He places his hand on my back and chills follow. "Then let's head out! I know the best joint."

Chapter Eleven

We sit awkwardly facing each other in the red booth that hasn't been cleaned since 1977. Nathan's eyeing me quietly, and I can't tell if he feels awkward too, or if it's just me.

I take a breath and decide to break the ice. "I used to come here all the time in high school. We came here after senior prom, and my date attempted to feel me up." My words cut harshly through the silence, and I immediately regret what I said. *What a weird way to start a conversation on a date-that's-not-really-a-date.*

"I'm a little jealous," Nathan chimes while staring straight into his menu. He flicks his gaze up to me for a moment, playfulness sparkling in his eyes.

S.O.S. What just happened? What is this exchange?

I turn bright pink and bury my face in the menu. So far this is the most awkward *date-that's-not-really-a-date* I've ever been on. Not that I've ever been fantastic at first dates, but this seems like an all new low for me, bringing up something that happened years ago in such an odd manner. I peep up over my menu, and instantly find his eyes. And just like that I'm locked in. Embarrassment floods my system. I quickly look back down at the menu. He is completely unreadable.

"So, what's your favorite thing here?" I ask.

"Usually, I just get a burger." He doesn't pick his eyes up from the menu. I wonder what he's thinking.

Thankfully at that moment we are interrupted by our server. "What can I get you two lovebirds tonight?"

My heart falls to my feet and I tear my eyes slowly from my menu to look up and see Larry standing in front of our table.

"Oh, Catherine, I didn't recognize you! How are you tonight princess?"

Nathan makes a sound that might be a stifled laugh. "Oh, and Nathan! Good to see you not scraping your dad off the bar floor for once!"

Whatever laugh Nathan was hiding before dies in his mouth. "Good to see you, too, Larry."

"So, anyway, drinks?" Larry is so blissfully unaware of how awkward this makes things.

"Coke for me," I say.

"Water with lemon for me," Nathan says, then looks in my direction.

Should I have ordered water too? It's been way too long since I've been on a date. A stupid drink should not make me this uncomfortable. Marcus always used to order water, he thought pop should be reserved for whiskey, and even that was rare.

Larry nods and walks back toward the kitchen. Larry is such a steady figure in this community, I should've expected him to be here. I remember many times that if Cici couldn't pick me up from school, Larry was there. He would pull up in his beat-up old station wagon, his one good arm—well, only arm—on the wheel and a big smile on his face.

"Is there multiple of him? I'd assume twins, but I think it would be a little outlandish for twins to have the same name and same missing limb," Nathan says in an annoyed but endearing way. Everyone has a Larry story. I wonder what Nathan's is.

"Cici says the military cloned him, he's just too useful not to." I smile. "He's like everyone's wacky uncle. I remember coming to Cici's after one of my parents' fights, and he was on the roof fixing some shingles. I have no idea how he made it up the ladder with all those tools. I was sure he was going to fall off each time he used the nail gun."

Nathan laughs, and I smile because it is such a wonderful sound.

He matches my story with his own. "Larry knows my coffee order every time I come into The Grove on campus. So much so that sometimes I come in and it's already finished and ready to go!"

"HE WORKS AT THE COFFEE SHOP, TOO?" I giggle. "Is there anywhere he's not employed!?"

"I don't work at the strip club!" I turn and Larry is gracefully balancing our drinks on a tray. "I bet I could though, I look good with tassels."

All three of us laugh. God bless Larry.

"Do you guys know what you want?" Larry asks, but I don't have an answer.

"I'll have a cheeseburger, mustard, pickles, hold the onions and an order of fries." Nathan clearly knows his order by heart.

I don't have a clue. "Surprise me, Larry. I know I want a burger and fries, but that's it. I'm too hungry at this point to make a choice!" I laugh.

"I got you, princess." Larry begins his stride back to the kitchen.

Nathan looks at me and gives a big smile.

Ice successfully broken, thanks to Larry.

Nathan's dark eyes have me mesmerized when he asks "So tell me about you. I know Cici's your aunt and that you have great taste in poetry, but that's pretty much it. You must have parents? What about siblings?"

I feel myself cringe, I hate answering that question. It's such a normal question that everyone asks, but it sucks for me. I can tell he sees my discomfort.

"I'm sorry. We don't have to talk about anything you don't want to." Regret clouds his eyes.

"No, honestly, it's fine. I guess no one really ever asks about my family at all. They're a bit complicated. My parents divorced when I was in high school. My mom was never into the mom thing and went off to do other stuff. My dad remarried shortly after and we moved to Georgia for my step-mom's job. And I have a five-year-old little sister, but there's not much of a relationship there." I try to find a good way to redirect the conversation to him. "What about your family?"

He becomes uncomfortable as well, but his eyes don't waver from mine as he speaks. "Maybe family wasn't the best place to start." He laughs uncomfortably. "You met my mom and one of the six sisters."

"SIX!" I gasp.

"Yep, six. My dad is a retired cop, and my mom has been a stay-at-home mother for as long as I can remember. I'm the oldest, and my youngest sister, Amaya, is seven, so my mom has had her hands full for years. That's about it, though." He pauses, taking a long drink of his water. "If you're officially from Georgia now, what brings you back here?"

Yikes! How to handle this? Oh, I was engaged, broke it off a month before the wedding, and ran away with no word.

"Well, I grew up around here, but Georgia is honestly too hot, and I wanted a fresh start. Atlanta is not as exciting as a one-armed superman, or Cici's bar during college football. Besides, Cici is really the only other family I have." I take a long drink of my coke. This is the most I've talked about my family in years. Between talking to Amber yesterday and Nathan today, I'm not used to feeling this exposed. "So, why do you work at a college library?"

"I like books." He says shortly, stirring the lemon around in his glass.

"No shit?" I exclaim. There's a mix of sarcasm and fake surprise in my voice.

Nathan's deep laugh brings shivers down my spine. " I mean, it's a nice job. The library is quiet and steady."

Larry returns, balancing the food on his tray. "One mustard pickle burger with fries and one *'The Works'* burger with Cajun fries."

I can't help but grin. Larry knows me and my love of spice too well.

We say our *'thank you's*, and Larry bows and heads off to serve the one other table that has people. I also know Larry brought me the biggest burger to mess with me. There is no way I can eat this gracefully.

Nathan starts eating slowly, waiting to see what I do with my massive burger. He somehow manages to do so very professionally, each bite controlled and calculated. How is this guy so put together even when eating a burger?

I look at my burger. "I'll be honest, I have no idea how I'm going to eat this without making a mess."

"Don't worry. I'll clean you up."

I look at him, wide eyed. He is so forward. I like that, though. I'm tired of people playing games. I laugh, enjoying the flirty banter he's been throwing at me all night. "Promise?"

He turns beet red. I can tell it caught him off guard that

I just rolled with it. I take a big bite. Are we seriously flirting like this over burgers?

I look at my phone as we eat. So much time has elapsed but it feels like only a few minutes.

Larry brings the bill, hands it to Nathan, winks at me, and walks away. *Oh, no…how much did he hear, and what will he report back to my aunt?*

We pay and Nathan holds the door for me as we head out.

I slide my hand into his. "My hand is a little cold." I feel like an awkward teenager, trying to find any type of way to make contact with him, but after our afternoon together, I just want to know what it feels like to touch him for a moment.

I sneak a look up at him through my lashes, but he is looking straight ahead to where his car is parked just up the street slightly. But his fingers lace perfectly through mine, and he holds on tight, causing my heart to leap around in my chest.

He pulls his phone from his pocket and frowns at the screen.

"What's wrong?" I ask carefully, hoping it's nothing serious.

"My mom said dad called her three times, but every time she answered, he didn't say anything." He lets go of my hand, and I am uncomfortably aware of how cold I feel when the physical contact is broken. He sends a quick text back and sighs. "It's still early, but I think I need to swing by the bar and see if he's okay."

"Alright," I say quietly. "I guess we should go then."

He studies me for a moment, then stops walking and grabs my hand so that I stop as well. He pulls me back to face him, so that our bodies are mere inches apart. "I had a good time tonight."

I hope I'm not blushing as much as I feel like I am. "Me, too."

He pauses for a moment as if he's thinking about something. Then, in a heartbeat, he closes the rest of the distance between us, resting his free hand on the small of my back.

I feel as though the oxygen has been pulled from my lungs as I stare up at him. His eyes haven't left my face, his gaze wanders slowly over me, and then settles on my mouth. My throat feels dry and constricted, but I don't dare to move.

Just then the moment is shattered by the sound of Nathan's phone ringing. He huffs, and steps back.

"Hey Mami," he pauses. "Yes, I'm on my way… okay… okay. Sure, I can do that." He runs his fingers through his hair as he shoves his phone back in his pocket.

"Are you okay?" It feels like a silly question, since it's very obvious on his face that he isn't.

He sighs. "Mom is just worried about dad. I need to go get him."

"Well, let's stop wasting time, then." I turn and head toward his car.

"I can drop you at your aunt's house first," he says. We reach his car, and he opens the door for me.

"And miss all the fun? I don't think so!" I try to sound lighthearted, hoping to boost his mood a little.

"Catherine," he starts quietly. "Tonight has been great, but you don't need to come with me. I can't predict how he's going to be."

"If you're worried I'm going to get freaked out, don't. I can handle it." The determination in my voice surprises me. I don't know why I'm fighting this, It's none of my business, and I know it. "I'll still like you." The words slip out before I can stop them.

He looks at me momentarily before starting the car. "Alright, don't say I didn't warn you."

Chapter Twelve

We pull up to Cici's bar a few minutes later.

"Well, here we are. So here's the plan—if I come back out without dad, he's not here and we have to go hunting at the two other bars in town. If he is here, the best case scenario is he is not super drunk and just butt-dialed mom. Worst case scenario… Well, just be ready to open the car door and lock it after I toss him in."

I can see how visibly embarrassed Nathan is. My heart breaks for him. "Whatever you need, I've got your back."

Nathan takes a deep breath and looks down in shame. "He wasn't always this way, I wish…" He sighs. "Alright I'll be back."

I watch him open the door and head into the bar. I feel anxiety as the minutes pass by. I wonder what's going on. I haven't experienced Nathan's dad sober or at all really. His mom seems extremely nice, so he can't be all that bad.

"*AY! AY! BE AMABLE, GORDITO!*"

I turn and Nathan has his father's arm pinned behind his back. I hop out of the car and do as I was told and open the back door.

"*I WOULD BE GENTLE, PAPI, IF YOU DIDN'T TRY TO BOOK IT OUT THE BACK DOOR WHEN YOU SAW ME!*" Nathan yells back to his father.

"*CAROLINA, CHICA, TELL GORDITO TO GET THE FUCK OFF!*" Nathan's father is visibly trying to slide out of his arms. The slur of his words makes me uncomfortable.

I try not to focus too much on the name Nathan's father used. *Carolina.* I wonder who he's talking about. Maybe one of Nathan's sisters.

"*PAPI, THIS WILL BE EASIER IF YOU STOP FIGHT-ING! CHARLES WAS ABOUT TO CALL MAMI AGAIN CAUSE YOU STARTED THROWING SHIT AT THE TV. I CAN'T FUCKING AFFORD TO BUY CICI A NEW ONE AGAIN!*" Nathan essentially tosses his father in the car. He turns to me and takes a moment to calm himself, mussing his hair and rubbing his face. "Worst case scenario it is then. Can you lock the doors until I get in? Dad's too drunk to unlock the doors from the inside."

I hop in and lock the doors. Nathan pulls out his phone and makes a call. His back is to me, but I can tell he's agitated.

Nathan's dad is drunkenly singing loudly, "*Para bailar la bamba ,Para bailar la bamba se necesita una poca de gracia, Una poca de gracia pa' mi pa' ti y arriba y arriba.*" *At least he can carry a tune?* "Ay, Carolina, did your mama ever sing *'La Bamba'* with ya? To dance the bamba, to dance the bamba you need a little grace!"

Nathan hops in, turns to his father, and yells

"*ENOUGH!*"

His father stops and turns to me. He squints real hard.

"Ay, you ain't Carolina! Who the fuck are you, *gringa*?" He hisses at me.

Nathan sighs. "*Papi*, this is my friend Catherine. Catherine, this is my dad, Oscar."

Oscar gets wide-eyed and looks at Nathan. "Does Carolina know about your little friend, *gordito*?" He smirks a little at his son, and I can feel a deep blush spreading across my chest.

Nathan starts up the car. "I would assume not since Carolina and I have been broken up for TWO years." He is clearly frustrated about his ex being brought up. I can see the white of his knuckles from grabbing the steering wheel so tight. He sighs heavily, turning down a side road to head back to his house.

"Oh, yeah, I forgot she got bored of you. I'm so sorry, *gordito*." Oscar starts sniffling. "I'm so sorry. It's not fair. You thought she was the one." Sniffle. "I love you so much. It'd be like *Mami* leaving me." He groans "NATHAN, WHAT IF MAMI LEAVES MEEEEE!?"

Nathan rolls his eyes and smirks at me. He mouths something that looks like '*I'm sorry*' before responding to his father. "Mami isn't going to leave you."

I offer the best reassuring smile that I can, trying to keep myself from analyzing everything this drunk old man is saying. I wanted to see into Nathan's life a bit, and I am not going to let myself step back because of this. I remind myself that this changes nothing about the nice dinner we just had.

"SHE IS! NELLIE! *MI AMORE*! I'M SORRY! SHE'S GOING TO LEAVE ME LIKE CAROLINA LEFT YOU! I'M AN OLD, FAT DRUNK AND SHE *ES MUY HERMOSA!*" Oscar is sobbing in the back of the car at this point.

"No, she's not gonna leave you, *Papi*." Nathan reassures his father. His voice is quiet and void of emotion, as if he's practiced these lines before.

Oscar pops his head between our seats "Listen, listen *chicos*. Don't ever, ever let them get in your way. You love how you wanna love, and when you find it, grasp it and don't ever let go. You, *chica*, what's your name again?"

I smirk since Nathan already told him, but he's so drunk he can't remember "It's Catherine."

"I hate it. I'm gonna call you *Catarina* because of your *rojo* hair. Don't you dare break my sweet *gordito's* heart. THAT BITCH CAROLINA HURT HIM! YOU... though... I can sense you have a good heart. Nathan, don't let her go. I would never let Nellie go, BUT SHE'S GONNA LEAVE MEEE!" He begins to sob again and throws himself back into the seat dramatically.

"NELLIE!" he shouts, then he slurs, "*Me amore.*" And then whispers, "Don't goooo…."

Then all I hear is snoring. I look at Nathan. His expression is stoic as he stares straight ahead. We ride in silence for a few minutes. I want to give him plenty of space if he doesn't want to talk, but I have so many questions. I turn in my seat, leaning against the car door so that I can look at Nathan. He peers at me out of the corner of his eye, but still says nothing. Oscar's snoring takes up all the space in the car, bouncing off the windows.

Nathan sighs and rests his hand on my knee in such a soft way I feel my heart become a puddle in my chest. I place my hand over his, rubbing my thumb gently along his knuckles. After a moment, his shoulders relax, and he exhales quietly.

"So," I say casually. "That was exciting."

Nathan releases a puff of air in what may have been an attempt to laugh, but it falls flat in the space between us. "There is rarely a dull moment when my family is involved."

I think the comment was meant to be light hearted, but it lands heavily on the mood, and I wonder just how long Nathan has had to deal with this.

As if he can read my mind, he continues, "You know, my dad wasn't always like this."

He turns his hand palm upward, and I rest my palm against his. The warmth of his fingers around mine is comforting, and I take a moment to appreciate the strength he exudes both physically and, now that I've met his dad, emotionally as well.

"What was he like before?" I hope my question doesn't push too far.

"He was a cop. He worked here in town, but it wasn't enough to support our family. So we moved and he worked in Philly after my younger sister Mariposa was born. Then some things happened, then my mom and him moved us all back here." Nathan sighs deeply, and looks like he's contemplating his next words. "I don't really know when things changed, exactly. He's a great dad. My childhood was happy and he was present. Then something happened shortly after I got my bachelor's and everything changed. He left the BGPD and has never been the same since."

"My dad was a cop here in town as well for a long time before we moved." I don't know what else to say. I want to ask more questions, dig deeper into understanding him, but I can't. This is not the time or place. I squeeze his hand, unsure of how to say more, or even what to say.

We drive in silence the rest of the way back to his house. Every few minutes Nathan would look at me and offer a small smile or squeeze my hand gently. When we pull up the drive of his family's brick farmhouse, Nellie, and another woman are standing on the porch. Nathan's mom has a cigarette between her fingers, and a big fluffy blue housecoat draped over her shoulders.

Nathan parks and steps out of the car. I wait a moment and then step out cautiously. Nellie and the other woman have made their way down toward us and are now standing quietly in front of the car. I keep my eyes fixed on Nathan, unsure of what to do next.

"Dad's in the back." Nathan speaks to his mom quietly. Nellie nods and walks around to the driver's side back door and opens it carefully, speaking to Oscar in hushed Spanish, coaxing him out of his sleep.

Nathan looks at me quickly, offering a sad smile before walking over to his mother to help Oscar up.

"Oh Nellie," Oscar mumbles. "*Lo he vuelto a hacer*... I did it again."

Nellie flashes him a sad smile and takes his hand. "*Está bien, mi amor*. Let's go inside and get you a shower?"

Between Nellie and the other woman, Oscar is ushered inside. Now it is just Nathan and me.

Nathan shoves his hands in his pockets, still watching his family retreating into the house.

For the first time tonight, the depth of my invasion hits me, and I feel terribly out of place. "I think I'm going to head home." I say, offering a weak smile.

"I can take you." Nathan starts toward me, but I take a step back, hoping the next few words come out as sincerely as I feel. "I think you have your hands full, I'll see you at work tomorrow. Go be with your family."

I try smiling again, hoping it doesn't give away how many things I'm feeling right now.

A range of emotions flicker in his eyes.

"Nathan, it's okay. I can find my way." I allow myself to reach out and touch his forearm reassuringly. "I'll see you in the morning."

Before I can hear his reply, I smile one last time and turn to walk back toward my aunt's house. Everything about this man pulls me in, even as his father drunkenly cried in the back seat of his car, I wanted more time. And I think I need to take a serious look at myself at the moment and tread carefully. This man does not need my drama on top of his own.

Chapter Thirteen

As I'm walking up to the porch of my aunt's house, my phone starts to ring. Cici must be calling to ask for something or see if I made it home okay. I pull my phone out of my pocket and hit the green button as I put the phone to my ear.

"Hey, what's up?" I say, pulling my keys out of my purse to unlock the door.

"Catherine?"

I drop my keys, and my blood turns cold inside of my veins. Every good feeling I've had tonight dies in my chest.

"Catherine?" My name sounds slurred coming from his mouth.

"Marcus? What are you doing calling me?" I fumble for my keys, looking around before unlocking the door and stepping into Cici's house. I bolt the door behind me and stand in almost total darkness. The light over the stove in the kitchen casts the smallest bit of eerie light down the hallway.

"Catherine." He says my name for the third time. I feel sick. "Fuck, I've been trying to reach you for weeks."

I hear him exhale unsteadily into the phone, and something sounds like glass clatters in the background.

"Have you been drinking?" I hear more glass clatter on his end, and a mumbled string of curses that I can't quite make out.

"Kitty, I miss you. I need you to come back." His voice sounds childish, and it causes something inside of me to stir.

Annoyance courses through me, and I can't seem to string words together around the swirl of emotions that are pushing their way through my blood, bringing a new kind of cold into my body.

"Marcus," I start slowly, measuring my voice. "You cannot just call me out of nowhere."

"I need you… to come home," he says slowly, matching my tone.

"Atlanta is not my home anymore." I'm surprised when the words leave my mouth.

I hear glass shatter in the background of the call.

"Fuck!" he yells. "YOU CANNOT DO THIS TO ME!"

"Marcus…" I say, my voice unsure.

"No, no. This cannot be happening. You were just going on a vacation. YOU ARE COMING BACK!" He sounds deranged and frantic, and something about it causes a surge of strength to run through me.

"No, Marcus. I am done. I am not coming back. I can't do this anymore. It's over." The words bounce around the hallway as I straighten my shoulders. "I don't want to marry you. I don't want to work through it anymore. Nothing has changed between us, but I am changing. This is not the life I want anymore."

Marcus is quiet, and I pull the phone away from my ear to see if the call was ended or not.

"This is not over, Kitty," he spits the words drunkenly across the phone, but unlike before, he cannot control me anymore.

I refuse to be pulled back in.

"Yes Marcus, it is." This time I hang up before he can say anything else. I drop my arms to my sides, feeling the adrenaline leave my body, and suddenly I am exhausted.

I walk to the bathroom and splash water on my face, staring at myself in the mirror. A single silent tear runs from my eye and splashes down onto the counter.

§

"You look stunning tonight." Marcus leans on his elbows, and smiles shyly across the table at me.

My cheeks flush slightly at his compliment. I've been crushing on this man from work for the last few weeks. He's tall, handsome, and interesting. I've made every excuse in the book to talk to him or end up beside him for the last few weeks, changing around my work schedule, and even working a little extra in hopes of having a conversation with him.

Then last week he asked me on a date and I couldn't

say 'yes' fast enough. My heart beats a little faster remembering the way he had placed his hand over mine that evening, making me stop what I was writing to look at him. When his words registered in my brain, I stared at him for a minute without answering, trying to figure out if he was serious or not. When I finally agreed, he warmly smiled and went back to what he was doing, but I could no longer focus on my work.

"So," I say, realizing I still hadn't answered him yet. "What do you do in your free time when you aren't at work?"

Marcus looks at his drink thoughtfully. "I don't do much besides work right now, but I do like nice cars." He leans back in his chair casually. "My dad has a collection of them, and sometimes on weekends we will drive around to car shows and look at what's for sale. He really likes vintage muscle."

"That's cool. When I was a kid, my dream car was a 1963 Corvette Stingray convertible in yellow. I saw one once at a car show with my dad and fell in love."

He chuckles. "My dad has a 1969 Stingray in white, I know it's not quite the same, but I could take you over there sometime and show you. I bet he would even let us drive it."

Our food arrives moments later and we talk for the next two hours about cars and work among other hobbies we shared an interest in. By the time he pays the bill I am content. With a full belly and good conversation still min-

gling around us, we head for the door. The drive back to my dorm is relatively quiet, and I enjoy the comfortable silence between us.

When we arrive back to campus, he walks me to my building's front door, holding my hand and talking about all of the things he has to do at work before the next week is over. I listen quietly, enjoying his confident air in conversation and the way he led us through the evening.

We stop a few feet from the door, and he pulls me gracefully against his chest. Butterflies spring to life at the feel of his hands resting gently on my lower back.

"I had a really good night with you." He says quietly. His blue eyes search my face as if seeking reassurance for the events of the evening.

"Me, too." My brain feels fogged over and I can't seem to manage any more words than that. I hope that the sincerity in my voice conveys all of the things I'm feeling after our night together.

He stands for another moment, studying me before he slowly leans forward. I close the rest of the distance, and our lips connect. He's sweet and gentle, not overly demanding, nor does he push farther than a kiss.

When he pulls back to study my face I can't help but smile.

"So, can I take you out again?" he asks almost sheepishly. His uncertainty is just as charming as his confidence.

§

Ping.

I pull out my phone and look down at it.

Nathan:

Sorry tonight didn't end quite as planned.

I stare at his text, butterflies pushing through the swirl of emotions I feel after my phone call with Marcus. Before I can think of a reply, the three little bubbles pop up to signal he is typing again.

Nathan:

I had a good night with you. Thanks for going to dinner with me.

Every reply I can think of sounds lame, so I stare blankly at my phone. After a few moments, I type back a simple message thanking him for tonight and saying I had a good time, too. I avoid using an emoji this time and close my phone.

I strip down and turn on the shower. Tonight has been very eventful, and after my phone call with Marcus, I'm left feeling drained and gross. Right as I am about to get into the shower, another text comes through. I check my phone one last time to see what Nathan said.

Nathan:

I really like that lip gloss. Sleep well.

I smile to myself, reveling in the feelings Nathan brings up in me as I stand under the hot spray of water.

Chapter Fourteen

The next morning I rush to get ready. Sleep wasn't easy. I am reeling from the night I spent with Nathan followed by the impromptu conversation with Marcus. I take a little extra time this morning to apply my mascara and lip gloss and pick out a comfy but cute outfit. I'm not working super long this morning since we are mostly just making sure everything is ready for the fundraiser tonight.

I walk quickly to campus and run into The Grove for some coffees before heading to the library.

Amber is seated at the front desk when I walk in the front doors. She looks up from her computer and grins at me. "Good morning, Catherine! You look extra cute today."

I smile back, pulling a coffee from the drink carrier and passing it over the desk to her. "I got you a caramel latte because I wasn't sure what you'd like."

"Aw! You're so sweet! Actually, caramel latte is perfect. But I love coffee so much I could probably drink just about any coffee." She takes a sip.

"Where's Nathan?" I scan the first floor, looking for him.

"He's been in his office since he got here. I think he's

in a bad mood." She shrugs and turns back to her computer.

I head to the elevator, nerves running up and down my back. I wonder if he's regretting last night, and taking me with him.

Before I can think too much, I head for his office and knock gently before cracking the door open.

"Come in." Nathan's voice sounds tired from the other side.

I push through the door. "Good morning. I brought you a coffee," I say quietly as I walk into his office and close the door behind me.

Nathan's big dark eyes stare back at me, but they're void of their usual sparkle. I set the drink carrier down on his desk, and hand him the coffee. He takes a sip, closing his eyes for a brief second and exhaling deeply.

"It's cinnamon vanilla."

"Thank you."

I stand awkwardly in front of him, unsure of what to say or do. I decide against my better judgement to stay and talk to him. If he wants me to leave I will, but until he tells me that he doesn't want me here, I'm going to at least try and be his friend.

"Is everything okay?" I perch on the edge of one of the chairs that is in front of his desk, taking my own coffee from the carrier.

His eyes droop at the corners, exhaustion filling his face. "Yeah. Last night just got a little rough."

I'm unsure if I should push for more or not. I'm sure it was a lot for him last night to have taken me with him when he went to pick up his dad, and I've gotten myself in trouble before prying where I'm not wanted. But the look on his face cracks a part of my soul. His shoulders are stooped, and his hair is mussed like he rolled out of bed this morning and barely got a chance to get clothes on before he needed to leave.

"Can I do anything for you?" I feel like the question is open-ended enough that he can choose to answer how he pleases.

"No." The word comes out harsh and he exhales again, raking his fingers through his hair, pushing it out of his eyes. "Sorry, it's just…" He sets his coffee down and rubs the palms of his hands into his eyes.

I sit quietly, holding my cup, waiting patiently to see if he says more. He meets my gaze, and it's filled with so much sadness.

"I just don't understand him. I know there's a lot of history that I don't know about, but man… sometimes it's just so exhausting." He props his head in his hands. "He wasn't like this before. I know PTSD and other mental illnesses can look different for a lot of people. And it feels unfair for me to say this, I just wish he was present again. It kills my mom when things get bad."

"I'm sorry." The words feel hollow leaving my mouth. I understand the hurt of a parent not being present. When my mom left, it broke something inside of me.

"If he doesn't think about changing what he's doing, there will be consequences. His health isn't great, and drinking himself shitless every night does more damage than he cares to realize. And when he drinks he has terrible dreams and spends more time up screaming or running around the house than actually sleeping. I hate the way my younger sisters look at him. They don't remember him like I do, they only see what he is now."

His words sting my chest. Even though I know they're not directed at me, his pain and irritation flow freely.

Nathan leans back in his chair, tilts his head back toward the ceiling and closes his eyes.

At that moment I make a choice. I stand slowly, inching my way around his desk until I'm standing in front of him with the back of my legs pressed against his desk. I stand before him quietly, before allowing myself to reach out and touch him softly.

His eyes open slowly, regarding me with a guarded expression, but behind his stiff features, I can make out both a sadness and exhaustion that mirrors so much of my own pain. My heart aches for him. Slowly, I lean forward, never breaking eye contact, and take his hands in mine. He doesn't fight as I step in between his legs and wrap his arms around my middle. I fight the urge to feel embarrassed about what he might think when I give him silent permission to touch me. This isn't about that, it's about all of the unspoken things I see glimmering in his eyes.

He stiffens slightly at my touch, but after a long second, he relaxes a bit and leans into it.

Without thinking, I settle myself into his lap, wrapping my arms around his shoulders and neck in what I hope is perceived as the comforting gesture I want it to be.

He lets out a deep, shaky breath, and I feel his big tense shoulders relax incrementally under my arms. He drops his head, allowing me to cup his cheek in my palm. Nathan's eyes close gently, and the worry lines around his eyes and across his forehead ease slightly.

I gently push my thumb along his jaw across the stubble that has grown overnight. His eyes open slowly, and he turns his head to look at me. Suddenly I realize the intimacy of our position in its entirety. One of his hands cups my back, while the other rests gently on the curve of my hip.

I think maybe I should move, put distance between us, but I can't bring myself to break the connection. I haven't been able to keep my mind from wandering to thoughts of him since the first night we met in the cold. His dark eyes swallow me up, and his expression changes to something I don't recognize, but I can't look away. My eyes roam his face, and I can see his pulse in his neck beating as quickly as my own heart. I gently move my hand from his cheek to his neck, placing my palm over the spot, reveling in the warmth his body brings mine.

"Catherine."

My name from his lips pricks goosebumps across my arms.

I bring my eyes back to his face, only to realize he is

looking at my mouth. I take a ragged breath, I bite my lip to restrain myself. His eyes darken, and it's all I can do to stay where I am. I don't remember the last time I ever wanted to kiss someone so badly.

Suddenly there's a knock on the door and I jump to my feet, turning to face the wall and compose myself. My cheeks flame red hot, and my heart is about to come out of my chest.

"Hey," Amber pushes the door open slowly and stands in the doorway awkwardly. She tries to meet my eyes, but I study the floor, unable to look at her right now. I'm sure if I looked at her now, she would get the wrong impression about what was just happening. " Sorry to, uh, interrupt, but the caterer is here, Nathan."

"Thanks Amber, show them to the conference room. I'll be down in a minute." He stands, so I follow his lead, walking around to the front of his desk to grab my untouched coffee cup as Amber turns to leave.

Nathan comes around to the front of the desk to stand in front of me, and I'm unsure of what is going to happen. "There are a few books behind the desk downstairs, I didn't get a chance to get them on the cart, but would you mind loading them up and putting them back? Then is it okay if you just hang out at the front desk for me?"

"Yeah, sure, that's perfectly fine." I nod, and before I can compute what's happening, Nathan sweeps a big hand around my waist and softly kisses my cheek. His five o'clock shadow tickles me. I blush and give him a meek smile.

"I'll see you tonight?" he asks, but he's already on his way out of his office.

"Yep," I call after him, my cheek buzzing right where he kissed me.

The rest of the morning passes painfully slow. I sit at the desk, half on my phone, half stealing glances in the direction of the conference room where I know Nathan is. My whole body tingles every time I think about our close-ness this morning. I feel more confused than ever, though. The more I think about him, the more I can't decide if I need to step back and take some space, or just jump him already. I feel like if he knew about Marcus, about how recently my last relationship ended, and how soon I was jumping into this, he might be afraid. The last thing I want is for him to feel like a rebound, or for him to see me differently given the fact that I just up and left my previous relationship with little warning or explanation.

When noon hits, Amber comes to find me.

"Are you coming tonight?" I ask.

"Yeah! I wouldn't miss it! This has been Nathan's baby for weeks. It would be the least I can do to support him." She smiles.

I wonder for a fleeting moment what their relationship is like and a thread of jealousy flashes through my chest. I know I'm being irrational because I don't really think it's anything romantic. More than anything, I'm jealous that they've been friends so long.

"What are you wearing tonight?" she asks, wiggling her eyebrows. "I think I'm going to wear this long blue dress that I got a few years ago for a dinner party. It looks a little like a prom dress, but I don't care."

"I honestly don't know yet..." I say truthfully. I have limited options since I didn't really plan for an event like this when I moved here, and I had such short notice that it's not like I had time to go shopping. "I used to go to events like this a lot. But I didn't really think about something like this when I left Georgia, so I didn't exactly pack my formal wear."

"That makes sense, I'm sure you'll look amazing no matter what you wear." She gives me her kind, reassuring smile that I've already come to appreciate.

"Who's going to look amazing?" Nathan wanders over, looking at something on his phone before putting it in his back pocket.

"Catherine will. What kind of dress are you wearing tonight?" She giggles at him as he makes a super exaggerated thoughtful face.

"Some little black dress I have lying around." He grins at us. "It really shows off my leg hair."

§

I stand in my bathroom in my bra and underwear. The few dresses I do have are strewn across my bed haphazardly. I've tried them all on nothing seems good enough.

They were either bought for me by Marcus and are too frumpy, or they were one of the ones I picked up at the mall last week and not nearly formal enough.

I sneak upstairs and into Cici's room. She's the queen of hoarding clothes. She picked this house solely on the size of the walk-in closet. And even that didn't end up being enough. A few years ago, Charles and Larry helped her knock down the wall between her closet and guest bedroom upstairs so that she had one massive closet, Hence the reason I was staying in the guest bedroom in the basement with the painted flowers.

I open the closet doors into a wonderland of everything from muumuus to elegant ball gowns. The blouses and dresses are crammed so tightly in there that it looks like pulling the wrong item will cause an avalanche.

I start to pull what might be a blue sleeve and am startled by an, "Excuse me young lady? What do you think you're up to?"

I spin around to see a grinning Cici leaning against the closet door "I thought you outgrew dress up in my closet nineteen years ago?"

"Oh, well, I thought I'd try and see if I still drown in your dresses?"

She begins to laugh. "I have not put on enough weight for that, you loser. Can I help you? Did you not bring any dresses?"

I hesitate "Yes to the help and… I didn't bring anything formal enough for this event."

"Ooooh, got it. It's a library fundraiser. Is it really that hard to pick out a dress for a bunch of fucking fuddy duddies?" She smirks.

I know where she's going with this.

"Or is because Naaaathan's going." Like a little girl she puckers out her lips and then starts making kissing noises.

"Oh, stop! I just want to look nice. For me. I haven't looked good for me since high school, I guess." Have I ever tried to look good for myself?

"Well then, Kitty, let's get you dolled up. *For you.*" She gives me a sincere smile and begins shifting through her clothes.

I join her and pull a black t-shirt dress.

"Oh no, honey, we want something spicier than that." She pulls out a green silky cami dress that looks more like a slip than a dress. She holds it up to me, sizing it up.

"It's winter, Cici. I don't want to freeze to death." In reality, even if it was summer, I don't think I would have the guts to wear a dress like that. With the better part of the upper half of my body exposed, and the inability to hide my extra fat, I would die.

"No 'Kitty popsicles'! Got it!" Cici begins to mutter "This? No, this?" She pulls out dress after dress, holding each one up to me before tossing it in a pile growing behind her.

I have the faintest memory of my mom complaining once that Cici would destroy an entire room in the process of getting ready. "No to frumpy. What about… nooo." I pull out a red dress.

It's the dress Cici wore to my dad's wedding.

"THAT! THAT'S THE ONE! PUT IT ON NOW!" She exclaims, she walks to the back of the closet and pulls out a black leather jacket. "Put it on with this." She's so giddy I think part of her likes having me be her dress up doll. She walks out and shuts the closet doors.

I pull on the dress. A snug mid length red dress with a black lace panel over the deep V cut that shows more cleavage than I'm used to. It has a slit that cuts high up my leg, revealing most of my thigh. I throw the black leather jacket on and peek around for some shoes. I see a pair of black converse and slide them on. I'm over wearing heels to every event.

I peek and slowly open the closet door to Cici's bedroom.

She's sitting at the end of her bed. She looks up at me and winks.

"Please don't make fun of me, does it make me look like I've gained weight? It seems a little tight in the stomach area…" I'm interrupted.

"You are so beautiful, that outfit looks great. It's spunky like you. You look like…" she sighs, "Well…you again."

My aunt has a tear in her eye. I think maybe she picked up that something was off with Marcus. It broke her heart to see me change but thought I was happy. It must've destroyed her to find out I wasn't.

"Come here." She wraps her arms around me. "Let's do your hair and makeup. I'm so proud of you, picking yourself up by your bootstraps. That's my girl."

I can't help it, I bury myself deep into her shoulder and sob. I cry hard—about Marcus, the friends I've lost because of him, feeling replaced by my dad's new family, never having a mom even before she left.

And finally I cry because I never realized I did have a mom, and her name was Cici.

"I love you so much," I sniffle, and she holds me tighter.

"I love you too Kitty." She holds me at arm's length, her hands on my shoulders. "Dear lord, child! Thank god we didn't do your makeup first." We both laugh. She ushers me into the bathroom "Let's add some final touches."

I sit down on her vanity chair in her big bathroom. It looks like a bathroom you'd find at the *Caesar's Palace* in *Las Vegas* with all its fake gold. She shuffles through her vanity, comparing foundations to my face. She finds one she deems close enough, and pulls out a thick brush with a gold handle.

"So," Cici starts to paint the foundation lightly over my face. "You never told me how your night was last night. How was your time with Nathan?"

Yesterday evening seems much farther away than just twenty-four hours ago. Between my awkward *date-that-wasn't-really-a-date* after setting up for the fundraiser and the impromptu trip to pick up Nathan's dad, I don't know what to think anymore. Then this morning… when I was so sure he was going to kiss me before we were interrupted.

"It was good, we got some food afterward." I hope the tone of my voice doesn't give too much away. "Larry was our server," I add, and my aunt chuckles.

"I still find it hilarious he took that job there," she says, turning her back to me, taking time to find whatever random eyeshadow pallet she's looking for.

"He does look a little ridiculous in that pinstriped polo they make him wear."

We both laugh again.

Cici pulls out some blush and rouges my cheeks. She applies some red lipstick, neutral eyeshadow and hands me the mascara. "I don't do mascara, I don't want to pay for your glass eye."

I roll my eyes and take the tube of mascara from her, bending over close to the mirror to see what I'm doing.

I take a deep breath, step back and look at myself in the mirror. The girl staring back is hard to recognize. My hair falls just below my collar bones in loose waves, and my makeup looks flawless. This dress is a little tighter than I'm used to. It stretches over my chest, pushing my breasts together. Running my hands down my sides, I hope no one will notice the slight creasing at my hips from where my underwear sits. I chose a silky red pair that I hoped would be smooth enough to hide the curves of the soft flesh at my hips and across my lower stomach. I suck in a little, unease filling my guts. Marcus would have hated that this dress didn't completely hide the fat I carry around my midsection.

I open the bathroom door and Cici lets out a low whistle. " Damn girl, can I get your number?"

I roll my eyes and laugh a little. "Would you mind dropping me off tonight? I don't really want to walk in the snow like this."

"Sure. Depending on when you're done, though, can you walk to the bar after? I don't know how late I'll be tonight."

I nod. "Sure, that's fine."

I grab the leather jacket and we head for the door.

Chapter Fifteen

When Cici drops me off before heading to the bar,
it's just after 5:00. The event doesn't start until 6:00, but
I wanted to come a little early and help. I am also kind of
hoping that I will be able to check in on Nathan after our
talk this morning.

I walk in the side entrance and head straight for the
conference room. There's a few decorations in the hall,
along with a makeshift coat room. I think usually it's just a
broom closet, but tonight it has coat racks lining the walls.
I find a hanger and put my coat in the back before heading in through the doors to where the main event will be
hosted.

The room is beautiful. The table clothes are a deep
navy blue with cream-colored plates set at each table. Balloons are set as the centerpieces tied down at each table
with a small bouquet of silk flowers. The stage is lined with
balloons and silk ribbons that flow down at each corner. It
is the perfect picture of elegance.

"Catherine! Hey!" Amber comes up to me, looping her
arms around my shoulders and hugging me for a brief

moment. "Wow! You look stunning!" She holds me at arm's length and smiles.

I can feel myself blush a little at the compliment. "You look amazing, too. that dress definitely does not look like a prom dress."

She's wearing a stunning royal blue tea length lace dress. It hugs her petite frame, accentuating the shape of her body. Her hair is swept back and tied in a low bun at the base of her head, and her bold eyeliner makes her look like she should be on the cover of a makeup magazine or something.

I peer around the room, looking to see who else is here, but all I see is the catering staff getting things set up.

"Nathan is upstairs in his office getting changed. I don't think he went home today. I'm sure he will be back any minute." She turns to survey the room, and I adjust my dress. "So, what was going on in Nathan's office this morning?" She gives me a pointed look.

"Oh, we had dinner last night. I was just checking to make sure he was okay, things were cut a little short."

"Dinner?" She gives me a funny look and raises her eyebrows.

"Yeah, after setting up we just went to the diner on campus for a bit."

"Was it dinner? Or, was it *DINNER*?" She smirks at me, and I roll my eyes.

"I honestly don't know. Maybe it was something, maybe it wasn't." I can't help but smile a little, thinking about how easy conversation came once we got over the initial awkwardness of being alone together.

"So are you guys a thing now? Are you going to have dinner again?"

I honestly hope we have dinner again, but I shrug, trying not to give too much away. I don't want to get my hopes up prematurely, or talk about it and jynx myself. After our shared moment in his office this morning I can't help but wonder what exactly will come of us. His quiet demeanor and snarky sense of humor makes me want so much more, but my past coupled with his current family struggles makes me nervous to move forward.

I'm wondering if I should go look for him when his tall frame strides through the doors. My breath catches in my throat as I take a moment to admire his dress shirt stretched over his strong chest and the way his pants sit low on his hips. He's got his hands shoved into his pockets casually as he scans the room.

Amber waves him over and my heart starts beating furiously as his eyes meet mine. I swear I see his throat bob as if he's nervous as well. I wonder if he can tell how knotted with unspoken feelings my stomach is when he's around.

"You both look stunning," he says, but his eyes never leave mine. His gaze drags slowly down my body. The heat from the look on his face leaves tingles all over me as if his fingers are actually trailing across my skin.

"Thanks, Nathan! You clean up nice as well." Amber

gives him a side hug and smiles at both of us knowingly.

Nathan still hasn't looked away from me, and I refrain from squirming under his gaze. "We're sitting over here If you wanna join us." I am transfixed by his gaze as we walk slowly to the table where Amber must have set her purse down when she arrived.

"I'll actually be sitting with my family for dinner, but they're not here yet it seems. I'd love to join two lovely ladies for a moment of conversation, though." He flashes a big smile at me, and then turns coolly to Amber, winking at me when her back is turned as if we have some sort of shared secret.

I can't help but blush at the way his eyes linger on the low cut top of my dress a moment before we follow Amber quickly to the table.

Nathan leans towards me and whispers. "You are absolutely breathtaking in that dress."

I jab him playfully in the arm as my cheeks turn bright pink. The look he's giving me makes me feel like he might prefer the dress on the floor. I glance at Amber, hoping she doesn't notice how hot my face feels.

Amber is already sitting down as Nathan pulls my seat out for me. I sit and he lowers himself in the chair beside me. Leaning forward slightly with his hands in his lap.

"I hope this isn't as boring as last year," Nathan says.

Amber chides him, "Don't you plan these events?"

Nathan smirks. "Every year, and I seem to forget every time how boring they are."

He brushes his knee against mine gently, glancing at me out of the corner of his eye. His knuckles drag lazily down the slit in my dress that seems wider than it should be at the moment.

I start to feel white hot within, I look over at Nathan, but he is deep in conversation with Amber. He's looking at her intently while she rambles on about some confusion earlier today with a group of students trying to ask for help with references. I can't focus. His hand moves up a little more, he slips his fingers under the hem of my skirt. *What are they talking about?* I think it has to do with work, but the only thing I can focus on is the feel of his fingers on the bare skin of my thigh. I can feel my center start to throb, and I cautiously brush my fingers along the back of his hand.

"OOOOH, *GORDITO! Hola*, Amber. *Hola,* Catherine. It looks so wonderful!"

Nathan's hand jumps off my thigh. "*Hola Mami!*" He stands to hug his mother and each of his sisters. Then he turns to us. "Catherine, you remember my mother from yesterday." He smiles at me, slightly apologetic. "This is Sofia, and her husband Carlos. They have two kiddos plus one that is half baked."

Sofia eyes me carefully, and I recognize her as the other woman who was standing on the porch when Nathan and I brought their father home last night.

"Nathan has told me about you." She keeps her voice quiet, reaching out to take my hand in hers gently. She smiles kindly, but her eyes sparkle with a whirlwind of emotions. "You seem to have impacted him greatly the last few weeks." She gives me a knowing look as she steps back to rejoin her husband.

Nathan clears his throat. "This is Lucia and Andria. You remember Nadia from yesterday, and this," he pulls the littlest girl close to him, "This is Amaya."

She smiles up at him, and her eyes sparkle with so much adoration.

"She's so pretty, Nathan," her voice comes out in a loud whisper, like she's trying to share a secret conversation with him and is altogether completely unaware that we all can hear her.

"You think?" Nathan chuckles and smooths her hair back on her head.

She eyes me and nods very seriously. "Definitely super pretty. Is she your girlfriend?"

He laughs again and Sofia steps in, asking about what table they'll be at. Nathan motions to a table up by the front of the room by the stage, and his family turns to make their way to their seats. Nathan's hand brushes mine as he turns to follow his family without saying another word to me or Amber.

"So what's going on with you two?" Amber turns to stand in front of me.

"After dinner last night, I ended up tagging along when Nathan went to pick his dad up from the bar. Then, this morning, we had a bit of a moment... I thought he was going to kiss me." I keep my voice low, making sure no one else around us can hear. After Nathan distanced himself from me when his family walked over, I feel like discretion is probably important to him.

"So is that what I interrupted this morning?" She steps in eagerly, her expression asking for details I don't have.

"I honestly don't know what you interrupted this morning…" All day I've been wondering what would have happened if we had been given a few more minutes alone.

"Do you think you want to kiss him?"

I shrug. After the way he introduced me to his family, and the way he just kind of walked off with them without saying anything else to us, I'm not sure what would happen. It definitely like like he didn't want his family to know anything, and despite Sofia's comment, I am a little worried that maybe he doesn't feel the same way I do. I've had a nagging fear since this morning that maybe I'm overstepping some boundary that I'm unaware of. Maybe I shouldn't have just assumed this morning that the kind of comfort or attention I offered was what he wanted from me.

The last thing I need to do is to throw myself at someone who wasn't nearly as interested as I was.

Amber and I make our way back to our seats. We watch people fill the room slowly over the next half hour, greeting each other and finding tables. Quite a few of the people go to Nathan's table to talk to him or shake his hand. Through the next hour or so, he doesn't look over to our table once. Amber and I are joined by a few other people who work around the library, and we make some small talk but mostly keep to ourselves.

I feel stupid every time I glance over at Nathan's table and can't seem to meet his eyes. He stays focused on his family sitting around him, talking and joking. Every now and then his laughter floats across the room, and a small pang of jealousy wells up inside of me.

I decide to push it down, I'll figure out where it's coming from later. It's been so long since I've been out with a friend, doing something I like. I should be enjoying my time with Amber. As dinner progresses, things relax a bit and she and I talk about school and things we have planned as spring approaches. When dinner is over, she and I both head to the back of the room to set up tables for the silent auction.

"So, when will you be done with your degree again?" I ask as we pull out the different pieces of art, boxes of goodies from local businesses, and gift cards

"I still have almost two years left, so not next spring but the one after." She follows behind me, leaving pieces of lined paper and pens in front of each object I put down.

"That's really not that far off! Are you planning to pursue a Doctorate, or do you think you'll be done?"

She shrugs. " I haven't really decided yet, but I think I want to pursue my PhD. So really, I'm nowhere near done with school."

"Do you know what you want to do afterward?"

"I want to teach. To be a professor. Here, I'd only need a Masters, but I love school, and my options would open up exponentially with a PhD."

"That makes sense. You'd be a great professor."

"Thanks, Catherine! That means a lot." She smiles at me and wraps her arms around her middle, leaning against the table. "What did you go to school for in Georgia? I don't think you ever told me."

"Political science. I minored in business administration, too. I actually worked in a nonprofit before I moved here."

"How did you get involved with that kind of job?"

"I got an internship there my third year of college, then I met my ex, and he helped me get my job when I graduated."

"The same ex you were engaged to?"

I nod. "Yeah, his family is pretty heavily involved and influential. It's actually one of the things that drew me to him. He was always great with people, and great at events like this. He really knew how to command a room. He also always knew what to say to get people to open their checkbooks for him." I try for a light laugh, but it falls flat and I purse my lips.

She studies me, her eyes gently grazing over my face. "So, if you don't mind my asking, what happened between you two?"

I am about to respond, that it was way more complicated than I wanted to explain, but I am saved when Nathan strides up.

"You guys did great setting everything up. Is it all ready to go?" I feel his eyes linger on me, dropping down to my cleavage for a brief moment before he turns to Amber. "Do you want to head to the stage and let people know they're free to mingle and check out the auction items?"

"Sure!" She bubbles, a wide smile spreading across her face as she looks back and forth between the two of us and walks up to the front of the room.

Nathan turns his attention away from her and settles back on me. "Have you been having a good evening?"

"Yeah, I mean, Amber is super fun to talk to. We've been enjoying ourselves."

"That's good." He turns back to the stage as Amber clears her throat into the microphone before letting people know the silent auction is beginning and they are free to move about the room and check out the items we have available. After a brief set of instructions on how the silent auction works, she excuses herself from the stage and soft music starts to play.

People stand and mingle, the room fills with conversation and laughter. Nathan presses his hand to the small of my back and guides me around to the back of the tables so that we won't be in the way of the auction pieces. I watch in silence as people start to slowly wander toward the table, taking their time to look at all of the options before stepping forward to write their names on the paper in front of the things they want. I glance over at Nathan, but his eyes are trained on the people in front of us, his expression unreadable.

"Are you okay tonight?" I ask. I mentally kick myself for feeling so weird standing beside him.

"Yeah, why?" He glances over at me for half a second before turning back to scan the crowd again.

Yeah, why Catherine? I realize I don't really have a response. I feel on edge tonight. After our weird moment this morning, I'm wondering if I'm making too many assumptions about Nathan's feelings toward me. I consider his weariness, compiled with how distant he has become since his family showed up. I feel weird. I worry that my feelings are muddled, maybe I am overthinking things. I feel exposed, and I am already kicking myself for being so drawn to a person I hardly know.

"Are you okay?" His attention is now turned to me.

I realize I haven't answered him. I wring my hands together in front to me, my chest tight under his gaze.

"Can we talk for a minute?" My voice shakes a little, and my cheeks grow hot.

He nods but doesn't reply. He turns and heads for the double doors that lead out into the hallway, and I follow behind.

Amber catches my eye, giving me a quizzical look. I smile in response, hoping it gives the illusion of confidence I don't feel.

When we are safely in the hallway, and the doors have closed behind us, Nathan steps to me. His eyes are studying my face intensely. I shove down the urge to shrivel at the expression on his face. He's still wearing an unreadable mask. I don't know what I honestly expect from him. He doesn't owe me anything. I feel guilty about pulling him away from his event, but I also have to know where I stand with him.

"Are you okay?" he asks again. His face softens, and little glimmers of concern dance in his eyes.

"Yes," I say firmly. "I just..." I don't know what I'm going to say next. Things are new between us, and I feel stupid for feeling like I'm pining for his attention. "Am I misreading the situation?"

"What situation?" His questioning tone sends my heart to my feet. I feel stupid enough asking in the first place.

My mind races. Maybe there really isn't a situation to misread. I should just be trying to enjoy myself. I don't even know if I'm looking for a relationship. I shouldn't be looking for a relationship. After my heated phone call with Marcus last night, I wonder if I'm just taking a swing at something that makes me feel alive. I should be giving myself space. But I also can't ignore the feelings I have right now.

"We went to dinner. And I had fun." I feel my chest squeezing around my lungs. "I know the night didn't end exactly as planned, and I feel like I may have overstepped this morning..." My voice dies in my throat. I could have sworn there was more between us than the stoic look he is giving me now. For a moment last night I thought he would kiss me. "And tonight, I don't know what I was expecting. I don't want to make you think I'm desperate. I'm not. I don't need anything from you. God, I feel stupid."

Nathan takes a step toward me, easing into my personal space. I have to tilt my head up slightly to keep looking at his face. Everything inside of me makes me want to close the rest of the distance between us, to thread my arms under his, and around his waist. But I will myself to stay put.

"You don't sound stupid," he says quietly.

I take a shaky breath. I wrap my arms around myself, feeling a slight chill from the turmoil of emotions swirling around inside of me. "I guess tonight I was just confused. You shot away like you couldn't distance yourself from me fast enough when your family showed up. If you're uncomfortable with this…" I wave my hand, motioning between us. "I get it. I just don't want to be left in the dark."

He catches my hand before it can fall back to my side. A jolt of electricity surges up my arm. "I'm sorry I made you feel that way." He brushes the back of my hand with his thumb. "I'm apparently not very good at this."

"Good at what?" My brain is having trouble focusing on his words as he takes another half step closer to me. There's maybe a hand's distance between us, and my pulse threatens to overpower the sound of his voice in my ears.

His eyes turn darker. "It was all I could do last night to let you walk away from me. I wanted you to stay so badly. I wanted to sit and talk the rest of the night. I wanted to walk you home." His eyes drag greedily down my body and back up to meet my gaze. "I can't seem to get enough of you. You showed up tonight in that dress, and I thought I was going to have a heart attack." He closes the last bit of distance between us, dropping his hands to rest lightly on my hips.

The pounding of my own heartbeat in my ears is deafening. I press my hands flat against his chest, unable to look away or move. I'm completely paralyzed by the lust dripping from his words.

"Oh," I say on an exhale. I can't seem to get enough air in my lungs. The ache I felt before, low in my stomach, starts to resurface again at his touch.

"Oh?" He repeats teasingly. His hands rub slowly up and down my hips and back as if he's testing the way I feel.

I'm trying hard to stay focused, but the longer he touches me, the more I desperately want him to kiss me. He grazes my stomach and chest with his knuckles as he slides a hand up to the back of my neck. "I had to keep my distance tonight because I knew if I was too close for too long, I would not be able to keep my hands off you." His fingers graze lightly down my neck and across the skin where my breasts swell in my dress.

I shudder pleasantly under his touch and his eyes drop to where his fingers leave a tingling trail across my skin.

"You are so beautiful." The words come out in a low rumble, his breath running along my shoulder.

My eyes drop to his mouth, and I find myself unable to look away from his full lips. His breath catches, and before I can register what's happening, he takes my hand and pulls me down the hall a few feet to the closet where I stashed my coat when I got here. He whirls around on me, closing the door behind us before gently backing me against it. I feel his hand trail down the side of my body before I hear the lock click into place.

His hands come up on either side of me, pressing into the door. Oxygen fills my lungs as his lips pass gently over mine. The first kiss is soft and tentative–almost reverent. He pulls back to study my face, as if checking for permission.

I meet his eyes and wrap my hands around the back of his neck, willing him to kiss me again. His eyes drop down my body again as a hunger coursing through me.

Nathan leans back in and this time his kiss is more demanding. His strong arms wrap around my torso, dragging me to him, pulling me against his chest. The action feels urgent, as though I might disappear if he doesn't grab on quickly enough. His warm breath sends shivers through my body as it brushes across my skin. Nathan presses soft kisses across my cheek and down my neck, lingering right on the sensitive spot where my neck and shoulder meet. I let out a puff of air, rolling my head to the side to give him better access.

His hands drop down my back running over my ass as he lifts me slightly to slide his firm thigh between mine.

My toes barely touch the floor anymore. A breathy moan escapes from my lips as he places a kiss on my chest, his hands moving to explore across my shoulders, slipping the straps of my dress down my arms. His mouth is on mine again, kissing me more confidently. He keeps one hand firmly planted on the door to steady himself as the other one finds the hem of my dress. His hand slips under, running up the outer part of my thigh to rest on my bare hip.

I arch under his touch running my own hands up his sides and under his suit jacket before pushing it off his shoulders. It falls to the floor and he meets my eyes again.

His eyelids droop as he peers at me through his dark lashes. "Catherine."

The sound of my name on his lips sends delicious waves of pleasure through me, the need I feel between my legs becomes a cry for more.

"You feel amazing." His hand travels back to my ass under my dress. His fingers dip under my underwear caressing my bare skin. He takes a deep shaky breath before following the line of my underwear around my body till his knuckles are grazing my stomach. He hooks his fingers in the front of my underwear, and leaves them there. My breath catches. I can't remember how long it's been since I've been touched so carefully. *Have I ever been?*

I take the opportunity to pull his shirt from his pants and slide my hands up to the bare toned skin of his stomach, but it doesn't feel like enough. His whole body shudders under my fingers as I painstakingly pull at the buttons on his shirt, exposing his strong bare chest. I free him of his shirt, pushing it so it rolls off his shoulders, and take a moment to admire his body. I run my hands over his chest, stomach, and sides.

He watches me, staying close, his fingers rubbing small circles under my belly button. He trials his nose across my cheek and down my neck before his hand gently cups the bottom of my breast.

My throat feels thick as I search for his mouth again, pulling him in closer to me as I take control of the kiss, parting my mouth to run my tongue along his lower lip.

He groans, returning the depth of the kiss, his tongue finding mine. His hand comes out from under my skirt to slip the straps of my dress farther down my arms, exposing one of my breasts. His hand cups me, grazing my nipple with his thumb, drawing circles around it, sending little waves of pleasure down my spine. I moan as he greedily moving my dress, exposing my other breast. Both of his hands are on me, working their way over me as if he's trying to memorize the way I feel under his palms. My breath comes in sharp gasps as he touches me, and the world falls away until all I can see is him. And it's not enough. I want more.

He lets out a shaky breath, pulling back but resting his forehead against mine. He stares down the length of me again, his hands still trailing over all of the exposed skin. "You are so absolutely beautiful." His voice is husky and filled with admiration, and suddenly I feel like I could come undone right here in his arms. My heart is hammering against my ribs, and I want to demand more from him, rip away the rest of our clothes, and let him have all of me right here. But his eyes are closed and he's taking slow breaths as if he's trying to calm himself.

Gently I lean forward, planting a soft kiss on his chest, and then brush my lips upward finding his neck. When I plant my lips on the spot where his shoulder and neck meet, I feel him tense and his hands tighten their hold on me. I carefully wrap my arms around his shoulders, anchoring his body to mine. His fingers dig into my sides when my mouth moves up his neck to just below his ear, and then his mouth. We stay transfixed a moment, skin to skin. His mouth works expertly against mine, driving the insatiable need inside of me to new heights.

He pulls away slightly, leaving me panting and wanting more. "We should probably head back. I'm sure people are looking for us by now." He sounds like he wants to leave about as much as I do right now.

I nod, realizing I'm unsure of how long we've actually been gone.

He presses another kiss to my lips, and slips the straps of my dress back over my shoulders, gently covering what he exposed moments ago before he bends down to find his shirt and jacket.

When he unlocks the door and we step out I realize I must look crazy. "I'm going to run to the bathroom and freshen up."

"Okay," he loops his arm around my waist and kisses me on the cheek. "Can I walk you home tonight?"

"I'd like that." I smile, feeling like a little girl who just had her first kiss.

He turns and heads back toward the conference room and I duck into the bathroom.

Chapter Sixteen

When I find my way back into the conference room, Amber and Nathan are standing on the stage listing off the names of people who won items in the auction. Amber grins as she hands Nathan slips of paper with each person's name listed, as well as what they paid for the item they won.

There is clapping after each announcement, but I can't seem to focus on what Nathan is saying. His eyes catch mine and he smiles at me, causing my stomach to do flips. I smooth my dress over my stomach, waiting patiently in the back of the room for the announcements to be done.

"Catherine, *querida!*" Nathan's mom approaches me as the announcements come to an end and everyone moves to start claiming their goodies. "*Mi hijo* seems to have a bit of a crush on you! You should come to dinner sometime soon!"

"Oh, umm," I scan the faces in the crowd looking for Nathan. I don't want to make him uncomfortable by saying 'yes' or 'no' without him around. We still haven't really gotten to have a talk to define what we are or what we are doing. "I don't know. I don't want to intrude."

"Intrude on what?" Nathan appears at my side, his face glued to his mother's. Something unspoken passes between them, but it doesn't seem to deter her in the slightest.

"*Ella debe venir a cenar!*" She turns her attention back to me. " You really must come, Catherine! It wouldn't be any sort of intrusion. I would love to have you!"

"*Mami!* She may be busy."

I'm definitely not busy... but I don't want to make the situation awkward by saying that if Nathan doesn't want me there. We aren't exactly on 'meet the family' level.

"WELL, if you decide you're not busy, just come over with Nathan after work!"

I nod. "Okay, thank you for the invitation." I try for a smile, hoping it seems genuine.

She smiles widely at me before heading back over to her daughters.

Nathan and I stand in awkward silence for another few minutes, watching people mingle around and pack up to leave. The catering staff is already tearing tables down in the corner as well as the sound crew.

He turns to me. "Are you ready to go? Can I still walk you home?"

"Chivalry really isn't dead is it?" I joke. "Yeah, I guess, but I don't think anyone is going to try and kidnap me."

He chuckles to himself and pulls me to his side as we walk toward the coatroom. My face heats with fresh memories of what we just did in there, and I keep my eyes glued to the floor as I carefully shuffle past a few people to grab my coat from the back.

When I step back out, Nathan is standing against the opposite wall with his hands in his pockets. His gaze travels slowly from my feet, up my legs, before resting on my chest for two beats of my heart. When his eyes lock on mine and the corners of his mouth turn upward in a small smile, I feel the butterflies in my stomach do a victory dance. I can see clearly on his face that he was just thinking the same thing I was.

He untucks one of his hands from his pocket and holds it out to me. I close the distance between us with a few steps and lace my fingers through his, feeling the warmth spread up my arm and through my body from the contact. We head for the door.

As we step outside, my phone vibrates inside of my jacket pocket. I pause to read the text.

Cici:

Slow night at the bar. Charlie let me off early. Lol. Brought home takeout, currently looking for some cringy chick flick. See you soon, Love.

"Everything okay?" Nathan looks back at me from a few steps ahead.

"Yes, Cici just texted and said she was home and she has takeout."

"That sounds nice." He looks at me again as I take his

191

big hand back in mine. "So…" He pauses awkwardly.

"Sooo..?" I mimic giving him a silly smile. "Are you always this great at conversation?"

He lets out a small puff of air, and I can't tell if he's nervous, uncomfortable, or amused. "Sorry if my mother made you uncomfortable tonight. She can get a little ahead of herself sometimes."

"Oh." I say flatly. I'm not really sure what I thought he was going to talk about, but I guess this is as good as anything. Even though we had a steamy moment a little while ago that totally made me feel completely unraveled, we still haven't really figured out what's going on between us. "She didn't make me uncomfortable. I was just surprised, I guess. And you weren't there. I didn't want to agree to anything that would make you uncomfortable."

He's quiet for a few steps.

I feel my stomach slowly deflating like a balloon, leaving a hollow feeling below my ribs.

He rakes his fingers through his hair with his free hand, and it takes everything in my willpower not to shrink away from him. I know I really don't have any right to feel hurt about this conversation, but I still do. I don't know what our relationship is–I shouldn't even call it a relationship.

"It's not that I'm uncomfortable." He says finally. "I just…" he sighs again. "My family is complicated. They're loud and nosy and curious. And my dad… Well, you've seen him. He marches to his own drum. I don't like complications, and my life at home is so complicated."

I hear the vulnerability in his voice.

"I appreciate your honesty." I give his hand a small reassuring squeeze trying to squelch the disappointment I don't have any right to feel. My mind wanders back to the other night when we drove his dad home from the bar. I feel even more like I intruded on something I shouldn't have. He didn't want me to see his family then, and he still doesn't now. And I can't even blame him, because I mostly feel the same way about my family as well.

He stops and turns to me, irritation flashing across his face, but I can't tell if the irritation is with me or the conversation. But as soon as the emotion registers on his face, it's gone again and he pulls my chest to his.

"I really like you Catherine." There's force behind his words. "I just don't want to overcomplicate us too quickly."

"What exactly are we? We got a little distracted earlier." I give him a cheesy grin, alluding to our steamy time back at the library.

His eyes turn dark around the edges and his gaze rests on my mouth. I feel my stomach heat as he locks his hands behind my back, trapping me against his chest. I allow myself to sink into his warmth bringing my hands up around his sides under his heavy winter coat.

"I like you," he says again. "But I also want to take my time getting to know you because you make me feel things I haven't felt in a long time." He rests his forehead against mine and breathes deeply. "I also think you deserve more than hasty closet make outs."

My insides flutter. His words bounce around inside of my chest, causing the sadness that had built up for years to slowly start to crumble. Before I can respond, he's pulling away, leaving my body cold everywhere that he was touching me moments ago. He pulls me against his side as we slowly resume our walk. His pace is steady like he doesn't want to get me home any faster than necessary. I relish the peace of the night, and the warmth his touch sends through me.

I don't really know what to make of what he's said. Part of me is disappointed because I have always jumped right in. With Marcus there was never any hesitation. He expected from day one for me to be his. Spend my time with him, meet his family, know his friends, and spend nights at his house. There was never any question of where we were in our relationship.

But it wasn't until I was too far in that I realized how stuck I was. Maybe it's good we are going slow. As much as my feelings seem to be present, I don't want to treat this man like a rebound. He is far too good for my stupid baggage.

"I was engaged." His voice drags me from my thoughts.

Engaged... At one point he was engaged, too. I don't have time to really process my relief at this thought because he continues talking.

"We met in high school. I was seventeen and she was sixteen. I had never really dated anyone before her, and

I fell hard. By the time we finished high school, I decided to propose." He pauses. "I just thought you should know. I understand whatever it is you're going through."

"Carolina?" I remember his dad calling me by that name.

"Yes," he says blandly. There's a melancholy look in his eyes. "We both stayed here for college and decided that we were going to wait until after we finished school to get married. But then college came and went, and we moved in together. Then the plan was to save for the wedding. Her family wasn't super well off, and we didn't want to expect them to pay for it, and my family wasn't in a position to help either. But then another year passed, and we still hadn't set a date. Life just became a routine. We worked, we came home, we talked arbitrarily about wedding plans, and then we repeated the whole process. Before my eyes, our lives were falling apart. From the outside, we seemed fine. She wore my ring and came home to me every night, but slowly we stopped talking about the wedding, and then we stopped talking about other things, too." He blows out a deep breath, rubbing the tension in the back of his neck with his free hand.

I quietly wait for him to continue, wondering what it would be like to come home to him every day, wondering what he's like when he winds down after a day at work, what he watches on TV and how someone could be so unaware of what they have.

"Before I knew it, she was spending more time out

around friends, and basically anywhere that wasn't home with me. By the time I thought to ask her about it, she already had one foot out the door. And when we did talk, I realized I didn't even know her anymore. I had no idea what I did wrong. I tried to talk to her, tried to take her on more dates. I offered to take some time off work and take her on vacation, anything. I felt stupid for how much she made me beg, but she didn't want any of it. She didn't want a life with me in it anymore. One day I came home from work, and she had her bags packed at the front door, she handed me my ring back, and left."

"I'm sorry." My voice sounds hollow, floating and dispersing into the darkness. I know my words are meaningless against his sorrow, but I don't know what else to offer in the moment.

He shrugs. Some of the tension that had clouded his face before seems to slip away. "I've done my best to make peace with it. But I just wanted you to understand, I haven't done anything like this before. I don't know what is supposed to happen next. The last time I dated someone that I was truly interested in, I was a child."

"I don't really know, either," I say honestly. I haven't found myself in a situation like this before. I feel like in the past my relationships were convenient. The boy I dated before Marcus, and before I moved to Georgia, asked me out because our friends thought we would be good together. He was quiet and a little nerdy, but we never hung out alone, only with our friends or his family.

Marcus, on the other hand, felt like a breath of fresh air at first. He was successful and dedicated, and the perfect doting boyfriend. Shoes, clothes, flowers, expensive dates and vacations; he truly swept me off my feet. But eventually the fresh air between us turned toxic and suffocating and the doting turned into manipulation. I knew I was in the wrong place with the wrong person, but I convinced myself the false safety he provided would be enough.

"When I left Atlanta a few months ago, I was running away from my fiancé." I can't bear to look at Nathan after the story he just told. I'm terrified that he's going to see Carolina instead of me, but I can't manage to hide the truth. "We met because I worked for his family's company in college. He seemed too good to be true. Great job, great family, and I really thought he loved me." My stomach twists at the memories of our first few months together, the outpouring of affection he laid upon me, the family that he offered. "But the longer we were together, the more I realized that all of his affection had strings attached. Everything came with a price. And when..." The words catch in my throat and I can feel panic building in my chest. "When he asked me to marry him, I was somehow convinced that it would all be worth it, that the strings would cut loose, and everything would be better. I don't know exactly when, but at some point I realized the cycle wasn't going to end when we 'tied the knot.'"

In reality, I feel stupid for not seeing the signs earlier. I feel like there were so many red flags that I just stepped over, pretending I didn't see them.

I continued explaining it to Nathan. "Maybe I always knew, but I just didn't want to see it. The control that I once mistook for care turned into something more. Nothing would ever be quite enough. I would never be quite enough." I let go of a shaky breath, afraid to look anywhere but straight ahead. My heart squeezes at the flood of unpleasant feelings that flood my chest. The night chill brushes my skin and sends ice through my veins. "By the time I registered who he truly was, I was being buried alive. This man, whom so many around us loved and respected, had become my own personal prison. His words and his actions trapped me to him. I was cut off, and there was no one around who could see my misery. My family loved him, and my friends thought he was great for me. But they didn't see what happened when they weren't around. They didn't know the poison that laced his words, or the contempt in his eyes. No one could see the ways he devoured me."

Nathan stops and I have to steady myself before realizing we are standing in front of Cici's house. For a moment we stand next to each other without speaking, and I can't bring myself to look at him, wondering if I've said too much.

He turns to look at me, grabbing my hand, forcing me to turn and look back at him. His eyes graze over my face, studying every piece of me.

I can't read his expression, but I get the feeling that he can see way more than just the words I'm saying. I fight the urge to look away, or back away, allowing myself to feel exposed in this moment; hoping he understands the vulnerability I feel, and how much of my soul I feel like I've bared to him tonight. I don't know why it matters to me, but it does. I'm done running.

"I don't think I'm quite ready to head home yet," he says softly, taking my hand and pulling me up to Cici's porch where the old swing sits on the end.

"Hold on." I duck into the house as quietly as I can, grabbing an big old blanket from the front closet before heading back out the front door, hoping that Cici can't hear anything over the sound of the tv. I don't bother turning the porch light on as I hand Nathan the blanket before settling into the swing and motioning for him to sit as well.

Nathan spreads the blanket around us, tucking me into his side as he gently pushes off the porch with his heels, causing the swing to sway gently in the quiet night air. I allow myself to melt into his warmth, and we sit quietly, both consumed by our own thoughts and heartache.

The quiet around us feels safe, though, like the broken pieces inside of me have the space to be broken without the expectation to tape it back together.

The hinges of the swing creak and I finally muster the courage to steal a glance up at Nathan's face. He's studying me quietly, and I realize he still hasn't said anything since admitting he didn't want to go home.

"What are you thinking?" I turn toward him a little more, trying to get an even better look at his face in the dim light.

His eyes roam freely over my face and down my neck to the swell of my cleavage that I know peeks from the neckline of my dress.

"I think your ex was a damn fool." he says quietly. "You're only given the chance to have someone truly special maybe once in your life. And he was stupid to make you lose sight of your worth."

"Oh, is that all?" I say lightly, because his words seem like too much for me to handle at the moment. I stash them away to pick apart at a later time because right now I don't have the courage to ask him what he means, and I don't have the ability to express what it makes me feel.

"No, it's not." He shifts slightly to rest his free hand on my thigh under the blanket. "I'm also thinking about how much I want to kiss you again."

My breath lodges behind the lump forming in my throat, and the need from before makes my belly hum with anticipation. Time seems to stop completely the moment his lips brush against mine. The kiss is soft and I ache for more the moment his mouth isn't on mine. My eyes flutter open and lock on his.

His arm that is draped around my shoulders gently slides down my back and he scoops me into his lap. My legs settle on the swing on either side of his hips, the skirt of my dress bunching up around my middle. He pulls the blanket up around my shoulders, shielding my body from the cold winter air before he slides his hands up the tops of my thighs.

I shiver and arch into his chest, unable to tear my eyes from his. One of his strong hands comes up to the back of my neck, gently guiding me closer to him as the other hand finds the small of my back. His chest rises in short measured breaths that hitch and become ragged the moment my hands touch his cheeks. He pulls me in closer still and his lips brush mine again, once, twice, three times before he deepens the kiss. I sigh against his mouth, my hips rocking closer to him, trying to soak up his heat, feeling his hands roam up my sides until his thumbs brush just under my breasts. He trails careful kisses along my cheek and jaw, the stubble on his cheeks brushes against the sensitive skin of my neck as he nuzzles his way down to my shoulder and back up to find my mouth again.

I nip at his bottom lip, playfully relishing the sound he makes in the back of his throat. His fingers sink into the soft flesh of my hips and he pulls me even closer. Threading my fingers through his hair I pull back slightly to look at him.

If my aunt wasn't sitting right inside watching tv, I'd invite him in. Given our moments together tonight, I can only imagine what a night alone with him in bed would be like. His body feels solid, and practically vibrates with the same need I feel pulsing through me. I kiss him again, running my hands down his strong arms, urging him to hold me closer, giving his hands permission to wander more.

When he pulls back, I have to bite back a moan of frustration.

"I should probably get going," he says, though there isn't much conviction in his voice. His hands rub slow deliberate circles over my hips like he's trying to feel my skin through my dress.

"Do you have to?" I sound like a sad child who isn't getting her way.

He studies my face for a beat and then kisses me again, wrapping his arms around my middle and standing. We stay there for a minute before he lowers me to my own feet, pressing one last small kiss to my forehead. Something about his tenderness brings strange feelings into my chest.

"I'm afraid so," he says reluctantly, leaning his forehead against mine and taking his time to regain composure. "You have no idea how much I don't want to, though."

Breathing deeply, he wraps the blanket around me, stepping away carefully and runs his fingers through his hair.

"Thanks for walking me home tonight."

He gives me a small smile that sends the butterflies in my stomach tripping over themselves.

"I'll see you at work in the morning?" He brushes a few stray hairs from my face and trails his fingers gently down my cheek.

"I'll be there."

As he turns and walks back off the porch and down the street toward his house, he doesn't turn back to look at me, but I can't take my eyes off him as I watch him go. My mind wanders to what he's thinking as he disappears around the corner and is gone from view.

I know that this is all still new, but I feel hollow without him here. I turn toward the door to head inside, my mind full of images of his hands on me and the feel of his breath against my neck. I don't know what is happening between us, but I am already looking forward to seeing him in the morning.

I close the door quietly behind me, making sure that I fold the blanket back up and stuff it into the closet before stripping off my coat and shoes. I walk carefully through the kitchen taking care to make sure that Cici doesn't hear me come in.

When I'm safely on the stairs of the basement, I relax a little, heading to the bathroom to strip off my clothing and take a hot shower. After the night that I just spent with Nathan, I am exhausted, and I really don't feel like hashing out my feelings around what happened. I can't squelch the giddy feeling in my stomach that he brings to life. I haven't felt so equally cherished, listened to, and needed as much as I did tonight with him. I think I might be going crazy, standing in the shower, doubt starts to creep in. Nothing is this good without a cost. I should know better by now.

I know Cici will ask me how the night went, and I am horrible at keeping secrets, but I also don't really want to know what her thoughts on my exciting closet make out are.

Chapter Seventeen

The fragrant aroma of sizzling, smokey bacon wakes me up. This could only mean one thing; Cici is trying to draw me out. Lying underneath my warm comforter made me consider hiding in it to avoid her forever. She knows something's up, and I can't miss work. I find the courage to lift the heavy blanket of warm safety off my shoulder and figure out what to wear.

I slide out of the bed and stand in front of Cici's old dresser. I open the top drawer and on the very top is a pair of lacey, lavender underwear. I bought them shortly after moving in with Cici to make me feel better.

I like them. Maybe Nathan will, too.

I chastise myself for thinking something so inappropriate before even having my coffee in the morning. I slide the panties on, then a pair of jeans, and I dig through the drawers to find the matching lavender bra. I pop it on and grab a black v-neck and throw on a long gray cardigan. I stand at the bottom stairs to head to what I know will be an interrogation.

I walk into the kitchen with Cici in an orange pajama

set with long sleeves and smiling cactuses adorning it.
She has a sky blue shawl thrown over her shoulder to
keep her warm. She hands me a plate with a bacon and
cheese sandwich and smirks. "Ah, Kitty, do you have work
with Naaaathan today?"

"As a matter of fact, I do. I see you're up early for a
work day. Thanks for breakfast."

Here it comes. I brace myself, waiting for the lecture
I know I'm about to receive over ditching out on her last
night.

"Well, you see, luckily I came home early for my dear-
est niece to tell me all about her fundraiser and fell asleep
on the couch since she never came in. So I got plenty of
rest and decided to get up and see my hooligan." Her attitude gives her away—she is not happy with being ditched.

"I'm sorry. Nathan walked me home and we just ended
up talking."

Cici crosses her arms. She's not buying what I'm giving her.

"I love you, I really fucking do, but are you making
good choices? You just met him and you just broke up with
Marcus after how many years? I've known Nathan since
he was barely old enough to talk, and he is not the type to
willingly be a rebound." Her voice is the sternest I've heard
since I broke grandma's urn in high school. "That boy has
a lot of complications. Do you need that right now? Are
you okay with hurting him? Because he has enough hurt."

I feel a bubble of anger start to creep up in me. "Funny

coming from a woman who never settled down. We were just talking, I let him know about Marcus, and we don't even know where this is going. It's just nice to be wanted, my relationship with Marcus was dead for so long that this doesn't feel like a rebound."

Her eyes soften "Kitty, I know you've seen enough to fucking write a book. You deserve to be happy, I just don't want you to find any more hurt. I have had a lot of hurt in my life, I'm fucking old and bitter. Kitty, you don't need that bullshit."

Just in that moment, Charles walks into the kitchen in a pair of dark wash jeans and a cable-knit brown sweater. "Good morning," he says cheerfully. He stops just inside the doorframe and stares at the both of us.

I look at him, mild shock brushing across his face as he picks up on the tension between the two of us. I turn my attention back to my aunt. I know she only means the best for me, but I can't help feeling like I'm being belittled.

"It looks like you had company last night after all." I don't mean for my tone to be as harsh as it is, but at the moment I can't hear any of what she is going to try and say. "I really appreciate breakfast, but I think I am going to finish it on my walk."

Her face looks defeated.

"I know you want what's best, but my mistakes are my own. I need to make them." I peck her on the cheek, "I promise to actually come home and talk to you about work and the fundraiser. But I'm headed out."

"Love you, Kitty." She goes back to making her breakfast as Charles closes the distance between himself and her. I head to the front, I'm feeling good about what's happening. I won't let this conversation ruin what's going on for Nathan and me. I can handle myself and I always have. I open the door and walk out into the bright winter sunshine.

Twenty minutes later, I pull open the door to the library and am greeted by Amber's bright shining smile.

"GOOOOOD MORNING, CATHERINE!" Her grin is big, stretching ear to ear. She puts her hand next to her mouth and pretends to whisper "I've been waiting to hear about your walk home." She snaps back into her normal speaking voice. "I'm also going to be experimenting with your different nicknames to see what fits best."

I'm so excited to finally have someone excited for me and not just worried. "Good morning. It was nice. I'm a little tired. We stayed up pretty late talking."

She goes to respond as the elevator pings and Nathan strides out. He's dressed in his normal slacks and green sweater, and my heart does a little pitter patter

"Good morning, ladies." Nathan nods at both of us and then turns his attention to Amber. "Amber, I need you to send thank you emails to everyone who came last night." Then he turns to me, his normal unreadable expression plastered to his face. "And Catherine, I need you to come to my office to help me pack up a few of the silent auction pieces to send them out."

Amber winks at me, then looks at Nathan and does a little salute. "Right! On it, sir!" Then she begins typing away at the computer.

Nathan shakes his head and nods for me to follow him into the elevator. I follow and study his strong back, his green argyle sweater is a touch too tight across his arms and chest. I can see the curve of his muscles moving underneath as he walks, longing to drag my hands down them. He's wearing tan slacks that show off his tight ass as he walks, and I have to work really hard not to stare as I follow him to the elevators.

The elevator doors open and he ushers me in front of him to enter, he follows behind.

"Up we go. How was your walk this morning?" He turns to me, his eyes leisurely roam over my face before dropping to my cleavage.

"Hey, big fella. Eyes up here."

His face flushes. "I was looking at your necklace! "

"I'm not wearing a necklace." I grin.

He knows he is caught. A small smirk twitches in the corner of his mouth. "I know."

We both giggle like high schoolers as the elevator dings.

He pulls on the bottom of his sweater nervously. "Let's head to my office and get started."

We walk past the meeting rooms and into his office. He opens the door for me and I brush my fingers teasingly across his stomach as I pass, flashing him a smile that I hope is as flirtatious as I feel this morning.

Something flashes across his face that I can't quite read as he turns to close the door. My heart flutters when I hear the lock click into place, but I pretend not to notice as I lean over his desk to look at the pile of addresses and miscellaneous items strewn across it. I vaguely feel Nathan shift until he is standing behind me, but I absently keep my eyes on the stack of papers on his desk, rummaging through them, taking time to pick up each individual thing.

His hands settle on my hips, and he takes another step closer bringing his front to my back. My breath catches at the way his hands migrate from my hips and up my shirt. His fingers drag lazily over the skin of my sides and stomach, sending pulses of electricity coursing through me. Heat pools between my legs as he brushes my hair off my shoulder, and his lips find the soft spot under my ear, pressing a soft lingering kiss there before trailing down my neck to my shoulder.

"How did you sleep last night?" He asks between breathy kisses.

"Just fine, I guess." I tilt my head to the side, giving him better access to my neck and shoulder. "How about you?" My voice catches on the last word when his hands roam higher and graze the soft cup of my bra.

He sucks softly on my shoulder and I have to swallow the moan that creeps up in my throat. Nathan guides me around to face him, pressing his palms to the small of my back and stepping even closer to me. My lungs can't seem to draw in enough air when I meet his gaze.

"I had a little trouble falling asleep," he says huskily. "I couldn't stop thinking about you."

"Oh yeah?" I smile at him, ducking under one of his arms, taking a few steps around to sit in his chair behind the desk. I don't want to put space between us, but I'm afraid if I stay in his arms too long, I will end up pulling all of his clothes off.

"What were you thinking about?" I try to keep my voice casual, leaning back in the chair and crossing my arms over my chest. But inside I am already on the verge of coming undone from the intensity on his face.

He stalks around the desk, leaning down and turning me in the chair to face him. His eyes lock on my mouth as I pull my bottom lip between my teeth. My own heartbeat in my ears is deafening, and it takes all of my willpower to not close this distance between us and kiss him.

"I can't seem to keep my mind off the way you tasted last night." His thumb traces my bottom lip and I shiver into his touch. He drops his hand to my leg, parting my thighs before dropping to his knees in front of me. His eyes never leave mine as he hooks his hands behind my knees, pulling me to the edge of his chair.

My nipples pull tight against my bra as my chest rests against his. He runs his hands up my thighs before grasping firmly onto them. He leans forward, agonizingly slow until his lips are barely a breath away from mine. "I'm going to kiss you now."

I don't wait. I close the last of the space between us, pressing my mouth to his with more intensity than I intend, but he instantly matches my passion with his own, wrapping his arms around my torso, pulling my body impossibly closer to him. A breathy moan escapes from my chest when he opens his mouth against mine and sweeps his tongue along my lower lip before taking it between his teeth.

"Yep," he says, his lips brushing against mine at every word. "Just as good as I remember."

I'm lost. Everywhere his hands touch me sparks fire, his kisses tying knots in my stomach. I fist my hands into his sweater, clinging desperately in an attempt to keep the world from spinning out from under me.

Nathan presses greedy kisses down my neck and across my chest. I tilt my head back, biting back another moan as his thumbs graze roughly across my breasts through my clothing. I arch into him, threading my hands into his hair, guiding him back to kiss me again. But as soon as our lips meet once, he pulls away to study my face. I miss the feel of his mouth on me as soon as it's gone.

"What are you thinking?" I ask, trying to catch my breath.

His face is unreadable, but his hands are slowly making their way down my body, running over my thighs as if he is trying to memorize every inch of me.

"I'm thinking we should probably stop…" But even as he says it, his hands roam to the button on my pants and I drag in a ragged breath.

"You're probably right."

In the next second he has my pants unbuttoned, and he tugs them lightly. I lift my hips off the chair letting him pull them off completely. A small bubble of anxiety tries to push its way through my mind, but I feel too cloudy with need to give it much thought. A wave of heat rushes over me as he takes in my bare legs and light purple underwear. His knuckles graze my center through the thin fabric and I feel like all of the oxygen has been sucked from the room.

"Nathan." His name escapes from my lips like a plea, and I don't even know what I'm asking for at this point. All I know is that I need him closer, I need to feel his mouth on mine again.

"I like these," he says, hooking his thumbs into the hips of my underwear. He slips them down, painfully slowly, exposing the most sensuous part of me. "Did you wear them hoping that I'd see them?"

"Yes," I admit.

He makes a sound in the back of his throat that sends chills down my spine. His mouth is back on mine at that moment, hungry and searching. He works his hands up my shirt, pushing my bra up and out of the way to expose my breasts. He kisses the top of one of my exposed nipples, and then the other before drawing slow circles around them with his thumbs. He takes my hips pulling me even closer to the edge of the chair, pressing kisses down my stomach, sending tremors through my legs.

I bite my lip, hoping he can't feel the nerves pooling in my stomach. I can't remember a time I've ever been touched like this. It's like he's not just touching me for himself, but as if he finds pleasure in the way he makes me feel.

He nips at the sensitive skin of my inner thigh before kissing the abused spot softly. "You are so beautiful." His voice is raspy and desperate. "Can I kiss you here?" He trails a finger down my center, causing my body to shudder and my hips to lift off the chair involuntarily in response to his touch.

His eyes meet mine, and I nod, unable to make my voice work. Something about the veneration in his eyes sends emotions gushing through my body. There's a momentary pause, where he looks at me, and I feel my skin prickle in response to the intensity in his eyes. When his mouth finds the most intimate part of me, I can't stifle the moan that forms in my chest. The knots in my stomach simultaneously loosen and clench, and he presses my thighs farther apart, adjusting his angle and sending spasms of pleasure rolling through me. It's both too much and not enough all at the same time. I roll my hips into him, and he hums his approval. I feel myself winding tighter and tighter as Nathan's hands come to my hips, anchoring me in place, making it impossible for me to squirm away. I bite my lip, swallowing the moan that is bubbling through me.

"Please." I'm overwhelmed by the intensity of his mouth and my own needs. I know I'm close. He responds to my plea, sucking and running his tongue over me, and when I think it's too much, and I'm wound too tight, he slides a finger inside of me and I come undone. When my orgasm hits I feel like I'm being ripped apart. Nathan doesn't move, he pulls the coils of pleasure from me, slowly bringing me back down from the peak. I can feel my legs shake, and I lock my knees, hoping to surpress the trembling. Only when I have fully come back down does he reverently trail kisses back up my body to my mouth. I wrap my arms around his shoulders relaxing into the contentment I feel sitting in front of him.

"That was amazing," he says against my lips. He holds me there for a few moments, gently rubbing his hands along my hips before wrapping his arms around my back, pressing me to him. His kisses are slow and deliberate, grounding me back in the present and bringing the surge of emotion I felt just before back to the forefront of my mind.

"You're telling me." My breath is shaky and I feel unsteady when I pull away to straighten in the chair. Suddenly, awkwardness pulses through me, the gravity of what he just did weighing on me. I pull back to meet his eyes, running my hand down his torso, and hooking my fingers into the waistband of his pants.

He takes in a sharp breath through his teeth, but places his hand over mine. "As much as I want you to do what you're about to do, I think we should probably get you dressed…"

My face heats in embarrassment. I know he isn't rejecting me, but I feel weird about being the only on the receiving end of what just happened.

"Okay," I say quietly, studying where his hand is over mine so that I don't have to look at him.

He tilts my chin up, so that I have to look him in the eyes. " I'm okay," he says plainly. "As much as I'd love to spend all day locked in here with you, we do need to make it look like we've worked a little bit." He smiles at me, planting a sweet kiss on my lips.

"Sorry," I say when he pulls away to grab my pants and underwear from the floor behind him.

He hands them to me, studying my face. "Sorry for what?"

Sorry that you took care of me, and I didn't take care of you.

"I'll make it up to you," I say, plastering what I hope is a seductive smile on my face. "Because no one has ever done something like that to me before. It was amazing."

He is still studying me with a look on his face that makes my stomach twist into uncomfortable knots. I slide my underwear back on, pulling them up as I stand. I hate that I can't tell what he's thinking, and I'm starting to question if maybe I shouldn't have said anything.

Marcus wasn't one for foreplay, at least not a lot of it. He liked to get to the main event as quickly as possible. It never really bothered me, sex was good with him usually. I typically enjoyed making him feel good, too.

"Never?"

I try not to flinch at the inflection behind his question. But his face softens when I look at him. "Yeah, I mean, it's not a big deal. It just wasn't something my ex was into. I never pushed it any farther than that."

"I thought you had been with other people before him? Didn't you date other guys?"

I stand awkwardly pulling my pants on and buttoning them, feeling more exposed by the conversation than what just happened a few minutes ago. "Not really." I start absently flipping through the stuff on the desk, restacking piles I had already messed with, trying desperately to avoid the conversation. "I dated one other guy before my ex, and we did stuff, but I just didn't really like it. And Marcus just…"

"Just what?" He's leaning against the desk listening to me intently, his face looks patient and open, but it doesn't change how weird I feel about having this conversation.

"He just didn't." I shrug. "I don't want to make a bigger deal about it than it was. I just wanted you to know." My face is burning, and I realize as I talk that maybe my relationship experiences weren't exactly normal. Or maybe my lack of experience just made me oblivious.

"Well, I'm sorry you missed out so long." He winks at

me and comes around the desk to stand next to me, turning my body into him so that I have to crane my neck up to keep my eyes locked on his. "I hope you didn't mind then. I really want to do it again sometime."

He gives me a wicked smile and I have to fight to not let him see that my knees start shaking at the idea of a repeat performance of what just happened.

Nathan cups my face in his big hand and kisses me gently, stepping so that my legs hit the desk behind me. I melt into him, wrapping my arms around his neck, urging him closer still. His second kiss is more demanding and he inhales sharply when my hand tightens in his hair.

"Hey, Nathan?" Amber knocks loudly on the other side of the door, causing both of us to jump.

Nathan steps away from me quickly, heading around to the door. He throws one last look over his shoulder, sending those silly butterflies in my stomach dancing around.

"Hey," he says casually. His voice betrays nothing of how I feel or what was just happening as he opens the door to let her in. "What's up? Did you finish the emails?"

"Yeah, I did. I was just checking to see if you guys still need help?"

"Yeah, actually, that would be great." I say, kicking myself for the slight tremble in my voice.

Amber gives me a look as she steps into the office but says nothing.

I brush my hair back over my shoulder, trying to be casual. "If you want to address envelopes and boxes as I separate the things out, that would be awesome."

She nods, grabbing a sharpie off of the desk and leans on the desk waiting. Nathan grabs the list of names from last night and reads them off as I grab the items and package them up. We make a great team and the entire process takes us barely an hour.

When we are done, Amber retreats to sit at the front desk to work on some homework, Nathan goes to finish cleaning up the conference room from last night, and I head to my respective corner to put some returns back on the shelves.

The rest of the day passes really uneventfully, and I don't see Nathan again until the end, but that doesn't keep my mind from wandering to the events of our time together this morning. I'm deep in a fantasy of what might have happened if we had gotten more time together when he comes around the corner of the aisleway and sweeps me against the bookcase, planting a firm kiss on my lips, leaving me breathless.

"Can I take you out tomorrow evening?" he asks breathlessly, resting his forehead against mine.

"Sorry, I actually already have a date."

Nathan backs up a few inches, trying to conceal the shock I can see on his face. "What? I mean, okay... uh." He stumbles over himself, awkwardly looking away from me, trying to compose himself.

I giggle, turning his face back toward me. "I'm kidding. I don't have any plans. What time are you gonna pick me up?"

Relief washes over him. "How about 7:00? I have some stuff to do in the morning ,but I will for sure be done by then. Does that work for you?"

"I can't wait." I finish up my work for the day and get going on my way home. The walk is chilly but not completely unpleasant. It would already be warming up for the year in Georgia, so the snow and cold are a fun change of pace after years of constant warmer weather.

§

When I reach the house, Cici's VW Bus is gone so I assume she must be at work. Stepping onto the porch, I see a box by the front door. It's not super big or heavy, but when I pick it up, my heart drops to my feet. It's addressed to me, and I recognize the handwriting all too well.

Marcus sent me something.

My mind briefly flashes to an image of my childhood cat bringing me a dead bird when I was nine. I was horrified, but I remember my dad telling me it was my cat's way of showing his affection. I head into the house, and practically throw the box on the dining room table. I retrieve a pair of scissors from the kitchen and return to the table. Perching on one of the chairs I delicately cut into the box. The sound of my own heartbeat whooshing through my ears is deafening. Inside, there is a shoebox, and an envelope.

Dread pools where my stomach should be, twisting and curling itself around my organs. I can't seem to get enough oxygen in my lungs, and my hands shake as I pull a handwritten letter from the envelope.

My Catherine,

I hope this gift finds you in a better headspace than when you left. I have been biding my time, hoping that you will reach out or come back to me. But after waiting for weeks, agonizing about how we left things, I've decided it's time for me to reach out.

I miss you.

I've missed you since the moment you closed the door on the life we spent so much time building together. It destroyed me. Everyone here misses you, and I still don't know what to tell them when they ask me why you left. The house feels hollow and quiet when I come home at night, and I still find myself looking for you after work. I come home and expect to see you in the kitchen, or curled up on the couch with a book.

I know the last few months when we were together were stressful. I know that I wasn't the best, and I know that I took a lot of my frustration out on you. But I want to be better. I want to work on things between us. I hate the way we left things, and I want to make it up to you. I don't want this to be the end for us. I understand if you need more time, I want you to have it, we don't have to get married any time soon. But I do hope that you will consider coming back home soon. My family misses you. My parents ask about you constantly. They've been worried about you. And our friends from work feel your absence at parties and dinners.

Please tell me what I can do to make this right.

When you come home we can work on whatever you think we need to do. We can talk to someone. We can put the brakes on with getting married. We can talk this out. I believe it. We've been through so much together, I know you better than anyone else. We are both guilty of a lot, but I am willing to work on it if you are.

I love you always,

Marcus

I feel hot tears burning the back of my eyes as I gingerly fold the note back up and slide it into the envelope. He must've sent this before that drunken mess of a call.

I open the shoebox to reveal a pair of black stilettos. Diamonds run along the top, framing the toe, making the tops sparkle. I close the box back up and set it aside, sinking fully into the chair. I haven't allowed myself to think about Marcus much since I left him, but firstthe phone call and now sitting in front of the gift he sent me, my mind absently wanders to the last few years.

I feel more lost now than I have since making the choice to leave. I miss parts of my life from before, and it terrifies me that I left so much with no thought or explanation. When I was confused after my dad and stepmom had my stepsister, Marcus's family made me feel loved. His mom took me in and treated me like her own when mine was nowhere to be found. I knew when I left that I would inevitably hurt them too, but at the time I was so scared of getting married I didn't care. I thought it was him, but maybe it was me too. Maybe I am the one who gave up trying and just let myself be afraid of what was happening. Maybe if I had been more up front with my concerns about getting married, we could have worked on it and I wouldn't have had to run away. Things were definitely far from perfect, but what relationship actually is?

Doubt starts to creep up in my chest, squeezing my heart.

My mind jumps to Nathan. Even in the beginning, the best parts of our relationship, Marcus never made me feel the way Nathan does. Marcus always expected something of me, he was always bringing up things I could change, and things that could be better. But even in the short few weeks I've known Nathan, I have felt at peace around him. He doesn't expect me to change, or treat me like changing would make him like me more.

I think I need a drink.

I walk to the door without thinking or throwing back on my coat and head out to Cici's. The cold air stings my face and prickles my arms through my sweater. But the farther I walk, the less I can feel it.

Chapter Eighteen

"Catherine, MY LOOOOOVE!" Larry calls from the kitchen when I walk into Cici's Pub fifteen minutes later.

Charles spins and gives me a big smile, his blue eyes so warm and caring.

"We have a new Nitro beer. Tall or short?"

"After the day I've had, I think I need the biggest glass you have."

He chuckles as he fills a glass and slides it across the bar at me. I take it, and take three long drinks, draining half of the dark liquid before I set it back down.

Charles furrows his brow "I know you and Cici are struggling, but maybe you two…"

"Are you hungry?" Larry pokes his head through the window behind the bar.

I feel right now is not the time for a heart-to-heart with Charles, so I'll just ignore him. "Fuck, yes. I've only had a salad for lunch. Give me the greasiest food you got."

Larry smiles and nods before disappearing again. I sit silently, Charles looks at me, shakes his head, and goes to a customer waving for him. I can't help but watch Charles quickly snap into bartender mode and laugh with some regulars down at the other end of the bar, but my mind wanders back to earlier in the night, and to Nathan.

I pull my phone from my purse, planning to text Amber, but there is an unread text from Nathan that I didn't notice from a few minutes ago.

Nathan:
Where do you feel like getting a bite? I need to up my game from the diner.

As I'm contemplating his words, another text comes through, this one from Amber.

Amber:
Turn around Goof!

I turn to see America's sweetheart sitting surrounded by books and giving a little wave. She pats the booth seat next to her, signaling me to join her, when Larry plops a basket of greasy fried goodness down in front of me. He smiles and heads down the bar to serve a few other people.

I stand up and meander over to her table.

"Hey! What are you doing here?" she exclaims.

"This is my Aunt Cici's bar. Are you studying? I'm puzzled. I didn't peg you as the bar type." Especially with dive bars like Cici's.

She smiles a cheesy grin. "Well, when you work where

people study..."

Charles walks over to the table that Amber and I are now sharing. He gives me a sheepish smile and then turns to Amber. "Can I get you anything to drink?"

Amber giggles. "I'll have what she's having, please." She nods toward me.

Charles turns back to the bar and fills a glass for her before heading back into the kitchen. She takes a big drink of the rich dark beer and her face flushes even more as she swallows. "Wow, I don't know what I thought you were drinking, but that is strong!"

A laugh bubbles up from my belly at her reaction to the drink in front of her. "It's an acquired taste for sure. Are you a beer drinker?"

"I thought I was." She giggles. "But this stuff reminds me more of an espresso than a beer. Why is it so thick?"

"That's what makes it good." I take another big gulp of mine, watching her nurse hers carefully. "You know you can get something else."

She nods and pushes her drink back a few inches. I wave Charles back over and Amber orders a vodka and cranberry juice instead. I slide over, situating my food and drinks, trying not to knock over the stacks upon stacks of study work and notes.

"I have a ridiculous exam tomorrow, it sucks, it's not even for a fun class." She grumbles and shrugs her shoulders. She is definitely slaying the grey sweats and messy bun.

I raise an eyebrow and smirk. "You mean you procrastinated studying till the last second?"

She pouts like a child. "MAYBE! Are you here to see your aunt? You seem a little off. Is everything okay?"

Am I really that obvious? I must have a cloud clearly over me.

"I'm unfortunately bad at poker faces. My ex sent me a gift and letter, and I am having a lot of conflicted feelings over it." I start to pick at my fingers, an old habit that I thought had died off. "It's just, like, a reminder of everything we had in Georgia. But now I have stuff here."

"Like Nathan?" Amber takes a sip of her drink, studying me over her glass. "I mean, I don't really know anything about your last relationship, but...do you think it's too soon? Maybe everything with Nathan is making it more of a struggle?" Suddenly all of the giggly school girl energy is replaced by something much more somber and intense. Amber's eyes don't leave my face as she waits for me to talk.

"Honestly? I don't know. I feel like my relationship with Marcus was dead long before we actually split up. Things had been weird for more than a while. I just couldn't live anymore pretending it wasn't doomed. The last few months that Marcus and I were together were basically just a whirlwind of stupid arguments, wedding planning, work, and sometimes sleeping in the same bed together." I grimace thinking about all of the quiet lonely nights I spent in his house by myself. "Maybe I didn't try hard enough, but he didn't either."

She nods, shifting her clothes around so that she can pull her legs up to her chest. "That makes sense. Sometimes I think we know the end is coming way before it actually does. What are you afraid of?"

"I don't know." I answer honestly. "It's just been so long. And all of the feelings I have right now are new, and a little scary with Nathan. Marcus was stable, always there, and I always knew what to expect."

"I don't think scary is always bad. Nathan is a good guy, and he seems to really like you. How did you leave things with the ex, though? You should tell Nathan what's going on and how you're feeling."

She's right, Nathan deserves to know that Marcus wants to fix things.

"I ran. I saw the problems and ran. I really like Nathan. He's smart, funny, and so very hot. I've never really dated, and everything has happened so fast the last few weeks." I can't help but think back to Nathan's office. I never felt that connected with Marcus during our entire relationship.

"Catherine, you're only twenty-five. Love is confusing and hard. I think you should go to Nathan and tell him how you're feeling. He's very kind and understanding."

Amber is extremely wise for her years. She grabs my hand and squeezes it. "Mistakes are okay. Not taking risks and avoiding all conflict is where regrets lie. Conflict builds relationships if done correctly, and it sounds like you avoiding conflicts is destroying those relationships."

"UUUUGH, you're right. I know you are. I think maybe I should go to dinner and explain things. He asked me where I wanted to go. Maybe Italian. This situation is a little spicy." The words surprise me even as I say them.

She giggles into her drink as I pull out my phone.

Italian would be amazing!

I send the text before I can think too much or try to cancel.

"So, you never got to tell me earlier—what happened between you and this ex of yours? You said his name was Marcus, right?"

My body involuntarily flinches at his name. "It's really complicated. We were together for a long time. And we worked together. I told you he's one of the reasons I got to keep my job at the nonprofit after my internship was up. I moved in with him before graduation, and I guess getting married seemed like the next logical step."

"So, why didn't you follow through with it?"

I study her face, looking for the normal judgement or condemnation I had expected to see from someone who found out I ditched my fiancé a month before the wedding, but instead there is just kindness and concern looking back at me.

"I was young when I met him. Heartbroken over my mom, and uncomfortable in my new family. He offered what looked like stability. It was a breath of fresh air to be with someone who seemed to genuinely want me, someone who knew all of the things he wanted in his life. It felt good to be included in his picture. But then came the stipulations. There were rules, and expectations.

"At first I thought they came from a place of love. I thought he was trying to motivate me. I had never had anyone so personally invested in who I was. But then if those expectations weren't met, there were consequences." I take a shaky breath, finishing my drink in one big gulp.

"At first he just got a little irritated, telling me he just pushed me to be better because he loved me. But slowly over the years, it got worse. He expected me to only hang out with certain people, preferably with him at my side. If I didn't, he would be pissed. Then it was my weight or my clothes. When working out didn't help, he changed my diet, watching what I ate. When I didn't perform around his friends the way he wanted me to, he would keep me away from them. God forbid I have a drink or two, or have fun."

Amber reaches out and takes my hand across the table. Her eyes are full of sympathy and understanding. I take a shaky breath, and wipe at my face. I don't remember crying. I'm thinking that I should stop talking now, but it's like someone broke the dam and now that I've started, I can't seem to keep the words inside me any longer.

"When he proposed, he said things would get better. He said we could go to counseling and he loved me, so he wanted to work on us. But that never happened. Things honestly got worse. He was holding me to an impossible standard, and when I didn't reach it, we fought. We argued about everything. Any time I messed up, I was terrified of the fight that would come after. I walked around his house on eggshells, unsure of what the next thing would be that set him off."

Amber nods, her expression and everything about her offering solace. "I understand. my dad was abusive like that to me, my sister, and my mom."

I freeze.

Abusive.

Marcus isn't abusive. I'm not abused, am I? I feel a surge of anger in me and dismiss her claim. "Abusive's a bit of an exaggeration. Marcus wanted picture perfect and I just am not that. No matter how much either of us wanted me to be, it's not my style." I feel defensive and I think Amber senses it. "He was very loving and did a lot, he worked hard to provide for us. I have many wonderful memories of him and me snuggled watching old movies. He loved me too hard."

"Maybe 'abusive' is not the right word for it. I do think perfect is your style, look at you!" She stops. "I don't want to offend you, but I saw firsthand what that kind of behavior does to someone. My dad spent years controlling what my mom and my sister and I wore, how we did our hair, and where we went. I wasn't even allowed to start wearing makeup until college, and that's only because I moved out of their house. Once my dad saw my mom putting on lipstick before they went to a friend's for dinner, and he dragged her into the bathroom and made her scrub her face. He used to say that lipstick was only worn if you wanted to be a whore." She sighs deeply. "I thought my mom looked beautiful, and I always thought she should have fought back, but in the end when I asked her about it, she shrugged me off, saying she didn't need it anyway because my dad loved her. But she seemed so miserable."

"I'm so sorry." I see her shoulders sag a little under the weight of her words, like they physically hurt for her to say. I understand that feeling.

"My sister and I hated it. We always had to have long hair, and I was never allowed to get my ears pierced. We had strict curfews, and my dad didn't even let us get jobs in high school. When I moved out for college I had nothing but the cash money that I was given at my graduation. Any checks I got, my dad deposited it into an account for me, and I had to beg for the money. When my sister and my ex moved in together, my dad completely disowned her. At first I was thankful, like wow, he's taking my side in this. But then one night when we sat for dinner and mom brought her up, dad called her a whore, said she deserved to be unhappy forever since she thought it was okay to sleep with a man before marriage. She hasn't been allowed to come to a family Christmas or Thanksgiving since then. I kind of envy her honestly." She finishes her drink in a few big gulps. "I know you say that Marcus didn't abuse you, and obviously I wasn't there, so I don't really know. But I know the ways a person's actions can destroy your life and sense of self."

I nod slowly, feeling the buzz of the alcohol in my brain.

Amber continues. "I know your family wasn't perfect, and in contrast, I'm sure Marcus felt like the hero. Especially after your mom left... Those things affect us more than we realize. I know my family changed everything about how I perceived myself. My own value was so skewed, I allowed myself to believe a man loved me when he was really after my sister."

"Yeah, my dad is a kind, very serious, clean cut guy. All he wanted was a Leave it to Beaver life with a big family. Mom didn't want any of that. I'm not even sure what she wanted. I was a 'whoopsie' and, well, Dad tried to make it work, and since the day I was born, it was clear it wouldn't. She did stick it out for fourteen years, so I have to give her props for that. I think anyway... Maybe in the long run it would have been better if my parents ripped off the band aid sooner." I take a big swig and wave my hand for Charles to bring me another. "If we're diving into dear ol' mom issues, I need something to loosen up my inhibitions a bit more. I'm still too sober for this."

Amber smirks and puts on a very valley girl accent. "OMG, YAAAS! WE LIVE FOR MOMMY ISSUES!"

We both laugh. I feel genuinely happy, which I haven't felt in a long time.

Charles brings her another cranberry and vodka, then hands me my beer. "Behave, you two." He laughs and heads back to where Larry stands behind the bar.

"Is it weird that I find him attractive, like a grayed Colin Firth?" Amber looks longingly at Charles.

I snort. "He and Cici are platonically married. If anyone comes within a foot of him, she will bite."

Amber laughs.

I look at my reflection in my beer. "Cici is amazing, I didn't realize until recently how much of a mom she has been my whole life. I think my mom just never really signed up for it. I'm thankful I'm here, but her life was seriously derailed by my birth."

Amber tilts her head like a puppy as I continue. "My mom was on her way to greatness. She was super smart and really free-spirited. She was on a premed path, had a summer fling with her best friend's brother, my dad, and got knocked up. He said when she had me, it's like a switch flipped and her empathy got turned off. She suffered pretty severe postpartum depression. My dad always told me it wasn't me, that it's just her brain wasn't healthy."

Amber interrupts. "It's true. It really wasn't your fault. PPD really can mess someone up."

"I know that now, but as a kid, it doesn't matter what anyone says. When your mom doesn't want to be around you, it's your fault." I take a swig and continue. "I have great memories, too. She wasn't all bad. She wasn't mean. She really tried to fake it. My dad really loved her, and I did, too. I can remember every night she'd read to me, she told me that kids who are read to succeed more in life. She read until the night she left even though I was a teenager." I stare off.

§

She opens the door "Hey Catie, can I come read to you?"

I drop the game I'm playing and pull out Harry Potter and The Half Blood Prince. The only time my mom felt like she was there was at story time. She walks over and climbs onto my white four-poster bed, and snuggles up with me under the pink covers.

She pulls my head into her chest and she starts petting my chestnut hair. "I love you no matter what, Catie. I know your father and I fight a lot. I struggle a lot. I'm sorry, I wasn't better at being there for you."

I wonder why she's apologizing, but mostly I'm just enjoying her warmth. She wasn't the affectionate type.

"You are strong, funny, and so kind. Don't ever let anyone change that. Don't let someone convince you to accept less. I love you so much, Catie."

I look up into her hazel eyes. "I love you, too, Mom. Are you okay?"

She looked back down at me. "I think I will be. I just don't want you to hate me for following my dreams."

"No, I could never hate you, Mom. You can do anything. I love you."

"And I you, my sweet Catie bear. This is our last chapter to read together," she said solemnly.

"I know! I can't wait for the next book!"

§

I could hate her. I do hate her. Why didn't she tell me that was our last chapter together forever? That I would never read the next Harry Potter book because she wouldn't read it to me?

The thought broke me. My mom never held me like that again, and I didn't want anyone to hold me again either.

"Do you talk with your mom at all? I mean, I can't imagine how hard that was for you." Amber looked at me with sympathy but without judgement.

"No, that was the last time I saw her. I woke up the next day with my dad crying over his coffee with a note in his hand. My parents did their divorce long distance. I get holiday and birthday cards, but that's it." I feel bad and good at the same time. It's hard to air the pain out, but it gives me such a sense of relief.

"That's really hard, I can't imagine my mom just up and leaving. I think maybe you have a lot of thinking to do." She finishes her drink and gives me a sweet smile "You can do this."

Can I?

"Thanks. I think maybe I should go for a walk in the cold for a little bit to clear my head. Sorry to keep you, then suddenly leave."

"No! It's totally fine. I have to get to bed. I have that early exam tomorrow! Let's do this again soon!" Amber flashes a big sincere smile at me.

We get up out of the booth. She comes over and gives me a huge hug that I reciprocate. I feel I've truly found a friend here.

"Thanks for listening. I appreciate it." I let go and she waves a little 'bye' at me as I head out into the cold darkness of the evening. It's a little past 8:00 and I'm just walking up to my aunt's porch when my phone buzzes in my pocket.

Meghan:

I'm so sorry! I forgot to call you today when I was at the salon. Are you still wanting to come in tomorrow morning?

Shit, I completely forgot about the hair appointment. I type back a quick reply, double checking the time, and then agree to be in the next morning at 10:00. I rummage around aimlessly in the fridge for a few minutes before deciding to just grab a bottle of water and head to the basement. I feel restless still with Marcus's gift sitting on the table. I shove the feelings down and head to bed. Instead, I focus on my excitement for tomorrow. I can't wait to get my hair done, and I have another date with Nathan.

Chapter Nineteen

I pull up to the mall once again in the old VW Bus that my aunt let me borrow. She has a picture of my younger sister, Bailey Mae and I taped to the dash. I'm sitting in a big arm chair and shes standing in front of me. My arms are draped around her and we are both grinning. It is only from last Christmas, and if you didn't know any better, the obvious age gap between the two of us makes it appear as if I'm Bailey Mae's mom. It is painful looking at the smiling five-year-old. I love her so dearly, but I can't help feeling jealous of the life she gets that I didn't.

It's 9:50. Plenty of time to leisurely walk into the salon, but not too long to start overthinking.

I open the bus door and climb out. I turn to shut it and use as much force as I can. If I don't, then it won't actually close, which is what Cici gets for having Larry fix up the bus over the years. As they say, jack-of-all-trades, master of none… I think.

The lonely strip mall looks even more abandoned this early in the morning. The parking lot is completely empty besides four other cars, and I'm pretty sure the old brown

Cadillac has been parked there since I was in high school. I hold my breath for a moment and release, as if I'm a child pretending I'm a dragon as the fog leaks out. I smile to myself, feeling lighter than I have since coming to Bethton Grove almost two months ago.

Approaching the old structure I feel a rush of embarrassment. I have put absolutely no thought into what I want to do with my hair. I know I want to go back to my natural dark. I am totally clueless on what is 'in' right now. I pull open the doors, no preteens trying to get every temporary tattoo, and no screaming toddlers. It's an extremely eerie feeling. The food court isn't even open yet, the tables empty and the whole place nothing but quiet, dirty tile.

Time is ticking away. At 9:58, Simple Image is in front of me. I open the door and the little bell seems earth-shatteringly loud in the empty mall. I cringe at the fact that I broke the silence. I hate this feeling I have of being unwanted. I look around the room and see just Meghan prepping her station for me. I sit down in the waiting area and take the salon in a little more to try and ground myself. It smells like chemicals. It's a little warm, so I slide off my big black winter coat. The room is as blinding white as before, but this time I notice the plants adorning the room. A smile spreads across my face. You rarely see real plants in shops, but someone here really takes their time and cares for them. They have little tiny grow lights hooked to the pots that look like little halos. They're pink tinted and it adds an intersting flare to the salon.

"HEY, YOU! You should've said something. I would've brought you back here to chat. No one else is supposed to be in until noon. We've got the place to ourselves!" Meghan shouts to me.

I sheepishly smile. "Oh, I just didn't want to bother you, sorry."

"Nope, nope. We don't say sorry for nothing. Come sit, tell me about everything, I'm all ready." Meghan has always been that friend, the one who does everything to make you feel better.

I stand up and walk towards her. She could be a model. Even though she is wearing all black, and a black apron, I can still see her perfect figure under it. She has always been beautiful and kind. Meghan's blonde hair is in a tight ponytail. The color has been done really well, and you'd never know she was naturally brunette. As I get closer, I see her dyed fingertips splattered with purples and blacks, her nails kept short. She turns the chair towards me and gestures for me to sit.

"So what are we doing today, Cat? I know you were saying you wanted to dye it darker and closer to your natural color. You've got a good bit of length, but a lot of yucky stuff. I could probably take a couple inches off." She starts fluffing my hair and getting a feel for it.

Why do I feel so freaked out? Before Marcus took care of it. "I'm honestly not sure, Marcus always told me I should do my hair like this, so I do."

"Well, let's trim your ends and move on from there.

239

Maybe inspiration will hit us." Meghan smiles brightly at me.

I hope she doesn't see the absolute mess I am... I take a moment as she starts to brush and section my hair, to breathe and get into a better headspace. Once she's done, she holds up the last few inches of my hair and looks at me in the mirror. "I think the last three inches need to come off.".

"I think I want to take off more." I don't know why, but the longer I look at myself in the mirror, the more I need a change. I don't want to be Catherine from Atlanta anymore, I don't even want to look like her.

"Okay," Meghan moves her fingers up another inch or two. "Here?"

"I think I want more than that." I pull some of my hair to the front, measuring against my chest where I think I want it. I place my finger across the chunk of hair, motioning that I want the length right below my collar bone. "I think I want it here."

Meghan's eyes go wide, but she controls herself quickly. "Oh, a big, big chop."

I nod, determined now. "And I want the color to go dark, like really close to my natural color."

Meghan nods, looking in the mirror at me, scanning my face for a long moment before she gives me a big smile. "I think that will be perfect. I'll get the bulk of the length off, and then go mix color. Once it's done and rinsed, we can take care of the rest of the haircut."

"Perfect." My heart is beating like crazy in my chest, and I am anxious to see what will happen. "I trust you."

My emotions feel muddled, Somewhere between excited butterflies and fear. I stare into the mirror at the woman I am, except the woman staring back at me doesn't even look like me anymore. I don't think I've been her for quite a while now. I instinctively run my fingers through my hair, like giving an old friend a hug goodbye. I can't even remember what I look like without my auburn waves flowing down my back. I can remember a time I went too short with the cut, and that was when Marcus decided he'd set up my appointments for me. He said that short hair made my face *far too round.'*

Our eyes meet in the mirror and she raises her eyebrows. "Know what would be fun? Let's turn you around, then it will be a big surprise, like in the movies!" Meghan squeezes my shoulder a touch "You are beautiful. It's time to show it off." She spins me away from the mirror.

"You ready?" Meghan pulls my hair behind my head.

I squeeze my eyes shut and hesitantly say, "Ready."

I can feel the cut of the scissors tugging at my hair.

Meghan hands me a chunk of hair and softly says, "It already looks better, Cat. A few more snips then we'll dye and shape, okay?"

I grip the hair hard. It seems like so much in my hands, but there's no turning back now. "Thank you Meghan," is all I can squeeze out in between the tears welling in my eyes.

The weight starts to lift off my head. The slice of the scissors feel like they are cutting away the years.

"I would love it if you joined me for dinner."

SNIP!

"Have you thought about growing your hair out? I'll set it up for you, and how about red? Redheads are some-thing else, right, Kitty?"

SNIP!

"I love you."

SNIP!

"You are lucky I got you into this job."

SNIP!

"Are you actually that stupid?"

SNIP!

"HOW DARE YOU?"

SNIP!

"NO ONE WILL EVER LOVE YOU!"

SNIP!

"Wow, you are stunning with shorter hair!" Meghan must feel the change in my attitude, "You okay, Cat?" Meghan's tone has a hint of worry in it.

"I will be. Let's dye this bitch."

No turning back… *Ever.*

She starts painting the dye onto my hair, the sound of it sliding down my hair is less than appealing, kind of a wet, squelchy sound. Meghan stays silent, but I can feel her positive aura around me. I wonder over the years how many clients' hair she's done who are like me. She is strong and I can feel the push and pull of the brush. Meghan has always been so self-assured, and I feel it with each stroke.

She stops painting. "Okay, this needs to sit for a little bit." She gracefully maneuvers around the chair. "Do you want to talk? Or do you want space?" She squats to face me eye to eye.

Even though Meghan has always been a talker, she is probably one of the most perceptive people when it comes to knowing when to talk and when to stay quiet. I have always admired that about her.

"Either is fine with me, but I want you to know I'm here for you, always." She smiles and places a hand on my thigh. "You are so amazing and have been through some stuff recently. I just want to be here in a way you want me to be."

I put my hand on Meghan's. "Stay, I don't know if I'll talk, but I'm not ready to be alone yet." I don't even know how to process the swirl of emotions bubbling inside of me. It's been so many years of shit. The relief I'm starting to feel almost hurts.

Meghan smiles. "Let me grab a waiting chair real quick." She jogs over, grabs a chair that absolutely dwarfs her, and carries it and sets it down across from me.

I look at her kind smile, wise beyond its years, and ask, "Why are you this way? Meghan, you have always been such a rock. After my mom left, when Ashleigh would make fun of my weight, you'd stand up for me. And now I haven't spoken to you in years. I abandoned all my friends for Georgia, yet you're still here for me. I don't deserve that."

She laughs and smiles. "You have always had a flair for dramatics, haven't you? Nobody deserves anything. Life sucks. It's hard. I just don't want to add to your hurt right now. Does it sting that you left and didn't stay in touch? Of course! Why does it sting? Cause you were–are one of my best friends. Being gone for what, five or six years? It's got nothing on the fourteen years of our friendship and the hundred God gives us. I've held grudges in my short time, it's too much work. It's easier to unconditionally love you than hold onto any grievances I have."

My eyes begin to sting again. "I'm sorry I didn't stay in touch. I.."

She interrupts, "I don't need an explanation, or a sorry. It's not like I tried to, either. You are awesome and I'm so lucky that you've come back and still want to be friends with me. I don't know what has happened in our time apart. You have been hurt in that time and I'm bummed I couldn't support you then. I'm here now if you want to tell me about it. If you don't, that's okay, too." Her face is so open, and her eyes glitter with the swirl of emotions I've been feeling since I saw her in the salon a few weeks back. My chest aches for the friendship I wish I would have carried with me to Georgia. I try not to dwell on what may have been different….

I look at her gentleness and let it all go. I tell her everything over the hour of waiting for my hair to dye. How Marcus and I met, the hurts and joys of our relationship, and finally how I left.

She sits, nods, and only speaks to get clarification. She allows the dam of my hurts to flow onto her shoulders, and it's not only from my hair that the weight has been lifted, but also from my troubles. Over the last few years, I bottled so much of it up and gaslit myself into believing the lies Marcus fed me. Talking to Meghan makes everything feel real, but the transparency lifts my soul and rekindles life I didn't know I still had living inside of me. For years, all I've had were Marcus's friends, thinking no one else wanted to be friends with me. Never realizing that home is still home...

§

PING! PING! PING!

"Time to wash all that away." The way she speaks makes me feel like maybe she means more than the hairdye. "Let's head to the bowl, then style and do a reveal?" Meghan pats me on the leg and stands. She guides me to the sink, I sit down in the chair and she starts running the water and washing my hair "So what are your plans for later? My husband and I are going out with my friend Sofia and her husband. She's about to pop her third kiddo."

"Well, I have a date actually." I smile proudly.

"Shut up! With who? I'm so excited for you. You are so awesome and strong, rebuilding your damn life." Her excitement eases my nerves.

"It's with Nathan Alvarez." I can't help but flush.

"Oh, wow, Nathan is a sweetie. I thought I sensed some chemistry the other night!" Meghan has me sit up and she towels my hair dry. "Sofia, who I'm having dinner with, is his little sister. As a warning, she is very overprotective of her siblings."

A pang of fear hits me. "Oh, I've met her. She seems nice, though..."

"Just a warning, dude. Now, backwards to the chair.

NO PEEKING!"

Her maneuvering me backwards is going to kill me. I stumble a few times before we make it to the chair.

Meghan starts blow drying my hair and adding products. The warmth feels like the sun after swimming in a cool pool. The sound drowns out her voice. I nod along anyways. She pulls out the straightener and I can feel the tug and pull of her curling it while I stare at my black snow boots. "I'll be right back. I'm gonna grab my makeup bag to really give you some vavavoom!" Meghan skips off to get whatever tools she needs, like a girl playing with Barbies.

Meghan comes back and kneels in front of me. "Relax. A little mascara, a little lip and a touch of blush is all you need. I've always been so envious of how perfect your skin is. You're probably one of the prettiest people I've met. I hope this helps you see it, too."

She turns the chair towards the mirror after applying the makeup. I wonder who I will be. I'm not Marcus's fiancé anymore, and I won't be the auburn-haired pushover, either. The mysterious new girl in town? The rebel? The best friend who is outspoken?

I force my eyes open and I can't help but cover my mouth in shock. My eyes well with tears, and I have to hold back so I don't ruin my makeup.

"You can let it go. The mascara's waterproof." Meghan puts her hand on my shoulder. I start to cry out in the open freely.

I look like... *me*.

My dark brown hair is styled into loose curls that fall a bit above my collar bone. The curls frame my face in a way that slims me. My hazel eyes stand out like glowing orbs against the darkness of my hair. The hint of olive tone in my skin no longer makes me look sick but natural. Tears cascade down my face. I stand up and place my hand on the mirror to say hello to the girl I haven't seen in years. She looks so free, like the world has been lifted off her shoulders. She is no longer a memory of what was but what is.

I am free....

Meghan hands me a tissue and hugs me from behind. "I don't know if you realize this, but you are a spitting image of your aunt. I remember how beautiful I thought she was when she'd pick you up from school. How pretty she still is."

"You really think so?" I finally squeak out.

"I know so. I bet Nathan will see how beautiful you are tonight, too." She rests her tiny head on my shoulder. "Let's get you all checked out. You can get ready and I can actually open the salon."

I nod and wipe my tears. I pull my phone from my pocket.

Me:
I love you, sorry about the other day.

PING!

Cici:

I love you, too, loser

Chapter Twenty

I kick my legs to keep the porch swing going while waiting on Nathan. It creaks from rusted old chains, filling the silence and helping to distract me from my racing thoughts.

After my liberating morning with Meghan, I decided to be daring and scour Cici's closet. I settled on a dark forest green knee-length slip dress. It feels velvety and smooth against my skin, and I think it compliments my new darker hair well. It has intricate lace across the top that dips down into a slight sweetheart shape. I pull on a pair of dark stockings, and a pair of low black heels. Over the dress I put on a black kimono style wrap, and even throw on a pair of small teardrop-shaped gold earrings and a necklace to match.

I hope Nathan likes my new hair.

My breath is like little clouds floating up and away. I feel like a giddy school girl. I can't seem to settle my nerves as Nathan pulls up in his little blue Civic.

He steps out of the car, and I head toward him, trying to contain my grin. I can tell he noticed my hair, he's looking at me intently, but I can't quite seem to get a read on his expression.

"Something's different," he states, his brows furrowed dramatically as if in thought. I stand before him, and he makes a big show of looking me head to toe. "I'm not sure what it is… Spin for me." He takes my hand, spinning me slowly under his arm.

I can't help but giggle.

"I know what it is!" he exclaims. "You have on earrings! I don't think I've seen you wear earrings before."

I place my hands on my hips and sigh dramatically, but I can't help but laugh. His face lights up, and he steps in close, threading his arms through mine and around my back.

"Your hair looks amazing," he says in a low tone, I can feel the vibration of his words flow through his chest, and my heart jumps around in my chest excitedly.

"Thank you." My words come out breathy. "I needed a change."

"I like the change, you are glowing." His words melt my insides, and I wrap my arms around his shoulders, standing on my tiptoes to plant a soft kiss on his lips. He tightens his hold around my middle, pulling me tightly to him as he returns my kiss. After a moment we break away from each other, both seeming reluctant to break the contact.

He turns and opens the passenger door for me. He gives me a little bow and gives his words a slight British accent. "Milady."

I giggle and slide into the Civic. It smells like Clorox. He must've detailed his car before our date. A little pine tree air freshener swings back and forth from the rear view mirror.

He climbs in and slams his driver door.

"Sorry, it sticks," he says, referring to his car door. "It's about a ten minute drive to the Meatball Factory."

I try to stifle a laugh and fail. "I'm sorry, but the *what*?"

"I know, it's the worst name but the best carbonara I've ever had. And I would honestly kill for their garlic knots." He gives me a big smile. "Let's go! Can't leave the knots waiting." He hits the gas and pulls away from Cici's.

I spend most of the car ride staring out the window at the town I grew up in as we pass by buildings that once housed old bookstores and antique shops replaced by fast food and supermarkets.

Nathan rubs my thigh and smiles. I like being with him, I usually feel bad leaving people in silence, but this feels good, comfortable. I don't feel like I need to fill the void, and I feel like he just likes being with me, too. I put my hand on top of his and I can see a small smile spread across his face even though he's looking at the road. This town has changed and grown. I hope I have as well. I'm startled by him stopping, pulling me from this blissful *la-la* land.

"And we're here." His voice is warm, and he gives my knee a little squeeze, sending wonderful tendrils of warmth up my legs.

I look up to see a great big warehouse with a giant neon sign that just says MEATBALLS. I open the car door and the smell of garlic and bread hits me like a brick. The parking lot is filled to the brim with cars.

Nathan comes to my side of the car and extends his elbow to escort me into the restaurant.

"What a gentleman." I hook my arm into his. "This place looks terrifying. If the other cars weren't here, I'd assume you were turning me into meatballs." I give him a big toothy grin.

"Who says I'm not? This is actually a cannibal restaurant and you're the main course."

We both laugh as we make it to the door. He turns to me, smirks, and says smoothly, "I mean, I'd love to eat you again."

My cheeks flush, and I can't help to look away in embarrassment as we walk through and are greeted by the sixteen-year-old host.

"Two for Alvarez, please," Nathan says it like he practiced it.

"Right this way." The young man grabs two menus and starts to walk us towards our table. Instead of seating us on the main floor, he takes us to a large elevator, he hits the button, and the doors open. "The reserved seating is this way."

We hop onto the elevator, and I snuggle up to Nathan, feeling his strong body against mine. I feel like a little bunny next to his large being. It makes me feel safe. As we stand in the elevator, I am hit by the smell of his cologne. It's fresh and a little spicy, and I can't help but snuggle a little closer to his side, trying to soak up as much of him as I can.

The door opens and we're swept into a completely different environment than the crowded family dining below. I feel like I've stepped into a mobster movie scene. The lofted ceiling is painted with renaissance style cherubs and clouds. The tables are set with silk table clothes and golden silverware. Candles adorn the tables, the people up here are dressed to suit the environment. I feel extremely underdressed. Nathan looks ravishing in his black button down and black slacks. His hair is perfectly groomed, and it looks like he put a lot of effort into the scruff on his cheeks and chin. It's shaped to perfection, accentuating his strong jaw.

I try and hold my head up a little more, slipping my hand into his as we exit the elevator. He glances at me from the corner of his eye and a look of complete adoration softens his features, sending more tendrils of warmth coursing through me.

The host takes us to a table secluded in the back with a bouquet of roses waiting. He pulls out my chair and ushers me to sit. The host takes our jackets, gives us a small bow, and scurries off. Nathan sits across from me smiling, so proud of what he was able to provide. I am in awe of this hidden gem and the fact it's here in Bethton Grove.

"This place is amazing, Nathan! You really stepped up

your game, didn't you?"

He shrugs. "Well, after the less-than-stellar diner date followed by the most boring fundraiser of all time, I felt like I owed it to you."

"The fundraiser wasn't all bad…" My mind drifts to our steamy make out session in the closet.

He eyes me, and for a second I think I might see him blush. But before we can continue, a waiter comes to the table for drink orders. I order myself a glass of red wine and Nathan orders a water.

"Are you not a wine drinker?" I ask as the waiter retreats to grab our drinks.

"I don't really drink at all, actually." He shifts, slightly uncomfortable in his seat.

"Oh, gosh. Is it okay that I ordered wine? I mean I don't want to make you uncomfortable."

He adjusts his silverware next to his plate, lining the forks up so they are perfectly aligned. "No! It's totally fine. It's just with the way my dad is, I just prefer not to drink. I mean, I don't like the way most of it tastes anyway… So it seems like a waste of a drink to me." He gives me a reassuring smile.

I feel like an idiot for not thinking about his dad and how that might make him uncomfortable about alcohol. I make a mental note that if we go on another date, to watch a little more carefully what I order.

I pick up the menu, flipping through as I look at all of the options they have. "Oh, shit. This place is expensive."

I don't realize I say it out loud until Nathan chuckles and answers me. "Don't worry about it. This is a date, and I intend to pay. Get whatever you want." He smiles at me, stirring butterflies in my stomach.

We sit in silence for another few minutes before the waiter comes to check on us, saying he will give us a few more minutes to look over the menu. The menu is over-whelming and expensive... I peer over my menu and Na-than is sitting there smiling at me. He quickly looks away, flushing from embarrassment.

"Caught you," I tease as butterflies fill my stomach.

He smirks. "I can't help it, my eyes are like moths to a flame when I see a beautiful woman."

My cheeks heat up and I'm sure he can tell. "Smooth."

"Thanks. I actually practiced and wrote down some pick-up lines." He pulls a piece of paper from his pocket and we both laugh.

"Let me see that!" I giggle, reaching across the table to take it from him.

"Oh no!" he says, shoving it back into his pocket before I can grab it. "You're just going to have to sit here and wait for me to use them." He winks at me, turning his menu over and folding his hand on the table.

I can't help but study the large hands, all the work they do, the calluses that tell stories I've yet to hear. I open my mouth to respond as the waiter comes and sets the wine glass in front of me and water next to Nathan.

"Are we ready to order?"

I look up and feel slightly annoyed that we are interrupted. It always made me laugh how horrible all waiters' timing could be.

Nathan speaks first. "Garlic Knots and that heavenly carbonara. Please, sir." He sounds so kind speaking to the young man, unlike Marcus ever was. Marcus would've come across as belittling and stern.

"How about you, miss?" The young man turns to me. His blue eyes and soft smile give away his youth.

"I'll have the same! Thank you." I flash the young man a smile. He nods and strolls away to place our orders.

I look at Nathan and his shoulders relax a little. He is so warm, and gentle. Our waiter walks by, drops the garlic knots without a word, and goes to another table.

"Wow, that was fast! They smell so delicious." I take a big whiff of the garlic as the heat of the fresh bread circulates. I grab one, ripping off a chunk, and pop it into my mouth. "Oh my god, this is the best!" I take another bite, closing my eyes as I chew.

When I open them again, Nathan is staring at me, the edges of his eyes have gone darker, and he smirks. "I think I need to take you here more if that's the face you're going to make when you eat."

I blush, but just like that the sexual tension dissipates.

He smiles at me. "They are so great, I have ordered these to pick them up and eat them in my office all by myself like popcorn."

We both laugh and he pops one into his mouth.

"I love how this place feels, very Godfather-esque." I giggle.

He places his hand a little far from what I think is actually comfortable on the table. I lean forward, reaching my hand toward his, allowing his big hand to take mine, almost completely engulfing it. We sit in silence for a long moment, his eyes searching my face, and I allow myself to do the same.

"So, tell me, Catherine," he gives me an easy smile, "what prompted the big hair change? Not that I don't love it, I'm just curious. My sister always says that any time a girl changes her hair drastically, it's because something has happened."

I laugh, a tad uncomfortably. I can tell by his face that he knows he's digging, but I don't actually mind. I've never felt weird talking to Nathan, even when I probably should have. It's been a whirlwind the last few weeks, but since he's been present in my life, things finally have started to feel like they make sense. I can't deny this attraction we share, and I also can't deny how much his compassion and understanding has started to change me.

"Well," I say finally, realizing he's still looking at me, waiting for some sort of answer. "It was just time. I think in some ways, I've been holding onto my hair and my appearance as a means to stay connected to things I shouldn't be connected to anymore."

He nods, but doesn't say anything.

I can't tell if he's waiting for me to say more or not, but

I decide to explain myself further. "I feel like I've made a lot of changes since I moved here. It was time for me to cut ties, literally." I motion to the length of my hair and giggle. "I just didn't like that person anymore, and I didn't even feel like her. I wanted to do something for me, that made me feel like... well... me." I blush, realizing I'm rambling.

He's quiet for a moment, then squeezes my hand gently. "I'm pretty sure you'd be just as beautiful bald, but I do love whatever Meghan did for you this morning."

Just then the waiter comes over with our food, and I don't even realize how hungry I am until we dig in. The rest of dinner is spent talking about a little of everything and also nothing at all. Nathan tells me about each of his sisters, and I in turn offer the few stories I have of my own. We talk briefly about the library, and Nathan asks about my job before back in Georgia.

We finish our meal and he pays. We go back the way we came out to his Civic in a much emptier parking lot. I guess our evening ended later than everyone else's. The night sky is filled with stars, the air is cool, and Nathan's arm around my shoulder warms me to my core.

We get to the car and my heart starts to pick up. I feel an urge and follow it. I grab Nathan by his coat and pull him in. Our lips touch and my heart starts running a race. His lips are soft, and his hands go from his sides to mine. His hands envelope my hips and are firm holding me tight.

I open my mouth a little to welcome him in. Our tongues meet and do their own dancing, sending electricity down my spine. I wrap my arms around his shoulders and press my body against his, harder and deeper. I can't help but run my hand up through his black hair and tug a little on the soft strands.

He presses me against the cold Civic.

I pull back a little and smile "Did you steal a breadstick, or are you just happy to see me. Let's head back to my place."

"I may have stolen some, but I hid them in your purse." We both laugh.

He looks at me and smiles. "I can't believe how I landed someone as amazing as you. Now, let's hurry back to continue… this." He gives me a deep kiss that reassures me that his words were more than just words.

We hop into the car and get on our way. I feel so bubbly and light we keep stealing glances excitedly knowing what's coming. It's been a long time for me since I had my needs met. My hand feels like a delicate flower in his bear paw, and I wouldn't trade it for anything else.

The street light illuminates the car flickering on and off like a countdown to blast off.

Chapter Twenty-One

As my aunt's house comes into view, a tingle runs down my spine.

"Hey, Catherine. It looks like someone's sitting on your aunt's porch." Nathan parks and I get out of the car quickly before Nathan even has time to get his seatbelt off.

Once I'm out, I slow my pace, taking care to make sure I don't speed even though my entire body is telling me to run.

"I thought you fucking quit that shit?" I yell.

Marcus sits on Cici's porch. He lets out a puff of smoke and shoves the Juul back into his coat pocket.

"It's been a rough few weeks." He shoves off the porch and walks sheepishly toward me. "Hey, Kitty."

My stomach clenches, he closes the distance between us and sweeps me into his arms before I have a chance to process what's happening. He takes a deep breath, burying his face in my neck.

"Fuck, I missed you." His voice sounds raw and his hot breath by my ear sends involuntary shivers down my back. Marcus pulls away slightly, his eyes running over my face and slightly down my body.

I fight the urge to squirm under his gaze. His looks always made me the slightest bit self-conscious. Like he is appraising me, considering my value based on the way that I look rather than admiring what he sees. His eyes are cold as he takes in my hair.

A wave of discomfort flows through me, knowing he doesn't like what he sees. I place my hands on his shoulders, trying to put distance between us, bracing myself to step back.

"I see you changed your hair." It's a statement, bland and objective.

"Yeah, I did." I pull out of his embrace, taking a few steps away from him in an act of self-preservation, a million questions bubbling through my stomach and up my throat, constricting my airways. "What are you doing here?" I refuse to return any of his sentiment, but my voice shakes when I ask, and I hate it.

Nathan gets out of the car and starts towards us.

"I got this." Marcus moves me to the side, then addresses Nathan. *Senior, you es Uber no necesito tip tu vamanos ahora por favor."*

My face flushes with embarrassment.

Nathan looks at me and smirks, "Well, I'd love a tip, but I'm not her Uber."

Marcus extends his hand toward Nathan, a shit-eating grin spreading across his face, "I'm—"

I make a split decision, cutting him off before he can

introduce himself as my fiancé or something. "Nathan, this is my ex-fiancé Marcus Michaels. Marcus, this is Nathan Alvarez."

Marcus shakes Nathan's hand in a way that appears good natured, but he looks at me in a way that makes my skin crawl. "Well, I guess Kitty and I are in a bit of a disagreement on that whole 'ex' part at the moment. Lovely to meet you, Mr. Alvarez." He gives Nathan another *'charming'* smile, stepping toward me almost possessively as they break contact.

Nathan looks at me, his expression even but a million questions flickering in his eyes.

I just want to curl up in a ball and die. I'm mortified, but Nathan returns Marcus's smile. "Nice to meet you, too. Catherine and I work together at the library. I was dropping her off after our dinner."

"Well, that was nice of you," Marcus says. "It's good to know Kitty has had someone looking out for her while she has been here."

"Yeah, I think I've taken care of her in a way that she's never had." Nathan straightens his shoulders. "We've been having a good time, and I've given her something you haven't."

I flush as I think of the morning in Nathan's office and the way his tongue felt, the way my body opened up to his touch. With Marcus standing there, I feel guilty about it even though I know I shouldn't. He has no claim over me anymore. This is just more of his entitled bullshit, but I can feel his hooks digging deeper into me with every second the three of us stand outside of my aunt's house.

Marcus looks between the two of us, expecting details. "Kitty likes gifts."

"Oh, she definitely liked what I gave her," Nathan jabs.

Marcus is clearly starting to get riled. He's scowling at Nathan, and I swear I can hear him thinking about what to say to Nathan to get him to leave.

Nathan's face remains stoic, and I can't tell what he's thinking at all.

I take a step toward him, trying to put distance between Marcus and me. More than anything, I want to go to Nathan and let him protect me, but it seems unfair at this moment to expect that from him. I meet his eyes, hoping that he will see the apology there.

Marcus doesn't seem to get the message and steps up to me again, taking my hand in his. "Did you get my gift? And the letter?"

I step away, heat rushing to my face, and I see stars for a moment. I step again toward Nathan, willing myself not to touch him, but moving close enough to put distance between Marcus and me. When I turn back to Marcus, I see his face shift almost imperceptibly.

"I think I should go," Nathan cuts in, turning toward me.

I look at Nathan as my heart breaks. Seeing the look in his eyes threatens to rip me apart, and I feel panic welling in my stomach. "No, you don't have to go..."

Nathan places his hand on my shoulder. "I think I do. It

sounds like you guys have a lot of catching up to do." He gives me a quick peck on the lips and starts towards his car. He gives a tiny wave before unlocking the driver's side door, getting in. "See you later."

I flinch as the door slams, and something inside of me shatters at the sound.

Marcus stands there shocked and turns to me, furious. "What the fuck? I'm busy sending you fucking expensive gifts and you're out here fucking other dudes? Did you even get my letter?"

"Yeah, I did. Yesterday, actually." I try and step around Marcus and head toward my aunt's porch.

He sighs deeply, turning to follow me. I can tell he's fighting for control of himself. "Did you like the shoes?"

"They are pretty, but they don't really fit the current weather here." I look over my shoulder to the dark house. Thank god Cici is at work tonight. I can only imagine what she would have to say if she saw Marcus standing here in front of the house.

"I guess I was thinking you'd be able to wear them when you came home." Marcus is studying me, his deep blue eyes glittering as much as the snow. I forgot how perfect his face is. Even with a few days of stubble, and his hair mussed from sitting outside, he is picture perfect. He is at least as tall as Nathan, his broad shoulders strong from hours at the gym instead of hours of moving heavy boxes and doing manual labor. His hands are smoother, too. They're not nearly as calloused and rough as Nathan's. He's leaner than Nathan, his torso trims down to a thinner waist due to hours of ab workouts, and miles of running. I feel like I'm seeing him for the first time again, and so many feelings bubble to the surface—longing, heartache, affection.

"I know I fucked up and that's making you look elsewhere. I feel terrible about the way we left things, and I know I surprised you tonight. I just couldn't stay away any longer." He breaks the silence, pulling me out of my thoughts.

I don't know what he sees in my face, but he steps closer to me, wrapping his arms around my waist again. "I'm staying at a hotel in town for a few days." My heart beats faster as he leans his forehead against mine. "I would really like to take you to lunch tomorrow. Is that okay?"

"I have some things I have to do." Like work a job with the guy I'm seeing since we broke up.

He grins really wide. "Well, I'm here now, so you can cancel whatever it is!" His phone pings and he looks down. "I'll pick you up around 11:00 okay? My Uber's pulling up. I have a meeting I have to attend virtually from the hotel. I've arranged everything so I can focus on us."

A car pulls up behind me. He takes my face in his soft hands and kisses me deeply. He feels familiar and warm, and his kiss is full of passion, but I feel absolutely nothing.

"Ciao, my love!" And there he goes sprinting away like a child in love.

I stand in shock, and my stomach feels empty. I walk slowly to the front door, dumbfounded at what just happened. I cross my aunt's threshold and head straight to bed. I'm exhausted from the emotional storm in my head. I collapse as soon as I walk into my room, not bothering to take my clothes off or anything.

I pull out my phone and immediately text Nathan. There has been a gaping hole in my stomach from the moment that he left a little while ago. I hate the way the night ended. I was feeling so good about things with Nathan, and so excited for tonight, and fucking Marcus had to show up and rip everything to shreds.

Me:

Hey, I'm sorry for the way tonight ended, he's gone, and Cici won't be home for a while if you want to talk. I could come over, or we could meet up.

I lay in my bed, staring at the ceiling waiting for his reply. I hope he isn't too mad at me. I can't control what happened, and I don't know what to think about the things Marcus said. I'm sure Nathan has a lot of questions, and as much as I'd like to pretend nothing happened, I think I need to explain myself.

My phone pings, and I open the chat.

Nathan:

Thank you for the apology, but I think it would be better if we talked tomorrow.

My heart sinks, and I feel like everything is shattering around me. I don't know what to do. Part of me thinks maybe I should text Amber, or Meghan, but I can't bring myself to do it.

I lay in bed another minute, fighting the overwhelming feelings from tonight and the tears that are threatening to spill everywhere.

I need to find Cici. I get back out of my bed, not bothering to change or anything. I find my snow boots and head for the bar. My body feels numb to the cold, and I barely remember my walk across town.

§

When I push open the door, I'm taken back by how quiet the space is. I was prepared for a full bar, packed with college kids and locals. It's after 10:00 p.m., and the only people who seem to be in there are Larry and a man sitting in the corner alone.

"Hey, Princess!" Larry smiles at me, throwing the towel he was using to wipe down the bar, over his shoulder. "What can I get ya?"

"A shot of tequila, please." I plop down on a stool right in the middle of the bar and slump against the counter.

"Oh no, who broke your heart?" Concern creases Larry's brows as he takes a shot glass from the counter behind him and fills it with some top shelf tequila. "Need me to take care of 'em? I know a guy." Larry winks at me, sliding the shot glass across the counter to me.

Somehow I doubt Larry is joking. Even though his tone is light-hearted, and good natured, I don't doubt for a second that he knows people he probably shouldn't.

For a brief moment, I entertain thoughts about sending a hitman to Marcus's hotel, but I push them aside.

I throw back the shot, cringing slightly at the burn on my tongue. I've never been much for liquor, but in this case it's a good time to make an exception.

"No broken hearts," I lie. "Just a rough night. Where's Cici?"

"It was so slow tonight that she and Charles took off to do 'inventory,'" Larry makes air quotes with his one hand when he says *'inventory,'* "of the liquor that is in Charles's garage."

My heart sinks. I really needed her tonight. "Can I have another shot?"

Larry gives me another worried look but refills the shot glass.

"I'll take one of those, too." I hadn't noticed, but the man who was sitting down on the end of the bar had stood and made his way down to us, taking the stool right next to me and motioning to Larry to grab him a shot, too.

Larry chuckles and grabs another shot glass. "I wondered when you were gonna catch up tonight. You've been awfully slow so far."

I look at the man sitting next to me and realize after a moment that it is Nathan's dad, Oscar. He gives me an easy going smile, taking the shot glass in front of him, and shoots it back without looking.

"What's wrong, chica? You look like someone ran over your *perro*." He sets his shot glass back down, leaning toward me slightly. I can smell the alcohol on his breath, but unlike the last time we met at the bar, his eyes are still alert, and he seems in control of himself still. I can see in the lines of his face that he once was just as good-looking as Nathan. But life and probably the alcohol have drawn deep lines around his eyes and across his forehead.

"Oh, it was just a bad day," I say, unsure of how much I really want to share tonight.

"Is my son giving you trouble? You let me know if he hurts you, I'll beat him with *mi chancla!*" He laughs to himself, and I can't quite picture Oscar beating his grown son with a shoe, but the thought makes me chuckle as well.

"No, your son is a perfect gentleman. An ex of mine just showed up unannounced tonight, and I'm afraid Nathan is upset about it." The words are out before I can stop them and I cringe. Maybe two shots was two too many.

Oscar nods slowly, his eyes boring holes into me as some sort of understanding passes through him. "Ah," he says after a moment. "I see we are going to need another shot of tequila... Larry, pour us another, *por favour!*"

Oscar clinks his glass with mine before shooting it back. I follow suit, thankful that the first two shots have dulled my senses enough for the third shot to go down like almost nothing.

"So tell me," Oscar turns on his bar stool to face me. "Why is this ex an issue?"

I consider for a moment not saying anything, but then figure it doesn't matter at this point. The alcohol has already loosened my tongue so I might as well keep going. If I'm lucky, he won't remember this tomrrow.

"Well, I ended things a few months ago, and then again on the phone a few weeks ago, but he doesn't seem to understand. He sent me something, and I just tried to ignore it, but then when I didn't answer he showed up, and now I'm worried what Nathan thinks about how I actually left the relationship. I really like your son, he's become very important to me, and I'm worried this is going to ruin it." I gasp a little, realizing I don't think I took a breath during that whole time.

"Oh, I doubt that's going to ruin anything. If I know anything about my son, it's that he's already jumped in with both feet. I highly doubt you, or your ex, has ruined anything. But tell me," Oscar pauses, taking a drink of the beer that he brought with him when he moved next to me at the bar. "Why exactly is this ex leaving you so *frustadas*?" He looks at me, mild concern flitting through his very perceptive eyes.

"I guess we just have a lot of history. We were engaged for almost two years."

"Ah, lots of baggage I see." Oscar cracks a smile. "You know, I stole Nellie from another man. Looks like my son takes after me in at least one way!" He laughs to himself

271

good naturedly, turning back to the bar, placing his elbows on the ledge to lean forward. "You know, Catherine," he says slowly, and I'm surprised a bit that he remembers my name after our one meeting when he mistook me for Nathan's ex and then thought I was the other woman. "I know *mijo*, he may be a little thrown off, *pero* he's not so freaked out that he's done. Nathan values you enough to let you have your space to deal with *todos*. He's not going to push if he doesn't feel like you want it."

"I feel like I had the rug pulled out from under me, and I don't know what the fuck to do." I sigh, dropping my head down into my hands, feeling a bit defeated.

"You need to do what you think is best. Nathan will be there for you, that's the kind of *hombre mijo es*. He's all in as soon as he chooses you. Just make sure you're all in too, *chica, por que* he will be there until you tell him to go. So don't drag him around while you make your choice." Oscar drains his beer, and I can't help but stare at him open mouthed. "You seem like a *chica buena*, these things have a tendency to work themselves out exactly like they should. Just don't let yourself live in limbo too long, it's not fair to either of you. *Que sera sera...*" He studies his beer bottle, as if he hadn't just shaken me to my core. "Larry," he calls.

Larry emerges from the kitchen, drying his hands as he walks. A small smile pulls at the corners of his mouth like he probably just heard our whole conversation. "I think we each need one more shot."

Larry smiles at me, and pours me a half shot, and I'm grateful, I think if I have too much more tonight, I'll be crawling back to Cici's house.

I sit for another few minutes with Oscar while Larry absently wipes things down and puts dishes away. The silence is like a balm to my soul, bringing peace back into my body. The alcohol warms my limbs, and my head feels a little heavy. There is still so much uncertainty, but at the moment I just enjoy the false sense of safety that the bar has created.

Chapter Twenty-Two

I wake with a start in the morning, realizing I need to be at work in about thirty minutes. I groan, shoving my face into the pillow, memories from the night before crushing me— my fight with Marcus, and the way I left things with Nathan.

Work is not an option today. I can't face Nathan, and I guess I have a lunch date with Marcus that I don't want to have to explain to anyone.

I pull my phone from my pocket and open my chat with Nathan. The messages from the other night make my heart hurt. I hate the way dinner ended, and I feel like shit for how things ended. I close the chat and open Amber's. I know it's shitty to tell your coworker instead of your boss that you're not coming in, but I can't muster the courage to talk to him yet. Not with Marcus sleeping at a hotel down the street.

Me:
Hey, I know this is shitty, but I'm not going to make it in today. Bad night. I'll tell you about it later. Can you relay the message for me?

Before I can even put my phone down her reply comes through

Amber:
You okay? Nathan's in a pretty bad mood today, but I'll let him know. Did something happen between you two? Did you tell him about the note from your ex?

Me:
Something like that... I'll fill you in later. Thanks.

I head to the bathroom to shower, cranking the heat up to a temp just short of skin-melting as I strip out of my clothes from last night and let the water hit me. I put my face in the steamy spray, hoping it will wash away the feelings of dread I have welling up in my stomach. Today with a clear mind Marcus's face bombards me, overwhelming my senses. I scrub vigorously at my skin, trying to wash away the feel of his lips on mine and the feeling of emptiness it left.

When I step out of the shower and stare at myself in the mirror, I realize I look like shit. Mascara from the night before leaves dark circles around my eyes. My face is swollen a little from the stress. I get my makeup out and get to work. I look at my phone and realize I have about two hours before Marcus will be here. I can't handle the criticism I will get from him, so I have to use every one of those minutes to be pristine.

I sit on the porch swing waiting for Marcus to pick me up in whatever swanky rental car he got. He was always one to put on a show.

I can feel my anxiety bubbling deep inside me, as if I'm a coke bottle that got shaken up. I continue to run my hands down my grey sweater to make sure every bit is smoothed out as a black BMW pulls up. Two short honks signal that it's for me. I roll my eyes—nothing has changed. Even though we haven't seen each other in weeks, and he is saying he wants change, he can't even get out of the car and greet me like a decent human being.

I head toward the street slowly and open the passenger side door.

"Good morning, Kitty. I found the perfect luncheon place online for us to go to... It's so very rustic. Then maybe we can drive around this quaint little hometown of yours." His bright blue eyes beam with joy. Maybe our time apart has been a wakeup call to him. "I can't believe after all of these years literally nothing has changed!"

His chipper tone makes me want to roll my eyes.

"You know I grew up in such a nice suburb outside Atlanta that this little podunk town is like a culture shock. It looks like the only new buildings are fast food. It's so cute." He chuckles to himself.

I can't believe how much I hate the sound of his voice today. I used to love his little remarks and sarcastic jokes, but today all I want is for him to shut up.

"Tell me, does your aunt still run that little dive bar on campus?" He seems blissfully unaware of how uncomfortable I am, and completely oblivious to the fact that I haven't said a single thing since getting in the car. I forgot how much he can talk when he wants to. "Alyssa… you know Alyssa, my secretary who looks like a pug? She's been answering your emails at work so when you come back it'll be like you never left."

My blood freezes in my veins. I remember now he mentioned me coming back. I was so preoccupied last night with the fact that he was standing on my aunt's porch that I feel like I didn't actually hear half of what he said. I'm hit with the realization that he really thinks he's here to take me back to Atlanta.

Does he really think I'm coming back?

"I picked this place, Soups. Not a really catchy name, but I didn't have much choice somewhere like this." He pulls into a parking lot on the far side of campus, not far from the Italian restaurant Nathan took me to the night before.

I vaguely remember passing this little strip of stores and restaurants when Nathan and I drove home last night.

"Let's go in already, babe." Marcus hops out of his side and starts walking to the little cafe before I have a chance to get my purse.

I jog a little to catch up with him, impatiently waiting inside the doors. I pull open the door to a warm, relaxing environment. The walls are painted orange with hanging pictures of artistic looking soups, breads, and salads along with an assortment of fruits and vegetables. A few cozy booths and some scuffed up wooden tables and chairs fill the small room, and the smell of bread wafts enticingly through the dining area. A little fireplace sits on one wall with couches surrounding it and a coffee table in the middle.

We walk up to the counter.

"I'd like two harvest salads, no croutons, we don't do carbs. Then I also need two wheatgrass juices and that's all. Thanks so much." Marcus orders for the both of us, he always used to order for us. He was always too impatient to wait for me to decide. It never used to really bother me. It's nice in a way. I always liked when he would pick, even if it's healthy, because I never had to overthink it.

Today, though, it irritates me.

"Actually, I would like your broccoli cheddar soup, please." I say to the cashier who changes my order on the computer. "And I'd like it in a bread bowl."

I keep my chin up, not looking at Marcus as we wait for our food. I can feel him staring daggers into the side of my face, but I refuse to give in and look at him. I need him to understand that he no longer gets to make choices for me.

After a moment, he must decide my choice is not worth the fight, so he begins to ramble on and on about how it's stupid that we have to wait for our own food instead of someone bringing it to us, and then he transitions seamlessly into some new project he's working on for work.

I can't seem to focus on what he's saying. I used to hang on every word, thinking about how kind he was with all he did for the nonprofit. Now it sounds as if he really is just talking to hear himself brag about all of the random shit he thinks would make him look good.

A server slides our food across the counter, and we grab the trays. I'm so overwhelmed by my anxiety, I feel like I'm on autopilot.

I absently follow Marcus to a booth and sit across from him. When I finally shake the fog a little, I begin studying him. He is wearing what I could only guess is a grey fleece jacket from Nordstrom. He looks casual enough, but in the rich frat boy kind of way. Like his clothes are made to look like he might just be lounging around, but something about them still makes him look like a spoiled rich boy.

I stare down at my soup. My appetite is nonexistent, and I feel unsure of what to do next. I can feel Marcus studying me as he eats, but he hasn't said a single thing since we sat down. I peer up at him through my lashes. His face is pulled tight, the lines on his forehead becoming more prominent when he sees that I'm looking at him. His lips are pulled into a straight line, but there is a glint in his piercing eyes that makes me even more anxious. I know the whole air of ease he's been giving off since he picked me up is an act, and by the look on his face, the dam is going to break at any moment.

"Do you not like your soup? You should have just gotten the salad like I did. You haven't taken a single bite. I'll go speak to the manager and get you one." Marcus begins to stand, and in that moment I can feel my own walls fracturing inside of me.

"Does it not bother you that I haven't fucking spoken once?" I feel my fists clench under the table.

Marcus slides back into his seat, "Excuse me? Where is this coming from?" He rests his elbows on the table in a way that may look casual to anyone else, but it causes me to flinch. "Watch your language. We are in public," he hisses at me.

"No, I don't understand where you get the FUCKING nerve to show up out of nowhere and pretend as if nothing happened." I hiss back and my throat burns with contempt. I feel my nails digging into my palms under the table, and I work to relax my fingers.

Marcus folds his hands and takes a deep breath. "I was hoping we could at least enjoy one meal together before we had to have this conversation, but I understand now that you really need to talk." He leans in closer to me, and his eyes sparkle with a dangerous light. "I have the nerve to show up and retrieve my future bride. I get it you have cold feet. I am totally open to postponing the wedding. You said you wanted summer, we can do summer. You disappeared, Kitty, and left me with a mess." He runs his fingers through his hair, mussing it slightly.

He's right, I left, he didn't. He should be angry, not me. I left him with everything to deal with in my wake. To clean up and explain. But at the same time, I left because things were over, not because I wanted him to come looking for me, and not because I wanted a summer wedding.

"I told everyone your aunt was sick. I couldn't have the embarrassment of this mental breakdown getting around to everyone." He sighs in frustration, fidgeting with the sleeves of his douchey looking jacket. "Yeah, sorry my fiancé is nuts and disappeared, Alyssa, so do all of her work until she comes to her senses." His tone is filled with condescension.

I boil inside, the cracks in the walls fracturing farther and farther. The pressure in my chest is almost unbearable. "I don't want a summer wedding." My throat burns as the pressure in my chest surges up my throat. "And I'm sorry this was such an *inconvenience* for you."

"You have no idea. Your father was up my ass about your whereabouts. My parents were devastated. Do you even comprehend how much money they lost on our wedding? You couldn't have done your soul searching and returned a couple months before? What was I supposed to do? You've clearly gained weight, you changed your hair, you're practically crawling on top of another man weeks after you disappeared. You are a complete mess without me. Now enough with the nonsense and let's get back on track." He reaches for my hand, "I have been lost without you. I love you. It's time to be done with the drama. You're acting like your mother."

I pull my hand away from his quickly, burying it back in my lap.

Marcus crosses his arms like I'm a child to be lectured. His arrogance is infuriating.

And just like that the dam bursts. All of the anger, fear, and resentment flow out of me at the comparison to my mother. "I am not that fucking bitch. I am me and only me. There is no fucking return, Marcus. Have you even fucking taken a second to look at yourself? I got that letter and was reminded of all our good memories." I feel tears burning my throat, but I refuse to let him see me cry ever again. "But, after sitting here listening to your fucking arrogant attitude I'm reminded of all the shit memories. Nothing has changed, and no matter what you say, nothing is going to change. You haven't changed, Marcus."

"Get over yourself." He rolls his eyes in disdain, leaning over the table toward me and lowering his voice slightly. "Look at myself? Fine. I see a wealthy, well-bred, and determined future CEO of a non-profit who is willing to look past everything you are and give you my name. Not many would do that for you." Marcus shrugs his shoulders, dropping his eyes over me as if being with me was charity work.

I smirk with a touch of my own arrogance, unable to hold back any longer. "You know, Marcus, for a long time I believed that was true, but after being back here for a few weeks, I have realized that you are not the only person willing to look past all of the things that you think I am."

His face contorts, and I can see him struggling to regain control of himself. For a moment I'm afraid my words will send him over the edge, but I can't take it back now. I pull back my shoulders, looking him in the eye. I hope my face doesn't give away the terror I feel building in my guts.

"What did you just say to me? I'm pretty sure I'm the one actually willing to spend my life with you? Remember, I am your fiancé." He folds his hands. "I am even willing to look past your little indiscretions with *Nathan*."

The way he says Nathan's name feels as if he's spitting it at me.

"Ex-fiancé," I hear my voice come out a little louder than I meant for it to. "I left you, Marcus. I went on a date and I'm moving on. I have a job here, Marcus, and a life without you in it. I have new friends, and I'm happy. I don't want to come back to Atlanta with you. I don't want to be your wife. I don't want the life you're offering anymore. I don't know if I ever really did."

Here comes the tantrum. His eyes tinge dark and he blows his breath out through his nose. I swear I can see the veins in the side of his head thrumming unreasonably fast.

"Here's the thing, Catherine, You don't seem to get it. You don't get a choice. Could I get anyone else? Absolutely. I have women falling at my feet. I don't want to start over. I don't have time for that or this bullshit hoop you're making me jump through. You are just as naive as the day we met, Kitty. No one gets happy-ever-after. That's movie shit. You survive, get married, have kids and die; that's it, Kitty. You came up here to act out whatever fucking fantasy you wanted to, and enough is enough." His voice starts to raise a touch as he grabs my hand. When I try to pull away he squeezes hard. " You are stuck with me just as I am with you. So the one choice I will allow is to come home or else."

I free my hand and glare trying to stab him with my eyes. " Or else. I would take anything over you."

"You will FUCKING REGRET…" Marcus starts to stand up.

A manager shouts from behind the counter "HEY, PAL! COOL IT OR LEAVE!"

Marcus takes a deep breath and smooths his blonde hair back into place. His eyes never lose their intensity or leave my face, but he sits back down, pushing his tray of food roughly away from him and dropping his elbows on the table.

"Fine, it seems you forget that while you have a separate account from me, my brother owns that bank. He will be closing your account and sending your money to the address on the account, which is my apartment. I will be holding that check until you get your shit together and stop cheating on me. Your shit in my home is gone. I have wanted to turn the space you used into a home gym anyways. Since I'm your only previous employer, I'll have you black marked so if people call for a reference, we will advise against hiring you. I will also just generally have my father reach out to his connections in this area and make sure you never hold a job here. A nice little donation to the library should help in removing that obstacle. With all that said, I'm sure you are now realizing 'or else' is not a stellar option. If you stick with that, you'll have plenty of time to think about your choice with no job or social life."

I take a deep, shaking breath, steadying myself as best I can. I can't keep living in this limbo of always owing him for something, or waiting for him to let me go. It's obvious at this point that I am not going to leave this lunch with Marcus unscathed. "Fuck it, Marcus. So be it." I pull my purse onto my lap, slipping the ring, his ring, out of a pocket and pushing it slowly across the table to him. "I can't do this anymore."

My heart is racing, and I feel a bit like I'm going to vomit. The world starts to tilt dangerously on its side, but I hold firm. I've always had doubts about whether or not I made the right choice, but at this moment I am positive I could never agree to be anything for him or with him ever again.

"Well, Kitty, I guess what they say is true. We all end up like our parents." His voice is low and raspy as he takes his ring from the table and studies it in between his fingers. "I am meant for success. But you? Well, you know what you're meant for. So long for now, Kitty." He walks away, driving the final nail in the coffin on our dead relationship.

I don't think that could've gone worse if I tried. At least it's done and over with. I lay my head down on the table and sigh. Somewhere inside of me, relief starts to trickle in. It's like a balm to the raw parts of my soul that Marcus tore open.

My phone vibrates in my pocket. I take a deep breath before I look. Is it Nathan texting to fix things? Is it Cici? She didn't know I was going to lunch. She doesn't even know Marcus came.

Sarah:
Hey Girl! Let's go dancing! Ladies night at X and Mercedes Benz-Over is performing!

Thank god—an excuse to get absolutely plastered.
Me:
I'm there

I sigh, walk to the counter, and ask for a to-go box. I decide to take a car today since Marcus drove me here and I don't feel like a post-breakup walk of shame. And I need to get going if I plan to make myself presentable enough to get free drinks tonight...

Chapter Twenty-Three

My life right now is falling apart.

Marcus isn't done with me, but I'm done with him. I have no more things to fall back on. I can't change my mind. I can't go back. I can only move forward from now on, and I'm so scared. The ride-share home was frustratingly expensive, but at least I didn't have to be with Marcus any longer.

I'm going to have to call another car this evening to get to the club. Cici works, and even if she didn't, I don't want to worry about parking or finding a way to drive home when I inevitably get plastered tonight. The bill will be huge, but at this point it's going to be worth it to forget the shittiest twenty-four hours of my life. I spruce up my makeup and rummage through Cici's closet for another red dress for tonight. I decide on a pair of comfy, closed-toed flats and attempt to style my hair like Meghan had done for me the previous day.

I throw on the leather jacket that I wore to the fundraiser in hopes of still looking kind of hot, but will be comfortable through the whole night. For a brief minute, I eye the shoes Marcus sent a few days ago. Those would definitely be super appropriate for tonight, but the baggage that comes with them would be stifling.

I also think about texting Nathan, but then decide against it. It would be better to just wait till tomorrow because I don't feel like I can face him at the moment, and I don't want to unpack the total shitshow that today has become. For all I know, tomorrow I won't even have a job. If Marcus brings his threats to fruition, I will be broke and jobless by tomorrow evening.

It's a long, silent ride to X. I push away all of the insecurities and doubts I've been feeling the last few days. I plan to use tonight as one last 'hoorah' to my old self before forgetting her completely.

Sarah and Ashleigh are waiting outside for me when the ride-share pulls up. Ashleigh looks like someone hit *'copy; paste'* on a character from Jersey Shore. She's wearing a tight bodycon dress with cheetah print, fishnets, and Uggs. Her makeup draws from two decades ago with a heavy red lip and dark, smokey eyes. Her hair is up in a ponytail with what I can only imagine is a whole can of hairspray to make a little poof in front. Sarah contrasts this with a nice blue dress with one long sleeve and one bare shoulder. The skirt flares out slightly and swishes in the wind. Her hair is down in curls and has a lovely, more suiting natural look.

"Where's Meg?" I thought for sure she'd be here, too, but I don't see her anywhere.

"She's already in there. We've been freezing our asses off waiting on you. I told Sarah you're a big girl and could've found us on your own, but nooo." Ashleigh speaks with a snarl.

"You didn't have to wait with me. I just was trying to be polite." Sarah rolls her eyes, then turns to me. "I love your hair! Meg told us how good you looked and she was not wrong."

I feel like I am always an inconvenience to someone. I still smile at the compliment, though. "Thanks, well, what are we waiting for? Let's head in. I'm fucking freezing my ass off."

Ashleigh takes the lead as we approach the door. We navigate the smokers and show our IDs to the bouncer. He opens the door and gestures for us to hurry up. The club is dark and the music is thumping. I feel the vibrations in my chest. The girls motion for me to follow them to the bar.

The bar is lined with clear plastic chairs that have a neon pink under glow. The bar itself has a neon purple glow coming from a string of lights under the counter, and the actual counter is white plastic filled with scratches and dents. Behind the shirtless bartenders with six pack abs are shelves covered with every kind of alcohol you can think of. Each shelf is lined with a small tube of neon casting pink, green, and purple light onto the bottles of booze.

Somewhere next to me, I hear Sarah shouting something like 'vaccine' to the bartender with dyed green hair, a six pack, and neon green tunnel plugs in his ears. He turns around and pulls a tray of syringes filled with brightly colored Jell-O shots out of a mini fridge and hands it to Sarah. He winks at her, taking his time to work his gaze over her body before turning to the next girl down the bar, lining up a set of shot glasses out in front of her and dumping some sort of green liquid from a shaker into each one.

I follow Sarah with her tray of Jell-O shots to a high-top table where Ashleigh and Meghan are already standing. Sarah passes out the syringes and Meghan says something that I can't quite make out before she shoots the first one into her mouth. She's in a cute pink crop top and jeans. A little black purse is slung across her body, and her hair and makeup look perfect.

Meghan hugs me. "Hey, hottie! Your hair looks so good! I wonder who did it!" she shouts coyly.

"SOME HOT CHICK!" I shout back. We both laugh.

I take one of the syringes that Sarah handed me and squeeze it into my mouth. I've had Jell-O shots in the past, and they're usually more Jell-O than shot, but this one hits the back of my tongue and makes me cringe. The burn of cheap vodka catches me off guard.

"So, what's going on with you and your ex?" Ashleigh says over the music. "I'm positive that I saw the two of you today outside of Soups. I thought he was in Atlanta?" Her tone is accusatory. I wonder briefly how she would have seen us, but then I remember that she works at the Dental office in the same strip mall.

I take another shot. I'm prepared this time, and the

burn is less than the first one. I'm going to need about ten more of these before the night is over. "He showed up to get me to go back to Georgia with him, and we ended up fighting in Soups," I say drily, not really caring if my voice carries over the thump of the base.

"So, you guys didn't get back together?" Ashleigh moves a little closer, the smell of her cheap Bath and Body Works spray filling my nose.

"No, we didn't. It's definitely over." I take my third shot off the tray, studying it in my hands.

"I'm sorry," Sarah reaches out, placing her hand on my arm. Her fingers are cool and the look in her eye is sympathetic.

Ashleigh sighs loud enough to be heard over the noise of the room. "Okay, enough sappy shit. Let's get plastered!" She takes another shot herself, and then taps her empty syringe against my full one signaling for me to shoot mine.

I look over and Sarah has also taken a shot at this point, which is weird for her.

"Since when do you drink?" I ask.

Before she can answer, Ashleigh is chiming in, "She's nursing her own heartbreak tonight, too. Now, since everyone has had a chance to loosen up a bit, can we please go dancing?" Without waiting for an answer, she turns on her heel and heads toward the dancefloor, Meghan close behind. Sarah gives me a sheepish grin and throws her empty syringe on the tray on our table and hurries to catch up.

As I follow behind, I feel the effects of the alcohol setting in, warmth spreading from my stomach through my body. The dance floor is packed with scantily dressed girls and a few random men. Almost everyone is swaying to the music with a drink in their hand.

I push away the anxiety I feel rising in my chest and look for my friends on the dance floor. It's not long before I see Meghan and Sarah up at the front by the DJ, jumping and swaying to the beat. Sarah smiles and pulls me closer to them. I follow their lead, soon completely enraptured by the music and the movement of the people around me.

I throw my head back, basking in the feel of my buzz coupled with the repetitive boom of the speakers near us. I don't know how much time passes, but Ashleigh appears a few minutes later, elbowing her way through the thick crowd, balancing four big pink cups in her hands. I take mine as it's passed to me, downing two big gulps of the sweet liquid.

The music changes and the crowd gets louder and more enthusiastic. The girls turn their attention to the stage with everyone else, and I focus on finishing my drink while swaying to the music. I don't know how long we stay on the dance floor, but I do realize when my drink runs out. I look around, seeing Meghan and Ashleigh drunkenly grinding on each other to the music with Sarah laughing and taking pictures of them.

My head swims, and my stomach starts to churn. I

think I need to find the bathroom. I push my way off the dance floor. This is all too much. Suddenly, I feel crushed by the weight of everything that's happened the last few days. I need air. I need to get out of here. I dig for my phone in my little purse, stumbling into the bathroom. The only person I can think to text is Amber. I send a quick SOS and my location and lock myself in one of the stalls. My head is spinning, and the music doesn't seem any quieter from in here. I feel as if the bathroom stall is closing in on me. I need to splash my face with water. I feel sick and sweaty.

I run to the sink, grab the faucet, and turn it to cold. I splash my face a few times out of the porcelain pool I've created. I feel my phone vibrate, not bothering to check it, assuming it's Amber telling me she's outside. I wipe my face down with a paper towel, blotting the little bit of mascara that has darkened the skin under my eyes. After I feel like I am at least kind of presentable, I head back out to find the girls to let them know I'm going to leave. I step back out into the crowded bar area, trying to steady myself against the wall. My phone buzzes again, and I dig around again through my purse to find it.

"Catherine?" My hands still at the deep voice I would recognize anywhere. I turn, feeling my entire body flush red as Nathan steps around a high-top table full of college kids. His hands are shoved in his pockets and his jaw is set hard. "You didn't answer my text."

"What?" I find my phone, seeing two texts from him,

the first one saying he's on his way, and the second saying he was waiting outside. I scroll up a little farther, my stomach plummeting to my feet as I realize I texted him instead of Amber my SOS.

"Shit." The word comes out rough and slightly slurred as I look between him and my phone. "I meant to text Amber."

"Well, you didn't. So…" he holds his hand out to me. "Let's get out of here." It's a command, not a question.

And I dumbly take his hand, letting him lead me out of the club and onto the street.

We walk quietly down the street a little ways to where his car is parked. He doesn't release my hand until we are standing on the sidewalk next to it. He unlocks his passenger side door, opening it for me. His eyes are locked on my feet as he helps me step into the car, which I'm grateful for at the moment because my head is spinning from a mix of alcohol and sheer mortification. He walks around to the driver's side and gets in, turning the car on and cranking the heat, but he doesn't make any effort to drive away.

"Are you okay?" His voice is toneless, and he's still staring straight ahead.

I stumble over my own thoughts. Should I be honest that I'm not? Or lie and play it off that I just can't hold my drink?

"No, I just had to re-break-up with my ex because he showed up out of nowhere blindsiding me and pretending nothing was wrong. You two got into it. He claimed I was cheating on him with you, then I got a text from Sarah and thought, 'What the fuck? Why not?' You know? I guess I went into self-destruct mode. And I accidentally messaged you instead of Amber. Which is an actual nightmare come to life." I slam my forehead on the glove compartment. My stomach churns just from talking. Whatever Ashleigh brought me in that pink cup was a mistake.

"Glad to know I'm a nightmare?" He asked offendedly.

WHY DO I MESS IT ALL UP! I turn my head towards him, not allowing my head to lift up. "No, the nightmare is having the guy I like more than anyone show up and see me like this, drunk as fuck and trying not to throw up in his nice Civic. It's not like last night ended on a good fucking note." I turn my head back down towards my feet and grown loudly.

"Did you cheat on him with me?" Nathan looks solemnly at me.

"NO! Absolutely NOT! I broke up with him more than once. I tried and he wouldn't let me go no matter what." I feel an anxiety attack coming on and start to feel myself hyperventilate. "Now he's going to ruin my fucking life. He's closed down my bank account, he threw all of my shit in his apartment away, he told his dad I lost it and ran here, and now his dad is going to blacklist me so that I can't get a job if they call them as a reference. And I think I'm going to vomit."

A firm hand places itself upon my shoulder that brings me back to reality. "We can talk about it later."

Nathan pulls an old plastic shopping bag from the back seat and gently places it by my feet. I squeeze my eyes shut. I feel every inch of my body saying Run! "I just want to go home, Nathan."

He shifts the car into drive. "Of course, Catherine. I just want to do what you need me to do right now. We'll talk more when we get you home. Just rest for now." He rubs my back and puts his foot on the pedal.

I shrug out of his touch, which makes me feel like a child, and tonight I don't need that. As he turns the car to head back toward my aunt's house, my stomach threatens to empty itself of the alcohol I have consumed tonight. We sit in silence. It brings back memories of the night before when we were on our way to the date I so royally screwed up. I close my eyes, leaning my head against the cold window. Is this what rock bottom feels like?

"Why do you always have to be so nice?" I turn in my seat to look at him. "I mean, who shows up to rescue someone after their ex shows up claiming to still be with them when you're supposed to be on a date?"

He's quiet a few minutes. "I honestly don't know what you want me to say here. I care about you and this is how people treat people they care about."

I scowl. "No one cares about me. I've got years and years of proof to back me up. The girls I was with? All friends from high school. Think we still talked while I was in Georgia? No, I'm out of sight, out of mind. I've been gone for months, left no notice and no one has checked on me, not even my dad." I feel tears well up in my eyes. "I have nothing anywhere. I am just so exhausted from being an inconvenience."

"I think about you when you're gone, especially since I had to do your work today." He smiles, trying to lighten the mood. "I think about you all the time. Is it inconvenient rescuing you from a club twenty minutes away from where I was? A little, but I came because I care and I'm concerned." He stops at a stop sign "Dinner was great. The night ended shitty."

"Why did you leave last night? You knew I didn't want you to, and you just fucking left me there with him." I feel my stomach roll, and I take a deep breath through my nose to avoid the vomit I feel rising up in my threat. My pulse is beating wildly, and I can't tell if I'm going to pass out or cry.

He stiffens. "I didn't know what to do. I still don't. I like you a lot, but I'm scared of trying to force you to love me like I did with my ex."

Now I'm quiet for a few minutes. I don't know what to say back.

I don't know how he interprets my silence, but he continues, "I don't particularly care for scraping you off of a club floor. But I know you've had a bad few days."

"I'm sorry you had to come find me drunk. I know you already have one drunk to babysit, I'm sure you didn't want me added to your list too."

He shifts uncomfortably in his seat as we pull up in

front of Cici's house. He turns the car off and we sit there in silence. I feel sober at the moment, my mind trying to rationalize all of the muddled feelings I seem to have accumulated on the drive from the club to my house.

"If this is where you are right now, I get it." He turns in his seat, placing his hand on my knee.

My mind flashes back to the last time he saw me drunk and ended up carrying me home from Cici's bar. The feel of his strong hand on my knee confuses my already broken heart more. I hate being in this place, I hate feeling like I have for the last few months.

"Catherine, look at me." His voice is soothing, and as soon as I turn to face him, I'm met with his soul-piercing gaze. Every time I think I am unreadable, he seems to see right through me. My heart flutters as his hand tightens on my knee. "If this is ever going to work between us, I want all of you. Even the parts I don't like. But I can't take it from you. It has to be something you give willingly. I'm capable of dealing with it all. If that means picking you up when you've had too much to drink for a while, I can do that. Lord knows it's not my first time. But it can't be because you accidentally texted me. You don't get to hide the messy parts of yourself from the people you care about. If they truly care about you, they don't just want the perfect stuff."

My head is spinning again. "I don't think I know how to do that. I've been hiding so much for so long."

I remember his dad's words from the night before, and

realize I really need to figure out what I'm doing. Nathan has already jumped in with both feet, and I'm terrified to hurt him more than I probably already have.

"I know." His face is soft, and his eyes study my face in a way that feels so vulnerable. "Why don't we get you inside."

He pushes his car door open and then hurries around to my door, opening it and helping me out. I feel unstable, but it's not from the alcohol, it's from the weight of his words tonight. Nathan walks me to the door, and helps me find my keys in my purse.

"Come in for a minute?" *What am I saying? I'm saying I need Nathan. I need him to make me feel again.*

He fidgets a little "Are you sure? Your aunt isn't my biggest fan."

"She's at the bar right now...I'm not ready to be alone yet." My brain feels fuzzy as he follows me in. I grab his strong hand and lead him to the living room. I sit down on the mustard yellow suede couch and pat the spot next to me.

He wades the shag carpet and sits next to me. He extends his arm behind me and pulls me into a cuddle. His black cardigan is soft and so comforting. The smell of his cologne stirs the butterflies in my stomach. I can feel his strong pecs through his clothing as he drags his fingers through my hair.

I feel something I haven't felt in a long time—I feel safe.

His smell is intoxicating. The mix of laundry detergent and aftershave sends warmth down my spine. I didn't know that just someone's scent could spark so much inside of me.

I lean up and kiss his jaw, feeling his body tense beside me. "I need you."

The voice that I hear doesn't sound like my own. I kiss him again, this time just under his ear. I feel his chest rise under my hand, and heat starts to pool low in my stomach.

"Catherine." My name comes from him in a low growl as he runs his hand down my back. I shiver, and a small gasp escapes my lips. In the next moment I shift to straddle him, pulling my knees close to his hips.

He looks at me through heavy eyelids as I slowly close the distance between us more, brushing my lips against his.

"We really shouldn't," he whispers.

"Please." I take his hands and place them on my hips. My heart is beating wildly and I lean back in and kiss him again. This time he meets me halfway. His lips crash into mine as his hands tighten on my hips, digging into the soft flesh, dragging my body impossibly closer to his. In the next instant I'm pulling my dress over my head. He pulls back, running kisses along my collarbone and down my chest. A moan escapes my lips as I rake my fingers through his hair.

He breaks away and breathes against my neck, sending tendrils of pleasure coursing through my stomach.

"I think we should slow down."

"I think my bedroom is downstairs." I start fumbling with the buttons on his sweater and shirt, but his hands cover mine, stopping me. "I don't understand?"

"Catherine, this isn't a good idea tonight. You've had a lot to drink."

"So what? I feel fine. I want this." I draw back on his lap so that I can see his face.

He meets my gaze, sympathy filling his eyes. That's definitely not what I wanted to see. "I want this too, but not like this. Not after the week you've had, and definitely not after you've been drinking."

I slide off his lap, shame and embarrassment clogging my senses. If I thought having him pick me up from the club drunk was rock bottom, I was wrong. This feels more accurate.

"Catherine, look at me. Please?"

I can't bring myself to turn my head. My insides feel like they're crumbling.

Nathan stands, wrapping a blanket from the back of the couch around my shoulders. " I think I should go…" he says it so quietly I almost think I misheard him.

I nod, staring at the pattern crocheted into the blanket. I hear the door close behind me, but I don't make any effort to move from where I'm sitting or get dressed. I pull the blanket closer around my shoulders, hunch down and close my eyes.

Chapter Twenty-Four

I can tell when the door opens again that it's Cici. I have no idea what time it is, but Cici looks like she just did the final call and cleaned up.

"Did I miss something, Kitty? You're a mess! Where are your clothes?" She kicks her shoes off and comes to sit by me on the couch.

"I am a mess, Cici. I can't keep my life together. I push everyone I care about away. I am so fucked up and tired." I begin to tear up, a hard lump swells in my throat.

Cici shakes her head. "I can remember a young teenager saying that after her mom left. You're only twenty-five, I shaved my head at twenty-five. You haven't reached my level of mess." She smiles at me lovingly. "What happened that sent you off the rails?"

I tell Cici everything. All that has transpired with Nathan, the mess with Marcus and the threats that I am positive he will figure out how to bring to fruition, and how much I just fucked up more with Nathan.

It takes what seems like forever and she just nods and listens— handing me tissues as my eyes continue to sting and leak. I share about how I felt nothing with Marcus and felt everything with Nathan. How I found a friend like Amber and realized how I thought I lost all of my friends in Georgia. About being angry with my dad and how he never even reached out or called me, nor did he come looking for me. I tell Cici about my conversation with Meghan in the salon, and how much I can't stand the way I was for the last few years. I tell her about my conversation with Oscar at the bar after I went looking for her last night, and how he told me to tread carefully because Nathan would be all-in regardless of whether or not I was.

"Kitty, I'm always here for you." She wraps her arm around my shoulder, drawing me close to her chest like she used to do when I was a child. "That's a lot of emotional exhaustion in such little time. You're fucking wonderful and smart. But you need to find yourself, not some guy. Girls these days are obsessed with men. Join me Kitty, in sweet, sweet spinsterdom." She laughs to bring some levity to the situation. "Dear, enough chasing; you've been chasing your mom, chasing your place with your dad, chasing Marcus, and now chasing Nathan. When are you gonna stop and chase after yourself? It hasn't been long. You haven't even met yourself without Marcus. You need to start chasing you. Find yourself, go back to school, meet more people, and maybe get a new job. You can't find you if you're fucking around with your boss. I am old. Some would even say wise. I disagree with them, but you deserve more to life than being some guy's supporting character."

"It's just, I think Nathan's the one. He makes me feel like I have never felt before." I feel butterflies swell in my stomach.

She smiles. "Well that's nice and all. But you need to get your shit together. That young man isn't supposed to be fixing you. He deserves better. Fix yourself first, then try again in a few months. Try friendship first. You barely know him. What if he picks his teeth or picks his nose and eats it. Take a break. Nathan will wait, and if not, then he doesn't deserve you."

My mind wanders to what Nathan said to me in the car, and to what Oscar said the other night at the bar, and I smile. I don't know that I'd care if he picked his nose, or snored or any of that. But Cici is right. He deserves better than what I can give him right now.

"I think I need to quit my job." My heart pounds at the idea, but I don't know if I could control myself seeing him every day.

"Well, just so happens I might have somewhere you can work until you figure things out." My aunt winks at me and stands. "Now, I need to smoke, and you need to go find some fucking clothes." She laughs to herself, walking to the kitchen to retrieve her box of goodies.

I stand as soon as she leaves the room, clutch the knit blanket around myself and head to my bedroom. I change into a comfy pair of sweats and one of my dad's old college t-shirts that I stole from him in high school and never gave back.

When I walk into the kitchen, Cici is sitting on the counter holding a joint.

"Here," she says, holding it out to me. "I think you probably need this."

I take a small hit, reminding myself that I'm still pretty drunk. I had forgotten until I went to change. It seems like the effects of the alcohol decided to lay dormant until now.

Cici hands me a bowl of popcorn and a huge bottle of water before grabbing a bag of Hershey kisses from the pantry.

"Let's go watch a show about some woman who murdered her husband." She makes herself comfortable on the couch and I snuggle in next to her like I used to after my mom left.

"I should probably text Amber," I say through mouthfuls of popcorn. "I asked her to cover for me, and I haven't talked to her all day."

"I think that's probably wise."

Me:

Hey, sorry I never got to explain myself today. It's been kind of a bad last 24 hours.

I turn my attention back to the tv, hoping that Amber isn't mad at me for being kind of shady the last few days. Only a moment later my phone buzzes in my lap.

Amber:

It's totally okay, Cat. Are you alright? You said you talked to Nathan, I'm assuming it didn't go well?

Me

You could say that. Dinner went great, then my ex showed up when Nathan dropped me off, and he tried to say we were still together and Nathan left really fast before I could explain anything.

Amber:

Holy shit! I'm coming over. Text me your address, I'll bring wine.

Me:

FOR THE LOVE OF GOD PLZZ DON'T BRING ME ANY MORE BOOZE.

I send Amber my location and tell Cici we are gonna have a house guest.

Her only reply is, "I guess I should pack us all a bowl then."

Twenty minutes later, Amber is rushing into the living room and practically smothering me as she lands beside me on the couch, wrapping her arms around me so tightly I think my eyes might bug out of my head like the old cartoons would do when someone was surprised.

"God, Kitty! I'm so sorry! I would have been over here sooner if I had known!" She pulls back, smoothing my hair away from my face like a mother.

"Funny story. I tried to text you earlier and accidentally texted Nathan instead." I feel the back of my eyes burn with tears as a giggle bubbles up from my stomach.

"How is that funny?" Amber is smiling uncomfortably, and looks over her shoulder at Cici– who shrugs at her in reply.

I spend the next few minutes retelling my story to her, sparing no detail as Cici takes a few hits from the bowl.

When I finish, Amber almost looks as if she's ready to cry, too. "That sounds horrible."

Cici hands me the pipe and the lighter as she reaches for the bag of chocolates. I take a big hit and hold it in probably longer than I should, but my nerves feel fried and I desperately need to chill for a while. I pass it to Amber who doesn't miss a beat, taking a small hit then coughing vigorously for a solid minute.

"You okay?" I hand her my water, and she takes a few sips before giving me a dorky smile.

"Yeah, I think I'm good." She takes another drink before handing the bottle back to me. "I've just never smoked before."

Cici sputters and laughs out loud. "Look at me, sitting with two fucking babies. I am ashamed I could pull a whole bowl in one breath at your age."

"Yes, but you also had a shaved head, so who's better off?" I jab back.

"Probably still me. At least I was getting laid!"

This time Amber is the one who cracks up. A full belly kind of laugh that makes everyone around laugh as well.

We settle into the couch. I pass chocolate to Amber as Cici goes to make more popcorn. When we are alone I rest my head on her shoulder.

"I think I need to quit working at the library," I say quietly.

Amber drops her head on top of mine, sighing deeply. "As sad as that makes me, I think you're probably right."

"I'll miss not seeing you every day." I pop another chocolate kiss into my mouth. "I just think Cici is right. I don't know who I am without Marcus, and without the constant drama that is my family."

"You know…" Amber says thoughtfully. "I live alone right now. And I have an extra room that I'm currently using for yoga. If you wanted to move in, you could."

I sit up and turn toward her, feeling my head swim wildly from a mix of leftover booze and weed. But in that moment my heart feels like it's about to leap out of my chest.

"Really?" I say a little more enthusiastically than I mean to.

"Really what?" Cici says, walking back into the room and plopping on the couch next to me. She hands a bowl of hot popcorn my direction, and keeps a second one tucked in her lap.

"Amber offered to let me move in with her."

Cici studies us for a minute, and I start to wonder if

maybe my eagerness to move out is going to hurt her feelings. But then she smiles. "Thank God! I haven't been able to walk around naked in almost two months."

"I call bullshit. More than once I came upstairs and you were feeling the breeze between your knees," I tease.

She laughs. "Well, now I can do it all the time again, anywhere I want. I'm all for it. Get out, make friends with someone other than Charles, Larry, and me."

I think for a second. I wouldn't have to live alone right away. I'd have support but I'd still be independent. "If you're sure about dumping the yoga studio, I'm in!"

We both squeal like school girls "Not to be a downer but we all need sleep. Amber, you're not driving. A lightweight like you gets the couch," Cici orders.

"But MOOOOOM!" we say in unison, laughing.

I give Amber a deep hug and then head down stairs to go to sleep. I think I'm gonna be okay. I think things will turn around, as long as I start chasing me.

For the first time since leaving Atlanta two months ago I almost feel like things will actually be okay. I toss myself on the bed and only moments later I'm asleep with a better attitude.

Chapter Twenty-Five

What is happening? My bed shifts violently under me, and I sit up looking around. My stomach churns violently, threatening to empty itself right here on my bed.

"Good Morning! How did you sleep? I think I should start smoking more often. I passed out last night! I don't think I've ever slept so hard in my life!" I manage to focus on Amber's smiling face, and the memories from the night before start falling into place. Marcus, Nathan, the club. Shit, the club. I throw my blankets off, running to the bathroom. I barely get the toilet open before I'm vomiting.

"Shit! Kitty, are you good?" Amber follows me into the bathroom, doing the good friend thing and holding my hair.

When I'm confident my stomach is empty I close the lid and flush. "Yeah," I say weakly. "I'm good. Just forgot how much I drank last night." I've thrown up more in the last few weeks than I ever did in college. I stand and turn on the sink, rinsing my mouth and splashing cool water across my face.

"Are you sure?" Amber's concerned face appears in the mirror over my shoulder. "We are supposed to be at work in an hour and a half, are you going to be up for it?"

I groan. "I don't know if I'll be up for it ever, but I need to go in."

She nods and turns on the shower, pulling the towel off the back of the bathroom door and hands it to me. "Cici let me borrow her shower this morning, why don't you get in, and I'll bring you coffee."

Before I can say anything she turns and leaves, closing the bathroom door behind her. I strip out of my clothes and step into the warm spray, taking my time washing my hair and body. When I am finished I get out, brush my teeth, comb my hair, and I'm sliding on a comfy oversized sweater when Amber comes back in with two steaming cups of coffee.

"Cici made this one for you, said it was your favorite."

I take a sip and sigh. The taste of cinnamon and vanilla coats my throat. I can't help but think of that first time Nathan and I drove me to the Library and stole sips of my coffee. Sadness tinges the edges of my mind as I remember the conversation that awaits me at work. I only allow myself to feel it for a minute though, before reminding myself of the conversation I had with Cici and Amber the night before. This is what's best– for now. Nathan wants all of me, and I don't think he knows what that means. I don't even know what that means because I don't know who I am right now.

"Finish getting dressed and I'll meet you upstairs. Cici said something about home made muffins and I could smell them while she was pouring the coffee." She grins, backing out of my room as I sit on my bed in the silence another minute mentally preparing myself for what today has in store.

§

When I walk upstairs, I find Amber and my aunt sitting comfortably at the kitchen table laughing about some show they both watch.

"Good morning my love! How did you sleep? I made muffins!" She motions to the plate of warm chocolate chip and blueberry muffins sitting on the table.

I look at her puzzled, "How the heck are you awake enough to be baking muffins? And since when do you bake?"

"Hey be careful or I won't bake for you again!" She turns back to Amber "Well now I have to get dressed. Enjoy breakfast girls." She stands up, swishes her pink nightgowns behind her and heads towards her room.

I grab a muffin for Amber and I and plop onto the couch next to her. "Are you still serious about being roomies?"

"Duh, I may have been high but I really have been thinking about offering. I need to be saving more money and having a roomie will help with that." She grins ear to ear. "Then I don't have to pay for soap operas, I'll get it for free from your life."

"Bully, you need more spice in your life anyway." I stick my tongue out. "I see you borrowed some of Cici's clothes."

"She has like, a whole mall back there why does she have multiple sizes?"

"Oh I'm positive she keeps lost clothes from the bar, don't worry she washes them." I smile as Amber squirms thinking about what random person's sweater she's wearing.

Amber peeks at the clock on her phone. "Well I have work and you have a job to quit. Let's go." We both throw on our jackets and head out the door. There sitting in my Aunts driveway is the saddest beat up old gold camry I've ever seen.

"This is Betsy, she's old and clumsy but reliable." Amber pats the hood. "I need to climb through the passenger door to get to the driver's side, so, just a second." I watch as Amber climbs through knocking over an empty drive through cup out of its holder. "ALSO THE HEAT IS EITHER ALWAYS ON OR ALWAY OFF." She shouts from the driver's seat.

"No wonder you need to save money. It's not gonna explode on me, is it?" I climb into the car, cigarette burns speckle the passenger seat.

Amber starts the engine and the car sputters to a start. "Nope if it was gonna explode again that's when it would've done it."

I feel seriously concerned, "Again?"

"It's no biggie, let's go!" She turns around and pulls out. Betsy clunks when we hit the street. I'm starting to wonder if I should've just walked. Amber is so determined and so sure of herself. I aspire to have the confidence she does. Maybe some of that will rub off on me.

Our ride is filled with laughs and planning. Betsy clunks and squeals to a stop in the parking lot behind the library. I sit in the car, staring at the big brick building in front of us.

"I hate to be this way, but I can't get out until you do…" Amber smiles at me reassuringly.

I smile back, mustering all of the courage I have. We walk into the Library together and Amber squeezes my hand. "Nathan is probably in his office, do you want me to walk up there with you?"

"No, I think I'll be okay." As I walk slowly toward the elevator I remember the first day I came here for my interview. I had no idea what I was walking into, or who I was going to meet. I remember seeing Amber sitting at the big desk on the third floor reading her book. I was so afraid of her at first. And then when I walked into the office and was met with Nathan's dark eyes, I thought I was going to die. I remember him showing me around, and our mutual love for Max Ehrmann. At that moment a few lines from the poem come back to me.

Be yourself. Especially do not feign affection. Neither be cynical about love; for in the face of all aridity and disenchantment, it is as perennial as the grass.

Take kindly the counsel of the years, gracefully surrendering the things of youth.

Nurture strength of spirit to shield you in sudden misfortune. But do not distress yourself with dark imaginings. Many fears are born of fatigue and loneliness.

Beyond a wholesome discipline, be gentle with yourself. You are a child of the universe no less than the trees and the stars; you have a right to be here.

I find myself standing in front of Nathan's office. My hand shakes as I knock on the door. I hear muffled shuffling from inside, before the door opens.

"Good morning," Nathan's tall figure fills the doorway. "Oh, I thought you were Amber." He steps aside, waving me into his office. "I honestly wasn't sure you would be in today." He says, closing the door behind us. He motions toward one of the chairs in front of his desk before moving to take his seat across from me.

We sit in silence, Nathan stares at his hands folded on his desk, and I look at him, taking my time to study his face. He's got a few days of stubble on his cheeks, and his button down shirt is pressed perfectly. I can see the outline of his strong frame pressed against the fabric. My heart stumbles when his eyes finally meet mine.

"Are you doing okay today?" His deep voice shatters the silence around us. The butterflies in my stomach flutter as his gaze ripples over me. This is going to be harder than I anticipated. "Can I get you coffee?" He stands uncomfortably, walking over to the counter and makes himself a cup.

"I'm okay this morning." I feel like my voice sounds way more chipper than I feel.

He nods and returns to sitting behind his desk. "So, you didn't answer my first question." He sets his coffee off to the side, refolding his hands and directing his full attention to me.

"I'm okay." I say honestly.

I mean it. After my talk last night, and confirming plans with Amber on the ride to work this morning; I feel okay.

"So," I take a deep shaky breath, willing my voice to come off stronger than I feel. "I actually came up here to talk to you about something."

He nods, his eyes never leave mine, and something in his expression gives me the little bit of confidence I need to speak again.

"I need to quit."

His expression doesn't falter, but he does avert his eyes back to his hands. "I see," he says flatly.

"This isn't because of you, or us. I mean it is kind of– I don't think I can work every day with you and keep my hands to myself. But this is because I think I'm lost right now. Last night, you said you wanted all the parts of me, and the more I think about it, the more I realize I can't offer you that right now because I don't even have all of the parts of myself figured out." I draw in a deep breath, releasing it slowly while watching for his reaction.

He nods slowly. "I understand."

"I think I'm going to move in with Amber for a while. Maybe work at Cici's bar for a while, or get a job with Larry at the diner." I try for a smile, but I'm pretty sure it just looks like a grimace so I relax back into my chair, watching him.

His breathing is steady, his shoulders rise and fall in rhythm. The longer I sit here the more I just want to go around the desk and crawl into his lap. But I grip my hands together and resign myself to watching him breathe.

I want to tell him so badly that I don't want this to be forever. I want to tell him how much he makes me want to be the person he is asking me to be. But I can't make changes for him. I can't intertwine my life with someone else's right now. I need to figure out how to be me.

Nathan is the first to break the silence. "I think I like you even more than I did before."

"What? Why?" His comment throws me off.

His eyes bore into me, the intensity unmatched by any look he's given me before. "You are one of the strongest, smartest people I know. You deserve to find yourself. I hope someday soon, you can see yourself the way I can see you. And then I hope, when you get there, you'll let me take you to dinner again, so I can hear all about it." A smile tugs at the corners of his lips, and I can't help myself any longer. I stand and practically run around the desk, collapsing into him, letting his strong arms hold me tightly against his chest.

"I don't want this to be forever." I choke out. I feel tears pricking my eyes, blurring my vision as he rubs circles on my back.

"I'll be here when you come back. I've told you before, I want to be whatever you need me to be." He presses a soft kiss to my forehead, his lips are warm and soft against my skin.

I allow myself another minute of his comfort before I pull away, wiping my face on my sleeve. "I should probably go…" I say quietly.

Nathan stands and takes my hand, leading me toward his closed office door. He doesn't say anything else to me, but he kisses the back of my hand affectionately, his eyes full of promises that are both soul shattering and hopeful. When the door closes, and I stand by myself, the last few lines of Desiderata float across my mind.

And whether or not it is clear to you, no doubt the universe is unfolding as it should. Therefore be at peace with God, whatever you conceive Him to be.

And whatever your labors and aspirations, in the noisy confusion of life, keep peace in your soul. With all its sham, drudgery and broken dreams, it is still a beautiful world. Be cheerful. Strive to be happy.

I walk toward the front doors of the Library, and push outside into the cool morning air. Over the last two days the snow has started to melt, and the smell of spring is starting to cristen the air with hope of warm weather to come. I walk slowly back toward Cici's house, I have packing to do. Amber said I could be in her apartment by the end of the coming week if I want.

The prospect of the changes that are coming spark a mix of fear and trepidation in my mind, but for the first time in weeks I feel like I am breathing on my own.

I cling to that feeling.